CRITICAL PRAISE FOR
EDWARD MATHIS'S
ELECTRIFYING THRILLER . . .

The Burned Woman
A Dan Roman Mystery

"A SPELLBINDING NIGHTMARE OF A NOVEL
. . . *The Burned Woman* never falters. The tale is
near-perfect in its execution."
—*Booklist*

"INTRIGUING MYSTERY . . . Compelling char-
acters . . . fast-paced prose!"
—*Publishers Weekly*

"ENTERTAINING . . . SMOOTH DIALOGUE . . .
SOLID ENJOYMENT!"
—*Library Journal*

"DAN ROMAN IS A PRIVATE EYE WITH A
HEART AS BIG AS TEXAS."
—Dorothy Salisbury Davis

"MATHIS HAS A FINE SENSE OF PLOTTING
. . . a distinctive sense of place and characterization
that brings a vivid reality to small-town Texas life."
—*Pittsburgh Press*

"MATHIS IS A WRITER TO WATCH!"
—*Texas Books in Review*

Don't miss his explosive novel of suspense . . .

Only When She Cries

Berkley Books by Edward Mathis

ONLY WHEN SHE CRIES
THE BURNED WOMAN
SEE NO EVIL

SEE NO EVIL

Edward Mathis

BERKLEY BOOKS, NEW YORK

SEE NO EVIL

A Berkley Book / published by arrangement with
the author's estate

PRINTING HISTORY
Berkley edition / November 1990

ISBN: 0-425-12360-X

A BERKLEY BOOK® TM 757,375
Berkley Books are published by The Berkley Publishing Group,
200 Madison Avenue, New York, New York 10016.
The name "Berkley" and the "B" logo
are trademarks belonging to Berkley Publishing Corporation.

PRINTED IN THE UNITED STATES OF AMERICA

10 9 8 7 6 5 4 3 2 1

CHAPTER

ONE

Everybody dies. That's the absolute in Mother Nature's formula; the unknowns are when and how. Peaceful and easy or violent and hard, the end result is the same: the ultimate fulfillment of nature's decree at the moment of conception. Abandoned from that point forward, left to dangle perilously above the maelstrom, the final disposition of your insignificant span is relinquished to the tender mercies of capricious fate, Mother Nature's strong right hand.

But homicide Detective Sergeant Hamilton Pope, kneeling beside the sprawled body of the elderly black man who had died a hard and violent death, if asked, would have sneered at the suggestion of capricious fate and pointed to the young white man slumped against the glass at the front entrance of the store, pointed to the sawed-off shotgun and the fistful of dollars clutched against a bloody chest, and given his opinion of why in no uncertain terms—greed.

It was easy to read the signs, to understand what had happened. Hamilton Pope climbed wearily to his feet and looked around for Detective Milly Singer. Her voice came from the rear of the small fast-service food store and he walked in that direction.

She was talking to a frail black woman with wispy white hair and thin fleshless hands knotted and curled inward by arthritis and silent, deadly time. Milly's voice was soothing, almost a croon, and she alternately wrote in her notebook and squeezed the old woman's shoulders comfortingly. She looked up as Pope approached and shook her head.

"She was in the back, lying down," she said softly. "She heard the guns, but by the time she got out here it was over. They were both . . ." She let it trail away and grimaced. "This is their fourth robbery in six months."

Pope nodded. "I guess he'd had enough. He took on the punk as he was going out the door." He shook his head and ran a hand through thick graying hair. "We all have our limits." He unbuttoned his corduroy jacket and lifted a pack of cigarettes out of his shirt pocket. "Everybody's on the way, Milly. There's nothing here for me, I'll see you back at the shop."

Milly nodded, her eyes on the old woman, her face glowing. "They've been married sixty-three years," she said wonderingly. She raised wide hazel eyes to Pope. "Can you imagine?" She wrinkled her nose. "To the same man," she added incredulously.

Pope grunted noncommittally and lit a cigarette, marveling as always at this curious display of naïveté by a woman who had been a cop for ten years, who had survived two disastrous marriages and the loss of a small son to leukemia. At thirty-two she had the smooth, taut skin of a young girl, an appealing air of emotional immediacy, of eager expectancy, as if the next sixty seconds might well be the most important minute of her life.

Pope watched them a moment longer, then turned and

walked to the front of the store. He detoured around the black man and stepped across the widespread legs of the young dead bandit. A patrolman wearing the brown-and-tan uniform of the Merriweather Police nodded as he went through the door.

"Bad one, Sarge," he commented, his young-old eyes gleaming out of a young, cynical face.

"Bad one," Pope agreed, noticing the squad car idling near the front door, lights rotating, the small crowd of Blacks and Hispanics milling around the perimeter of the parking lot, held at bay by another uniformed patrolman. "They're all bad, but this one turned to crap. The old man was using a .45. He shot the boy twice. How the kid could fire the shotgun after that is beyond me."

The young officer shrugged. "High on something. Speed, probably." He turned as a large panel truck zipped into the parking lot and came to a stop behind the patrol car. "Channel Five," he said dryly. "Wonder what took them so long."

"Keep them away until Milly's finished in there," Pope said. "And turn off that motor. Gas is a dollar fifteen a gallon." He headed for his car, parked on the street. "Tell them Captain Roscoe Tanner will issue a statement," he called over his shoulder. He climbed into his car and drove away grinning. Captain Roscoe Tanner had as much affection for the news media as a cobra for a mongoose.

It was a beautiful day, temperature in the seventies, smogless, still, a benign cerulean sky with wispy puffs of cotton candy vying with lacy jet-vapor trails for a favored place in the warm Texas sun. A lovely day. Not a day for dying.

It was warm in the car and Pope shed his jacket at the first red light. He hummed along with Sinatra's "My Way" on the radio and tried to cleanse his mind of the residual effects of the horror he had just witnessed, the senseless violence that never failed to bring a stir of atavistic rage to the growing indifference of man to his most precious commodity of all: life.

As the ranking member of Merriweather's two-man Homicide Division, it was his job to investigate deaths other than those from natural causes or those that were traffic-related. As a matter of practicality, he became deeply involved only in homicides for which there was no readily apparent perpetrator—death by person or persons unknown.

Fortunately, for the sake of his peace of mind, Merriweather had always been a relatively peace-loving, law-abiding town. Located approximately midway between Dallas and Fort Worth, the small city was essentially a bedroom community, and he spent the greater portion of his time assisting the robbery detail or working an occasional rape or assault. But robberies were skyrocketing, as were residential burglaries now that the economy was scraping rock bottom, now that more and more marginally honest citizens were out of work and forced to steal to live. To a great extent both rape and assault were by-products of this ever-increasing human tragedy, the result of chance encounters during the commission of a crime.

Mugging, a crime formerly associated only with "up North" or "out West," was rapidly becoming a popular pastime with the local, out-of-work younger set. People were hurting, and when the pain became too great, they passed it along. For many the good life had become a velvet-lined trap. Big cars and big houses, even bigger debts. Confused and disoriented by vanishing jobs and dreams, they were further disillusioned by the callous disregard of an inept government, by leaders who tailored their words to fit the exigencies of the moment, blithely ignoring their specious rhetoric of last year, or last month, or yesterday.

And all these damn Yankees swarming down here ain't helping matters any, Pope thought gloomily, turning into the lot behind police headquarters. He parked among a scattering of marked and unmarked official cars. He lit another cigarette and crossed the narrow grassed buffer zone between the lot and the rear entrance.

"Aw, the hell with it," he muttered aloud. "One second after the bomb it won't matter a damn, anyhow."

He heard his office phone ringing as he came down the corridor. He didn't bother hurrying, certain it would be stopped by the time he got there. It wasn't. He sat down at his desk before yanking up the receiver. People who let a phone ring more than ten times annoyed him, and it showed in his voice.

"Pope," he said, snarling.

"Hey . . . Ham? Hey, man, how you doing?" The pleasant baritone voice hesitated. "Did I catch you at a bad time?"

"Hello, Hack. No, one time's about as good as another around here. What're you up to?" He shook a cigarette out of his pack and searched for his lighter, his mind's eye envisaging the dark, handsome face at the other end of the telephone line.

"Not a hell of a lot," Deputy Hackmore Wind drawled, a faint tightness in his voice belying his words. "I—uh . . . I'm investigating a murder right now," he went on self-consciously.

"Yeah? Anybody I know?" He found the lighter and put fire to his cigarette. He covered the mouthpiece and coughed lightly.

"I don't know," Wind said, making no further attempt

to hide the nervous excitement in his voice. "Clinton Fielder. Lives out here in Fox Hollow . . . just barely over the county line. Maybe you know him."

"I've heard the name," Pope said dryly. "I keep what little money I've got in his bank."

"Yeah, that's the one. Owns the Merriweather Bank and Trust." He hesitated again. "That wasn't why I called you, though, Ham. Do you know a woman named Nancy Lessor?"

Pope felt a tremor along his backbone, a faint tickle of movement in the pit of his stomach. "Yeah," he said evenly. "Yeah, I know her. Why?"

"Well, she just mentioned she knew you, is all. She just said—"

"Is she involved in Fielder's murder?" Pope discovered he had a death grip on the receiver and forced himself to relax.

"Well . . . Ham, I'm just not sure. She was here. She was the one found him floating in the pool with his head almost cut off. She was the one who called us . . . or rather the Merriweather Police. They called us when they found out it was in the county. It's a wonder you didn't hear about it."

"I was out on a case," Pope said mechanically. He cleared his throat. "Did she say . . . what she was doing there?"

"They were shacking up." There was a tinge of cynicism in Wind's voice. "She don't make any bones about that." He stopped for a moment and Pope heard the rasp of a lighter. "She said they got it on about midnight last night. Afterward he wanted to take a swim—he's got a heated pool—but she didn't. They took a shower and he went downstairs to the pool and she went to bed. That's the last she saw of him until this morning. And that's when she called the police.''

''Isn't he married?''

''Yeah. His wife and kiddies are in Atlanta, visiting her mother.''

''She didn't hear anything?''

''Not a peep, she says. Said she went to sleep right away—all tired out from the sex, I reckon.''

''Do you believe her, Hack?'' The tickle in his stomach had become a hollow ball. He stubbed out the cigarette butt and automatically reached for another.

There was silence on the line; Pope could hear the faint rasp of Hack's breathing.

''You know I'm new at this, Ham . . . but, you know, I kinda do—believe her, I mean. Not just that. I'm not sure she's strong enough to do the job that was done on Fielder. And, too, we never found the murder weapon.'' He paused. ''How well do you know her, Ham? Do you think she's capable of slicing a man's throat clear to the bone?''

Pope expelled his breath in a heavy sigh. ''We're all capable of anything with the right kind of provocation. Are you having the shower drain checked for blood traces? The sinks . . . ?''

''Yeah, we're doing all that now.'' He paused again. ''I don't guess you'd want to run out here and look around?''

''Do you really need me, or are you just looking for moral support?''

Wind chuckled. ''I guess you got it. I'm afraid I'll overlook something.''

''Remember the big three: relatives, friends, and . . . lovers.'' He listened to the line sizzle for a moment. ''Did she ask you to call me?''

''No, that was my idea. She just mentioned that she

knew you, is all." His voice became casual. "Old girl-friend?"

"Yes," Pope said quietly, remembering vividly pouting lips and an incredibly rounded, miniature body. "For a time."

"You got good taste, man."

"Yeah," Pope said dryly, "I can really pick them."

"Hey, man, I wasn't being sarcastic. I mean, she's . . . really something. I can see how an older guy could really go—" He stopped suddenly. "Aw, shit!"

Pope forced a laugh through the emptiness in his chest. "Old guys need a little love, too, youngster."

"Aw, shit, Ham, come on. You know what I mean. She could turn me on without half trying . . . and I got Wendy."

"Yes, you have, you lucky bastard."

"Yeah . . . well, look, I've gotta go. Okay if I come around and talk to you about this a little?"

"Sure . . . anytime. Just bring money." His attempt at humor fell flat. "You're not going to hold her, then?"

Silence again, then Wind's slow, drawling voice. "It'll be up to the sheriff, but I reckon after we get her formal statement we'll let her go. At least for now. She was here, but there's nothing to say someone else didn't come in and kill him between midnight and morning. The doctor puts it between two and four—what he calls an educated guess. And she's offered to take a lie-detector test." The sounds of his Zippo lighter came through again. "I don't know, Ham, but her story sounds straight to me."

"Is she still working at that hamburger place, the Hamburger Box?" What had happened to her husband, Pope wondered, the wanderer who owned her body and soul?

"Yes—hey, look, I'll see you later, okay? Somebody waiting on me."

"Sure, later," Pope said. He hung up the receiver and leaned back in his swivel chair, his mind slowly filling with unwanted memories, vivid imagery of soft, warm lips and a small lithe body squirming on his, bright shining eyes as blue as his own, radiant with an eager desire to please, to be pleased, a desperate hunger to be needed.

What had happened? he wondered again. The shiftless runner who had come back into her life and snatched her out of his arms before they had grown fully accustomed to the delightful contours of her body, the aimless young nomad contributing nothing, taking everything—had he run from her again? He sternly repressed a burgeoning spark of exhilaration at the thought, reminded himself that she had taken up with another man, another older man—a rich one, if appearances meant anything. A *married* rich older man. So what did that make her? He avoided the answer to that.

He rocked forward and leaned his elbows on the desk. He cupped his head in his hands. *So what does that make me?* he wondered. *Admit it, old man, you're willing to stand in line no matter how much you hate it, willing to grab your turn at the honey pot no matter how many he-bears have been there before you. Admit it, sucker. You're still hooked on a broad who's just one rung above a hooker—if that. Bluster and squirm all you want. You've swallowed her bait, and she can reel you in anytime she wants—if she wants.*

"Bitch!" The sound of his voice was muffled by his hands, the taste of truth like acid on the back of his tongue. He lifted his face. "Why didn't you call me?" he whispered hoarsely to the empty room. "You don't need anyone else but me! Dammit, you promised—" He broke off abruptly and shoved to his feet. He ripped open a new pack of cigarettes, his movements jerky and savage. He lit one and stalked out of the room and down the corridor toward Roscoe Tanner's office—he was halfway there before the tension began to dissolve from his stocky, well-knit body, the acrimony from his heart, the twinkle returning to sky-blue eyes along with an incipient stir of dry, caustic humor.

Everybody deserved a second chance, and who in hell was he to judge? The good book said it plain: It is more blessed to forgive than . . . or something like that.

CHAPTER

TWO

He lay facedown among the boxes and trash behind Dorrie's Flowers and Bouquets, his cheek pressed into the grimy concrete, and from a distance, as Pope approached, the wide ribbon of wine-red blood appeared as the loose end of a scarlet muffler. His eyes were stretched wide, his mouth open, his face drained, puckered and congealed as if he had seen the horror of approaching death and it had turned him to stone. His hands were crusty red with dried blood, the dirty nails ripped and shredded where he had scratched at the rough concrete in a helpless dying frenzy. His clothing appeared clean, though baggy, a mismatch of odds and ends that had long ago seen their best days. Even his cracked and worn shoes were of two slightly different shades of brown, and despite the turned-out pockets, it seemed inconceivable to Pope that anyone would have bothered killing this pitiful derelict for what they could find in his pockets.

He squatted beside the body and looked carefully at the face. Not old, somewhere between thirty and forty. Rough, callused hands—a workingman, not a bum as he had first thought. Ground-in grease on the fingers, black under the nails—probably a mechanic or someone who worked around greasy machinery. He touched the callused palm with a fingertip—it was hard and firm. If he was out of work, it hadn't been for long.

Reluctantly he raised his eyes to the gaping purple wound in the neck. Raw, red muscle and ghastly white ends of cartilage and ligament—the cut extended almost completely around the neck, as if the killer had started his cut at the spine and circled the neck in one swift, savage twist of the wrist.

Power, Pope thought. A cut like that would take power and a certain amount of knowledge. And a weapon with a good hilt and a razor-sharp edge. Maybe a razor, at that. The old-fashioned kind with a long blade and a thick handle. Not too many around anymore. Something to think about.

He heard footsteps in the alley behind him and rose to his feet. He recognized the clumping gait of Captain Roscoe Tanner and spoke without turning his head.

"Better cancel our poker game tonight, Roscoe. I don't think Clyde, here, will be able to hold up his head."

Tanner grunted sourly and ignored his subordinate's black humor. He knew from long association that Pope's sometimes gruesome sense of humor was a safety valve, a defensive mechanism to preserve his equilibrium in the face of violent death.

"That his name? Clyde?"

"Yeah. Clyde Burns. That's according to a driver's license and Social Security card. That's all he had in his billfold. Sheldon called it in to Sally. She's running a make on him now."

"Sheldon here? I didn't see him." Tanner slouched against the brick wall of Dorrie's Flowers and Bouquets.

Six feet four inches, two hundred and sixty pounds, he dwarfed everything and everyone around him. Because he was overly sensitive about his size, he usually sat when having a conversation, but there was nothing in Dorrie's alley to sit on except cardboard boxes, so he did the next best thing and slouched.

"He was working a robbery down the street when he saw the patrol car up here. He found the billfold near the mouth of the alley. I guess he's gone back to his robbery squeal."

"This a mugging, you think?"

Pope shrugged. "He's not the kind of guy I'd pick to mug, myself. He looks pretty damn strong for one thing, and for another he doesn't look like he'd have a dime."

It was Tanner's turn to shrug. "Can't never tell. Maybe he had a wad and somebody saw it. Maybe he just got paid or got his welfare check cashed—hell, some of these crumbs would open you up for a pack of cigarettes."

"I thought at first that he was a wino. But his clothes are relatively clean and I couldn't smell anything. Pretty young. Thirty-two or three, I'd say. Either works, or has been working recently, at manual labor of some kind. His hands are greasy and he has big calluses." He looked down at the dead man, his gaze moody. "Just another poor working stiff getting the shitty end of the stick." He fished a small glassine envelope from his jacket pocket. "He had fifteen cents in change—and this in his pockets, according to Sheldon. It's curious."

Tanner plucked the envelope from his hand with huge, bananalike fingers. He peered closely at the object through the transparent plastic. He scowled, then grunted and handed it back to Pope.

"Looks like a pocketknife to me. What's curious about it?"

"It's a Stockdale. Handmade in a small factory in Houston. Very expensive. I know, I've wanted one for a long time. This small penknife costs over a hundred and fifty dollars."

Tanner shrugged. "So? Maybe he found it or bought it secondhand from a hock shop or something."

Pope shook his head. "No. It has his initials on it. It looks brand-new, and the initials were professionally engraved."

"So?" The big man gave him a blank, distracted look.

"So I don't know. It seems out of place, is all. It's a very fine knife. One of the best, if not the best, made. The kind of knife you'd find in a wealthy man's pocket and not a guy's who looks like he's one stumble above a bum. Hell, I'm working steady and I can't even afford one." He put the envelope away and fished out a cigarette. He lit up and blew smoke at the big man holding up the wall. "Maybe what I need, by God, is a raise."

"Don't we all," Tanner said. He pushed away from the wall and thumped Pope on the arm. His grin was ingratiating. "Stay busy, fellow," he said. He turned and clumped away down the alley. "I'll send Milly and whoever else I can find down to help you canvass the area."

"Hey, thanks, Roscoe," Pope called after him. "You're almost all heart."

Hackmore Wind was waiting for him when he got back to the office, his long body slumped in Pope's chair, booted feet crossed at the ankles on one corner of the desk. His tan campaign hat was tilted over his eyes, a cigarette dangling from one corner of a wide sensuous mouth. As tall as Roscoe Tanner, he ran more to wide shoulders and narrow hips, a long rangy body well padded with muscle and covered by fine dark skin. A duke's mixture of Mexican and Indian, black and white, he had finely sculptured features, dark eyes, and a warm flashing smile that created fluttering in female tummies and set men's teeth on edge. He was good-natured, gregarious, and fun-loving, and more than a few men over the years had learned to their sorrow that male beauty does not necessarily equate with effeminacy. Born Hackmore Ryder Windinniquitta, he was eternally grateful to his half-Indian father for shortening it to Wind. He considered being a black Mexican Indian honkie in a honkie society burden enough without having an unpronounceable, unspellable name. But his father had a stubborn streak, too, and had flatly refused to do anything about the Hackmore Ryder portion of his name.

"Just about given up on you," he told Pope, his boot heels crashing to the tiled floor. He rose and stretched to his full height and ambled around the desk, a genial giant with a smile on his face. "Heard you got one of these unauthorized tonsillectomies, like mine."

Pope paused in the act of sitting down. "You think there's a connection?"

Hack shrugged elaborately and collapsed into Pope's visitor's chair. "Don't know. Thought we might compare notes, see what we got."

Pope nodded. He sat down and lit a cigarette. "You never did come by last week."

Hack crossed his legs. "Yeah, I know. I thought you might be busy. I heard you had a couple of homicides." He rubbed at scuff marks on the toe of his boot, his face gloomy.

"Not my type. Straightforward robbery and killing. That old black man handled the court proceedings for us."

"If more people would do what he did, maybe these assholes would get the message."

"It's a big price to pay for principle. There was only

twenty-seven bucks involved. The old man knew that. My guess is he was fed up with being robbed and decided not to take it anymore." He broke off and smiled faintly. "His way of yelling out the window, I guess."

Hack raised his eyes, his brow furrowed. "What?"

"Never mind. It won't make any sense if you didn't see the movie."

Hack bobbed his head and fished a low-tar, low-nicotine cigarette out of a box in his shirt pocket. "That neck job of mine. The county coroner's come up with some more educated guesses." He lit the cigarette and inhaled. He rolled it in his fingers and stared at it balefully. "Don't know why I ever started these sons of bitches again."

"Such as what?"

"The murder weapon, for instance. He thinks it was a curved instrument, a damned sharp curved instrument. Specifically, a linoleum knife. I think they use them on carpets too."

"Yeah. Utility knife. They're used for a lot of things." Pope pursed his lips in a soundless whistle, his sky-blue eyes thoughtfully hooded. Finally he nodded. "Yeah, that would have done the job too. Did you bring any pictures?"

Hack inclined his head toward the corner of the desk where his boots had been resting. "Try that folder there."

Pope opened the folder and shuffled slowly through the photos inside. Full-face shots and profiles: Everything had been severed except the spine and the thin strip of flesh covering it. Except for the broad, fleshy face and red hair, he could have been looking at Clyde Burns. His lips tightened and his head bobbed absently. He quickly scanned the coroner's report and noted the four-hour span allowed for estimated time of death. He felt a dry tingle in the back of his throat when he saw Nancy Lessor's signature at the bottom of her simple statement. He read it twice, then closed the folder and tossed it across his desk. He lit a cigarette and rocked back in his chair, his blue eyes narrow and brooding.

"Well?" Hack asked after a while, when it became apparent that the thick-bodied, somber detective wasn't going to comment.

"What about the girl?" Pope asked casually. "They're not mentioning her on the news anymore."

Hack started a grin, thought better of it. "The coroner says no way. He don't think she's physically strong enough to do it that way, and besides, she let them give her a chemical wash that would have picked up any traces of blood even if she had taken a bath afterward." He rolled the cigarette in his long fingers, his face noncommittal. "You haven't seen her?"

"No," Pope said curtly. "No reason to. Any suspects?"

Hack shook his head. "Nobody worth mentioning. DPS picked up a transient out on Loop 820 the next morning, but he was clean. No bad enemies that we've been able to find. His wife was just where she was supposed to be. No business partners past or present that show any possibilities. No record. No scandals. Except for a little huffing and puffing on the side, he's the original Mr. Clean." Hack sighed and took refuge in his cigarette, his face dejected.

Pope snorted. He leaned his elbows on the desk and stared at the young man. "Don't look so sad, cowboy," he said. "In this business you lose more than you win."

"Yeah, but this is pretty damn near my first case." He cut his eyes around at Pope. "I sure would like to crack it."

Pope grinned. "Ambitious, eh? Well, let's wait and see what we come up with on Mr. Burns."

Hack's face brightened. "You think they might be connected, then?"

Pope shrugged. "A little early to tell. They're on opposite ends of the economic ladder, that's for sure. By the way, was there any evidence of robbery at Fielder's?"

"No. His billfold and watch and personal stuff were in the room with Nancy Lessor. Mrs. Fielder didn't find anything missing downstairs."

"Burns was robbed of about fifty dollars, according to his wife. So I don't know, Hack. It has all the earmarks of a mugging except . . ."

"Except what?"

"The way he was killed. Muggers hit, kick, stab . . . they're not usually so precise and thorough. Chains, pipes, knives, and even the hands. This thing seems so . . . so deliberate somehow. Burns lived in that world down there in South Merriweather. It's hard for me to visualize him allowing a potential mugger access to his back, and I don't see any other way the cut could have been made."

Hack nodded. "That's another one of the things the coroner said. He thinks it was done from behind too." He glanced at his watch and lurched suddenly to his feet. "Damn. Wendy's gonna be pissed. I was supposed to pick her up at TCJC ten minutes ago."

"She going back to school?"

Hack shrugged and grinned. "Creative writing class at night. Creative art during the day. Last semester it was creative decorating. Since she's gotten rid of her migraine headaches she's a bundle of dynamite looking for a place to explode."

"Glad to hear it, Hack."

"I don't know," he said, his face sobering. He picked up the manila folder and crossed to the door. He stood there a moment, then turned abruptly and came back, his dark eyes glittering, his face set and cold.

"What I think, Ham," he said quietly, "I think she's fucking around on me." He stared hard into Pope's eyes, then wheeled and stalked out of the room before the stocky detective could think of anything to say.

Wendy wasn't at the appointed place when Hack Wind arrived at Tarrant County Junior College. He sat waiting for a few minutes, then got out of his pickup and went inside to the information desk. A young blond girl coyly directed him to a two-story building on the other side of the campus. He found the room and listened outside the door long enough to determine that the knowledge being dispensed inside the room now concerned mathematics.

She's pissed, he told himself as he walked back to his pickup. *She's pissed because I was late, and somebody offered her a ride home and she took it. Yeah, that's it. She's probably at home getting more pissed by the minute, and if I don't get my ass home, she's gonna be* really *pissed*.

He chuckled hollowly. He lit a cigarette and started the pickup. He picked up Longworth Avenue and drove west toward their small frame cottage just outside the Merriweather city limits.

Yeah, that's what happened, he told himself again. *She found a ride home.* He drove mechanically, his mind refusing to consider any other possibility. He turned on the radio, found nothing but whining country and raucous rock and turned it off again. He drummed on the wheel and fumed at the late-afternoon traffic. He cursed and yelled futilely at the rear end of an eighteen-wheeler that blocked his view and his passage and belched black smoke into his window. He drove recklessly and not well, spurred by an inexplicable sense of urgency. He pulled into his driveway with a feeling of relief that lasted only as long as it took him to drive the fifty yards to their door.

Wendy wasn't there, either.

CHAPTER

THREE

Pope heard it on the five o'clock news, on a Dallas station that gave it only a sentence or two. Another slashed throat. This time in Fort Worth. He switched quickly to Channel 5 and heard it again in a little more detail.

A derelict named Clarence Switzer, nicknamed Sonny. A panhandler on North Main, a well-known sight to the habitués of the porn bookstores, bars, and pay-as-you-go hotels.

A shot of a blanket-shrouded gurney and an ambulance, a few cynical words from a red-faced detective named Mobley, and the news dashed on to more relevant matters.

Pope watched the rest of the broadcast with growing disgust: the facile tirade of the OMB director remonstrating with an obdurate Congress because they couldn't understand the necessity for poverty, unemployment, continence, and disease in dealing with the nation's democratically induced ills—giving the impression that he no more believed what he was saying than men on the dais above him did. One bright spot. The weather was going to be good.

Pope switched off the set and heated a Hungry Man meat-and-potatoes TV dinner. While he fiddled with the hot aluminum wrapping he pondered the fact of the third cutthroat murder in little more than a week. Ten days at the outside. Three murders. All within the loosely defined confines of what the city fathers delighted in calling the Metroplex. If the Fort Worth killing matched the M.O. of the first two, then the outer perimeters of credible coincidence were rapidly being reached—had already *been* reached, as far as he was concerned.

He attacked the thin, stringy beef and mushy potatoes, wolfed down large chunks of dry shepherd's bread, and made the whole mess barely palatable by chasing it with milk. He threw the half-empty aluminum plate into the trash and washed his knife and fork and glass. Dinner was over. He went back into the small living room and read the paper until the six o'clock news came on. Nothing new. A rehash of the five o'clock broadcast. He almost fell asleep during the Secretary of Defense's low-key speech on aid to foreign countries and was debating the merits of a rerun versus something called *Entertainment* when the front doorbell sounded. He closed the *TV Guide* and wondered if he possibly could have forgotten a date with Milly. Often as not on their infrequent dates, she picked him up in her car and paid for dinner. A fierce advocate of women's rights, she considered herself his equal at work and in the bedroom and saw nothing wrong with paying her share of their relationship's expenses. He disliked the idea intensely, but since dinner and a couple of drinks invariably led to the bedroom, he had learned to keep his mouth shut about it. But that didn't keep him from feeling guilty, the way he felt guilty now as he padded to the door in his bare feet. *Jesus,* he thought, *I should have been a Jew—me and my guilt.*

He put on an ingratiating smile and swung open the door.

"Hi," she said, bright blue eyes gleaming at him from under lids narrowed in coquettish apprehension, blond hair tumbling around her pale face the way it had tumbled the very first time she stood there. She was wearing a navy-blue blazer with powder-blue slacks and a white blouse. A thin pink ribbon encircled her short sturdy neck, and lipstick to match had been applied sparingly to full pouting lips that were trying valiantly to smile. No effort had been made to hide her smattering of freckles, and they stood starkly against her unnaturally pale skin.

She wet her lips. "Well . . . are we going to stand here and look at each other, go inside and talk like grown-up adult people, or . . . or do I just get back on my horse and ride away and leave you alone?" Meant to be light and humorous, the words dragged painfully.

"No—I mean . . . yes, come in, Nancy." He moved back a pace, his expressionless face betraying none of the turmoil inside him.

She stepped inside the door, then noticed his bare feet. She tilted her head and smiled. "Unless you're expecting someone . . ." She let it fade away.

"No." He shook his head in definite denial. "No, I wasn't expecting anyone." He paused. "Least of all you."

She flashed a quick smile and ducked her head in understanding. She closed the door and walked past him into the living room. He watched the gentle sway of her shapely body, caught the clean, natural smell of her, and felt his body begin to betray him, a fierce, unwanted desire rising, heat and tumescence and a hollowness in his chest.

"Sit down, Nancy. Can I get you something to drink?" He managed a cool, courteous tone.

She dropped onto the edge of his battered leather couch.

"No thank you, Ham." She folded her plump hands in her lap and looked everywhere in the room except at him.

He sat down in the recliner across from her and let the silence grow as he busied himself with lighting a cigarette, making sure it was drawing well, and with replacing his lighter and cigarettes in his shirt pocket. He looked up to find a round face slowly coloring, downcast eyes absorbed in the intricate webbing of lines in the palm of her hand.

"What do you want with me, Nancy?"

She shook her head without looking up. "I—I'm not . . . I don't know for sure, Ham. I felt . . . I just felt the need to see you again."

"Does it have anything to do with Clinton Fielder's murder?"

She looked up, startled. "No! No, not at all. No, it was more . . . more of a personal thing."

"I see. All of a sudden you just had a compelling need to see old Ham."

She nodded abruptly, her face fully flushed. "Something . . . like that."

"After all this time."

"Yes." Her hands were battling it out in her lap.

"What were you doing at Fielder's, Nancy?"

She closed her eyes, her face beginning to pale again. "Ham, don't be a cop with me . . . please. I—I'm sure you know what I was doing there."

"What happened to your husband? The one who owned you body and soul? Did he run out on you again?" He fought to keep bitterness out of his voice and failed miserably.

She seemed to sway, opened her eyes. "Yes." Her voice was barely above a whisper.

"And you went to Fielder," he said harshly, accusingly.

"I met him," she said. "I was . . . low. I needed someone . . . I was ashamed to come to you."

"But you're not now."

"Yes—yes, I am." Her chin tilted, a brief flash of defiance igniting in her eyes, sparking blue fire. "But not for the reasons you think."

He mustered a sardonic laugh.

She looked at him steadily, her pouty lips pulled into a firm line. "I'm not ashamed of giving my marriage a second chance, Ham. And I'm not ashamed of having—well, not much ashamed of having—an affair with Clint Fielder. He was a very nice man and he needed me . . . something more than he was getting at home." Her face softened. "I am ashamed that I hurt you. I really didn't know how . . . deeply you felt. I didn't know until that day at the Hamburger Box . . . honestly. I thought it was just fun and games with you."

He shrugged thick shoulders. "What else?" he said lightly. He stubbed out the cigarette and reached for another, avoiding her eyes.

She smiled. "All right. I'm glad you weren't hurt. That makes it a lot easier to ask a favor."

He shrugged again. "Sure, why not?"

"You'd better wait until I tell you before you say yes." She took a deep breath. "I—I need a place to stay." She blinked slowly, lips parted, her eyes watching his face intently. "Only for a few days," she added hastily. "Until I can—"

He stared at her, stunned. "Stay? I don't understand."

She grimaced wryly. "I lost my job, Ham. The notoriety, I guess. Louie got some calls from indignant housewives."

"You mean, he fired you?"

She nodded. "I haven't found a job yet. Things are

terrible. I have to give up my apartment tomorrow . . . I
wouldn't ask you, Ham, but I don't know who else to turn
to." She swallowed audibly. "And you have that extra
bedroom . . . Oh, hell, this is stupid! I feel like a . . . a
. . . forget it, please, Ham. Dumb idea!" She leapt to her
feet, her face a burning red. "I don't know what got into
me. A little panic, I guess. It's not all that bad, Ham. I
have money. I can get by. Jesus! How dumb can I get?
You must think . . ."

"Are you finished?"

"No—no, really! It's not as bad as I made it sound. I
have money. It's only a matter of time until I find another—"

"Sit down, Nancy," he growled, his eyes squinted to
tiny slits. Without the twinkling blue of his eyes to soften
his square, craggy face, his features were truly formida-
ble, and Nancy sat down abruptly, her eyes wide.

"Hey," she said, "don't look at me like that, Ham.
You know I don't like it when you look like that." Her
voice was plaintive, her tone wheedling.

His lips formed into a grim smile. "You'd better get
used to it if you're going to live here."

Her eyebrows arched. "You mean, you want me to stay?
Really?"

"Yes. In the guest bedroom. I have plenty of room.
Why not?"

"In the guest bedroom?"

"In the guest bedroom," he repeated, suddenly self-
conscious. "Wasn't that what you wanted?"

"Sure. That's what I said, didn't I?"

"That's it, then. No reason we should bother each other
too much. I'm pretty busy, I'll be working a lot. You can
come and go as you please." He stopped. "You never
gave me back the extra key. Do you still have it?"

She nodded, smiling. "Yes, I have it."

"Okay, it's settled, then. Do you need some help with your things?"

"No, I only have my clothes and a few personal things. My apartment's furnished. I can move . . . in tomorrow, if that's all right."

"Tomorrow is fine." He stood up. "I'm going to have a beer. Sure you don't want one?"

She shook her head. "Maybe a sip of yours."

He stopped in the kitchen doorway, her words triggering a flood of memories: another time, the first time she had been there, a sip of his beer had led to unbelievable physical delight and virtual emotional enslavement.

He walked back a few paces with a crooked smile that transformed his stern face into incongruous boyishness.

"No sips, Nancy," he said almost gently. "No touching, no flirting, no accidental meetings in the hall without your clothing. Okay? I'm helping you because . . . you need help. I have other commitments."

"Of course," she said quickly, coolly. "Your girl . . . Milly, isn't it?"

"Yes, that's right. Milly."

She pressed a forefinger against the curl of her lower lip and gave him a quizzical smile. "But won't my being here make things . . . awkward?"

"Let me worry about that. She has her own place. Nicer than mine and a hell of a lot cleaner." He grinned suddenly. "She prefers going there. When we come here, she gets sidetracked into housecleaning."

Nancy's eyes swept around the room: overflowing ashtrays and last Sunday's newspapers on the couch, an empty beer can forgotten beside the recliner, a wrinkled, obviously dirty pair of socks on the fireplace hearth.

She wrinkled her nose and smiled. "I can see why. I'll clean it up for you."

"You don't need to do that."

"Yes, I do," she said pertly, rising to her feet. "If I'm going to be staying here, I do." She softened her critical tone with another smile. "You haven't changed much, Ham."

He shrugged. "Who changes in less than a year?"

She laughed and crossed to the door. "I meant your habits." She fussed with the mass of thick blond hair jumbled around her shoulders, her expression suddenly sober.

"Are you sure about this, Ham?"

"No, I'm not," he admitted. "I'm nervous as hell about it if you want the truth. But we're both adults. I see no reason why it can't work if we both . . ." He let it fade away, uncomfortable under her steady scrutiny.

Her smile was back and mocking. "I won't seduce you, Ham." She moved away, then looked over her shoulder. "But you still have the most beautiful eyes I've ever seen."

He watched her walk to her car, trim and jaunty, incredibly rounded, a perfect, miniature woman who had turned his life topsy-turvy for a time, too short a time, who had enthralled him with her free-spirited naïveté, enslaved him with the velvet fire of her body.

You're a sap, Hamilton Pope, he told himself. *A sucker. A glutton for punishment, a spineless jellyfish . . .* But maybe not. Maybe a conniving lowlife with a subconscious yen for another swipe at the honey pot—a hungry, drooling bear with his snout full of the irresistible aroma of the honey tree. But whatever, altruism or self-interest, acceptance of a possible ulterior motive did little to quell the rapid pounding of his heart.

CHAPTER

FOUR

"I told you, Hack," Wendy said, her plaintive tone diluted by a faint note of exasperation. "I told you about the seminar, honey. You just weren't listening to me—as usual." Tall, willowy, with a lovely heart-shaped face, she had recently changed the color of her hair to blond. Shorter, curly, arranged attractively around her face, the new color enhanced the pale smoothness of her skin, the dark gray sparkle of wide-spaced, steady eyes.

"I don't remember," Hack said. "Where was it?" He poured syrup over his pancakes.

"In Dallas at the Hilton. I told you we were taking our class time at the seminar, that I would probably be late coming home. They had lots of writers speaking. They said—"

"Where did you have the drinks?"

"At the seminar, silly. They had a kind of buffet . . . you know, with cocktails and . . . things."

"You shouldn't be driving when you're half drunk."

"I wasn't anywhere near drunk, Hack! And anyhow, I wasn't—" She broke off, apparently absorbed in buttering a piece of toast, a faint trace of pink creeping slowly up her neck.

Growing exasperation or guilt? he wondered. He cleared his throat of half-swallowed food and took a drink of coffee.

"Wasn't what, Wendy?" he asked.

She raised her head, her eyes defiant. She tossed her head, a holdover habit from when her hair was long. "I wasn't driving. At least from TCJC into Dallas. I—we went with Al Judson."

"Your teacher?"

"Instructor. Yes. He has a van, and several of us rode with him." Her lips drew into a firm line. "What is this, Hack, the third degree?" She managed to inject a thread of humor.

He chewed on his last bite of bacon, then swallowed and smiled. He reached across and took her hand. "Don't you think I'm interested in what my wife does?"

She eyed him dubiously. "No, I didn't. I thought you'd lost interest in my 'selfish improvement,' as you called it."

"I was just teasing, Wendy."

She shook her head. "Uh-uh. Be honest. You were irked because I wasn't at home every night with your dinner ready and waiting, a sweet little apron and a humble, grateful smile for my lord and master—"

"Cut it out," he said mildly. "We thrashed all that out. I'm glad you're interested in improving yourself. You know that." He studied their clasped hands, fascinated as always at the stark contrast between the pale ivory of her skin and the dark mahogany of his own. Fascinated and somehow almost repelled, as if the difference in pigmentation represented a subtle betrayal of something important, of some incomprehensible code of etiquette.

"Do you really, Hack?" Her voice was warm, as was the hand that reached impulsively to join the two clasped on the table. "I wish I could believe that. I'm twenty-six years old. I've been a daughter and a wife. I'm not even a mother. I can't find much purpose in my life."

"Making me happy. Isn't that a worthy cause?"

"It could be. If you were happy. But you aren't, and I don't know anymore how to make it happen."

"You do," he said awkwardly. "Just by being here you make me happy."

She shook her head slowly, her smile wistful. "I wish that was all it took. It would be so simple. But it isn't." She squeezed his hand and sighed. "You're so wrapped up in this black Mexican Indian honkie thing. I think you're beautiful, Hack. I think your skin is the loveliest color I've ever seen. But you're not all white, and you're never going to be all white, and—" She stopped, her face soft, her eyes moist. "And you're never going to get over it, are you?"

He shrugged and squeezed out a lopsided grin. "Maybe next time I'll come back as an albino."

She nodded, her face serious. "But not this time. And this time is what's important. You have the blood of four races in you, and I think you received the best that each had to offer. You're brilliant and witty and incredibly handsome . . . yes, you are! A lot of men would give everything they own to look like you—dark coloring and all. You have lovely eyes and a heartbreaking smile—"

"You keep this up and I'll have to take you back to bed just to prove this is a man you're talking about and not a woman."

She laughed throatily and wiggled her eyebrows. "Oh, you're a man, all right. And I'm the one who knows." She retrieved her hands and began clearing off the table, smiling down at him. "And you, cowboy, had better get on your horse. You're late already."

"Would you like to go back to bed, Wendy?" he asked quietly.

She bent and kissed him, her eyes startled. "Of course I would, darling! But you're late and I have those writing assignments and Carol is coming by for lunch." She ruffled his hair and gave him a Groucho Marx leer. "Tonight, huh, babe?"

"You have class again tonight."

"Oh! Well . . . after class, honey. Okay?"

"Sure, afterward." He got up and picked up his gun belt, hanging on a chair. He buckled it around his slim waist. He put on the tan campaign hat he hated with a passion. "Will midnight be early enough? Do you think you can make it home by then?"

His tone brought her around from the sink. She made a rueful grimace and slipped her arms around his waist. "Come on, honey. Don't be like that. You're acting like a little boy who isn't getting his Twinkie for lunch."

"Maybe that's the way I feel, Wendy," he said glumly. "It's been over a week."

"Has it? Oh, no, not a week already! You poor baby! I'll make it up to you tonight!"

"Thanks," he said dryly, responding automatically to her kiss, feeling a latent stirring of something akin to anger at the unbidden rush of gratitude.

She gave him another quick kiss at the door. "I'll miss you," she murmured.

He drove his pickup around the curving driveway in front of his house, past the cypress and the pines and the lazily whirling Dutch windmill. He lit a cigarette and tried to remember when she had begun substituting "I'll miss you" for "I love you."

• • •

Hamilton Pope was poring over the file of throat-cut victim Clyde Burns when Hackmore Wind stumped into his office. He looked up, irritated, ready to bark, then relaxed and leaned back in his swivel chair and smiled amiably.

"Hello, Hack."

"Hi." Hack Wind's face was somber, the usual sunny smile missing, and Pope decided it was not the right time to bring up the subject he was certain was on both their minds.

"How're things?" Pope asked tentatively.

"Fine, everything's fine." Wind dropped into the visitor's chair and threw his booted feet to a corner of the desk.

Pope cleared his throat. "You almost missed me. I was going out on the Burns case. And something else, I'm meeting Sergeant Globe from Fort Worth for lunch. Want to come?"

Wind frowned. "Sergeant Globe. Don't guess I know him."

"He's working the Switzer killing. You know, the guy they found with his throat cut."

Wind's dark eyes came alive. "I heard that on the news. You think it's another one like ours?"

"Could be, from what I've been able to find out. I thought we could compare notes with Globe, see what we come up with. First thing, though, I want to talk to Mrs. Burns."

Wind nodded. "You bet I'll go."

Pope stood up and picked up the manila folder. "Let's go. You driving your pickup?"

"Sure. Why?"

Pope lit a cigarette and allowed the younger man to precede him out of the office.

"I've got a problem with my Dodge wagon. Can we take yours?"

"Sure," Wind said. "What's wrong with it?"

Pope cut his eyes at the young deputy. "Gas. It's a dollar fifteen a gallon," he said.

It was a small frame house, the kind the realtors call a dollhouse or a honeymoon special. An ill-kept yard and peeling boards, a general air of disrepair, visible proof that the sieve had somehow become clogged on the new trickle-down economy.

She was a tall, spare woman wrapped in a threadbare nylon robe. An angular face and a pointed nose. A small, rounded chin and burning black eyes worthy of a saint. A face that probably had been beautiful once. Before time and life got to it, squeezed its juices and stretched its skin over bones too strong and bold ever to have been delicate.

She offered tea and Pepsi Cola and talked to them in the soft, nasal, mellow tones of North Texas, or possibly Southern Oklahoma.

"We was doing good for once. Clyde—bless his heart—was working two jobs and we was almost out of debt for the first time in . . . Lord, I don't know how long. Except for this house, of course. We still have twenty-five years to pay on it. But we'da made it. We're strong stock. We come through some mighty hard times, me and Clyde and the boys. They're all in school now. Now, I don't know how . . ." Her voice faded and she made a vague gesture, either of resignation or of dismay.

"Mrs. Burns," Pope said gently, "your husband, Clyde, do you know of any enemies he might have had?"

"Good Lord, no. Not Clyde. He was the most gentle man . . . a hard worker. Who would want to hurt Clyde?"

"Someone did, Mrs. Burns," Pope reminded her gently.

She made the vague gesture again, then brought her strong, worn fingers together in her lap.

"It was them thieves. Them thieves that hang out down there on South Wilburn. They're always hangin' around and waiting for honest men to come along with money in their pockets. Clyde had more'n fifty dollars on him that day."

"That's what it looks like, all right," Pope said. "How about relatives in Merriweather, anywhere in the vicinity?"

She looked at him vacantly for a moment. "Clyde's folks, his mama and daddy. They live here in Merriweather. I came from Oklahoma. Clyde was born and raised right here in Merriweather. His daddy and mama are his only kin that I know about."

"How about friends?"

She nodded vehemently. "Clyde had a lot of friends. He's lived here all his life. Everybody liked my—"

"Close friends, Mrs. Burns. Guys he went hunting with, or fishing, or maybe asked over for a beer."

The glow in her eyes dimmed. "He didn't do any of them things. We couldn't afford it."

Hack Wind cleared his throat and shifted in the soft, prickly confines of an overstuffed chair. "Someone he was especially friendly with, ma'am. Maybe a guy he worked with."

She nodded slowly. "Preston Small. I guess he was Clyde's best friend. They played pool sometimes together. He works out at the machine shop where Clyde worked."

"Does he live in Merriweather?"

"Yes. I can give you his address. We always sent him a Christmas card."

"We'd appreciate that."

She nodded vaguely, then seemed to shake herself. She

got up, clutching the old robe together in front, and went to the center drawer of a child's desk crowded into one corner of the small room. She came back with a tattered imitation-leather-bound notebook. She thumbed through it silently, lips moving as she read the names.

"Here it is," she said finally. "Under S. P. Small. The P stands for Preston. Preston Small. He lives at 903 Arrow Lane, here in Merriweather." She ran rough fingers across the book's binding. "Clyde kept everything wrote down in his book. He was a cautious, careful man. Like a woman in some ways." She looked up then, a ghost of a smile. "Not like a woman in the ways that counted. He fathered me six boys in ten years. I married him right out of high school. I'm only thirty-three years old. I got me six boys to raise. The youngest boy just started school this year. I wonder how in the world I'm going to do that." It was a rhetorical question but one she had obviously been asking herself ever since her husband's death. "Take them back home, I reckon." Her eyes were squinted, as if she could see the boundaries of her past, her homeland, and was wondering if there would be room for seven more.

Pope stood up and fished something out of his jacket pocket. He crossed to her.

"Do you recognize this, Mrs. Burns?"

She took the small glassine envelope and held it to the light from the window. Her face lit up. "Oh, yes. Clyde's knife. His new knife he was so proud of. I was wondering if the thieves got it." She turned it over and over in thin fingers, her face soft, her eyes moist. "See. It even had his own initials on it. That was lucky."

"Lucky?" Pope took the envelope from her reluctant fingers and returned to his seat.

Her head bobbed eagerly. "Yes. Clyde got it swapping. Clyde was the sharpest swapper. Everybody said that."

Her head lifted, her face beaming. "There was this one time. We lived in Tennessee then. He worked for the Tennessee Valley Authority. We lived outside a small town called Big Sandy. Clyde went into town one Saturday morning with three dollars and an old Barlow pocketknife in his jeans." She stopped and made a muted chuckling sound. "He came home about dark, leading this old milk cow. And my, my—did we need it. We already had three babies, and our milk bill was something fierce." She clasped her arms beneath her breasts and rocked, smiling at the memory. "He said he'd swapped all day, finally ended up with that cow. She was worth at least a hundred dollars. Nobody could beat my Clyde at swapping."

"And he swapped for the knife?"

"Yes. At where he works . . . worked. The B & K Machine Shop. Swapped it off a man named Charles Bottomley. That's how come the initials match." The smile was back. "He traded him a chipped bowling ball somebody gave him and an old .22 pistol with a barrel so crooked, you couldn't hit the ground with it."

"He sounds like a sharp dealer, all right," Hack said, smiling.

Pope coughed and moved to the door. "If you need help—financial help, Mrs. Burns—I can see that someone comes out."

"Thank you, Mr. Pope, I believe we can manage."

Hack Wind stood over her. He took one of her hands in his. He smiled his most charming smile, and a light seemed to flare briefly in her dark eyes.

"Thank you very much, ma'am. We're very sorry about what happened."

"Why . . . thank you, Mr. Wind." Her free hand fluttered near her unkempt hair, came back to her throat, and plucked nervously at the frayed edging on the robe.

"That's very sweet of you." Her burning eyes rose slowly, met his in a look as old as man himself.

Hack Wind straightened abruptly, then bent again and laid her hand gently in her lap.

"Good luck, Mrs. Burns." He backed toward Pope.

"Take care, Mr. Wind," she said, her voice following them through the door, as warm and vital as August rain on sun-baked earth.

Pope lit a cigarette and chuckled. He watched his companion's nonplussed expression as he fumbled the key into the ignition.

"Still got it for the ladies, I see."

Wind scowled at him. "I don't know what you mean."

Pope snorted. He puffed on the cigarette, a bubble of mirth rumbling in his chest. "One more of your high-voltage smiles and the bereaved widow would have been climbing your frame."

"Dammit, Ham! I wasn't trying to come on to her. I was just being friendly."

Pope nodded and stared at the passing cars. "Yeah, I know." He grinned and shook his head.

"To have it and know it and not use it is one thing. But to have it and not know it"—he sighed—"man, that's something else."

CHAPTER

FIVE

Hack Wind located Wendy's Plymouth by driving up and down the rows of parked cars in the lot nearest the building where the creative writing class was being held. He spotted the high-visibility yellow Snoopy aerial topper and pulled into an empty space from which he could see both the small car and the classroom entrance. He checked his watch: nine twenty-five. Much too early, but he had found it impossible to sit in the empty house alone with his suspicions. He lit a cigarette and settled down to wait for ten o'clock.

Five minutes later he stiffened and sat upright as the double glass doors of the building began spewing people. Nine-thirty. Too early to be Wendy's class. He watched, puzzled. The classroom was right, he could see the open door through the glass entrance, and unless they had changed classrooms . . .

He stepped out of the pickup and crossed between the next row of cars to intercept a trio of middle-aged women students.

"Excuse me, ladies. Is this the creative writing class?"

"Yes," they chorused.

"Al Judson's class?"

"Yes, it is." One of the women, slightly younger than the others, a brassy redhead with bold eyes and a clipped New Jersey accent, smiled coquettishly. "Did you lose someone?"

Hack smiled ruefully, his eyes searching the thinning crowd for Wendy. "I seem to be confused. I thought this class let out at ten."

"Oh, no," the redhead said quickly. "We go from six-thirty to nine-thirty."

"Oh, I see," Hack said casually. "You've changed your hours."

The three heads wagged negatively. "No," said the redhead. "We've always gone from six-thirty to nine-thirty. Some of the night classes are seven to ten, though."

"And this is Al Judson's class?"

Heads nodded, and the redhead volunteered, "But he wasn't here tonight. We had a substitute teacher."

Hack nodded and smiled, his fingers touching the brim of his hat. "Thank you, ladies," he said mechanically.

"You're very welcome, Officer," the redhead said warmly.

The van pulled up at five minutes after ten. It sat beside her car for less than a minute, the interior banked in shadow. Then Wendy leapt lightly to the pavement and into her Plymouth. Seconds later it roared away. The van drove off slowly.

Hack Wind followed the van.

A big Ford with large rear windows, draped; wild, psychedelic colors; and double-whip antennas. Hack could imagine the interior: plush carpets and padded walls, brittle flashy metal trim, a stereo, and, without a doubt, a dinette that would make into a bed.

He followed only long enough to get the license number, then swung out and around the leisurely paced van and caught a glimpse of long blond hair and a beard, a flowing mustache under a prominent nose. Hairy white fingers drummed on the steering wheel in tempo with a Barry Manilow tune blasting from the stereo.

Hack turned off at the next corner. He eased into the curb and shut off the motor. He sat for a long time, breathing hard, hands clawed around the wheel, knuckles shining in the dim light like smooth, dark stones.

She was freshly bathed and securely belted into the robe he had bought her for Christmas when he got home. He went in the back way, put the six-pack of beer into the refrigerator, hung his hat and gun in their accustomed places, then ran his hands through his bushy thatch of hair and went into the living room.

She looked up from the evening paper, smiling. "Hi, honey. Where in the world have you been at this time of night?"

He shrugged listlessly and dropped into the rocker-recliner across from her. "Got called out on the Fielder thing." He yawned. "Bum lead. Didn't pan out."

She put down the paper and came over to him. She sat on the arm of the chair and brushed back his tangled hair. "Poor baby. They work you too hard. They expect too much." She kissed him on the forehead, patted his arm, and went back to the couch.

He yawned again. "How was your night?"

She shrugged slim shoulders and turned the page. "Same old thing. Boring lecture."

"If it's so boring, why go?"

"It's not *all* boring. We're going through some dry technical stuff right now. I really enjoy the writing assignments, the little stories he makes us write." She lifted her head, her eyes sparkling. "He always reads one of mine aloud in class."

"Hey, that's great. You must be getting good, huh? I'll have to read some of them."

"Oh, it's really pretty silly stuff if you aren't involved. Descriptions of objects, people, things like that. Little short stories."

"This guy Judson a good teacher?"

She nodded indifferently. "So-so. He's a published writer, of course. Five novels and a lot of short stories, articles, like that. I guess you could say he's good. He's pretty interesting." She flipped rapidly through the newspaper, tossed it aside, and smothered a yawn. "Boy, I'm pooped. It's been a long day."

"Yes, it has," Hack said.

She rose and crossed to him again. She leaned down and kissed him. "I'm going to bed, hon." She hesitated. "If you want a little, you'd better hurry . . . or are you too tired?" She smiled and stroked his cheek.

He returned her smile. "I guess not, Wendy. I am pretty tired."

Her smile became sympathetic. "Poor baby." She kissed his cheek and moved away. "Good night, hon, I'll see you in the morning. Sleep good."

"Sure—you, too, babe."

He was totally immersed in the dream. A gift of his mind. Recompense for what he stubbornly refused to allow in the living world. A part of him watched distractedly, a small part that had to do with ego and pride, a part that was gradually diminishing as his senses became more and more attuned to the importunate demands of the wanton seductress who shared the dream with him.

Sweet, melting lips and clinging arms; a pliant, burning body, and magic sounds of entreaty, supplication, and eager submissiveness—he found himself drawn inexorably into the fire of her secret flesh, submerged in her sexuality, overwhelmed by her frantic need. . . .

The phone rang.

He sat upright, his mind reeling, disoriented, the edges of the dream fragmenting, fading.

The phone rang again.

The phone rang a third time. He yanked up the receiver, dimly aware of the gray light of dawn through the draperies.

"Hello, dammit!"

"Ham?" Milly Singer's voice, hesitant, faintly amused. "Sorry to break into your dreams, Ham, but we have another one."

How did she know? he wondered groggily.

"Another one?" he asked stupidly. "What do you mean, another one?"

"Another one like Clyde Burns. *Just* like Clyde Burns."

"Where . . . just a moment, let me get something to write on." Grimacing, he swung his feet to the floor and rummaged in the nightstand drawer. "Okay. Shoot."

"We're at 111 Gramercy Place, Apartment 4B. The new apartment . . ."

"I know where it is."

"Twenty minutes?"

"I—uh—maybe you'd better make it thirty. I—uh—have to get some gas."

"Okay, chief, thirty minutes."

• • •

He made it in twenty-eight, his black hair still wet around the edges from his shower. He pulled in behind a patrol car double-parked in front of the five-story brick apartment building. A small crowd had gathered, and two men in white uniforms stood smoking beside an ambulance. One of them, a beefy young man with sideburns to his jawline and a fiery red thatch of hair, watched Pope get out of his car, scowling truculently.

"Hey, man, are you this guy Pope everybody's waiting on?"

"My name is Pope, yes."

"They call us out here, and now that broad upstairs won't release the stiff."

Pope came to an abrupt halt, his eyes narrowing. "That what?" The twinkle was gone, a tiny slice of menacing blue all that remained.

The young man took a step backward. "That—uh—that lady detective up there. She—"

Pope nodded. "I'll let you know when the lady's ready to release the deceased, friend. Until then you just hang around and be nice and try not to let the citizens see you playing with yourself." He turned on his heel and went up the steps and into the building.

Milly was in the hallway outside Apartment 4B. She was talking to a somber young patrolman who watched her with avid eyes, one hand perched on the butt of his gun as if he expected to be called upon at any moment to defend her life. Approaching, Pope wondered briefly if the young cop's eager interest might not be directed more at Milly than at the crime she was obviously detailing. Vivid and vibrant at thirty-two, she had a lovely appealing smile, warm hazel eyes, and a compact, shapely body now that she had lost fifteen pounds and kept what was left firmed up with two nights a week at the Aerobic Shop.

She looked up and saw Pope coming, and her solemn face brightened as if by magic.

"Hi, Milly." He ran his hand over the wet edges of his hair and hoped she wouldn't notice. "What do we have?"

She nodded and smiled faintly. "Male Caucasian, name Jesse Bond, married but possibly divorced since he evidently lived alone. Age thirty-three, a loner according to the manager. No women that she's ever seen, ditto friends. Occupation . . ." She paused and brought back the faint smile. "Thief."

"Thief?"

"This is a two-bedroom apartment. The spare bedroom looks like a pawnshop. I'll bet we'll be able to clear up at least two dozen burglaries with what's in there, unless he's been operating in some other city."

Pope stared at her thoughtfully, his lips pursed. "And he was killed just like Clyde Burns?"

She nodded and turned. "Come see. I wouldn't let them move the body until you came. They're all finished, except Ainsley from fingerprints. The M.E. gave his usual educated guess. Midnight last night, give or take two hours. Film at eleven."

Pope nodded and followed her into the bedroom.

The body seemed to leap out at him: starkly nude. Sprawled on its back across the bed, arms and almost severed head dangling off the edge. A nearly perfect circle of blood gleamed darkly red beneath lank brown hair that had been matted into ropes by the seeping, sticky fluid. Pope walked around the bed and stared down at the gaping wound, the now familiar edges of white cartilage and raw, red muscle.

"No signs of a struggle," Milly commented from near the doorway.

"How about sexual activity? Did Paris check for that?"

"If he did, he didn't say, Ham." Her eyebrows lifted quizzically. "Are you thinking homosexual?"

"May be. He's naked, and by the looks of it, he got that way himself. I don't see any clothing. Was there any?"

Milly shook her head. "It was just the way you see it, Ham."

"No robe, no pajamas, no damn nothing. A man don't lay around naked for no reason."

The ghostly smile came back to Milly's face. "Some men do, Ham. Maybe he was into TM or yoga. They do some weird things."

Pope walked back around the bed and viewed the corpse from another angle. "It don't make any damned sense, Milly. The bedspread ain't even ruffled up. It looks like he just stretched out across the bed and let someone slit his damned throat. Without a struggle. No blood anywhere but that pool under his head and just that little splash on the bedspread. That coulda happened when the guy slashed him. Jesus Christ! You sure there ain't a razor under that blood on the bed? Looks more like a suicide than a murder."

"There's nothing, Ham. We've gone over it with a vacuum. I thought of that myself, but Dr. Paris said he didn't believe anyone could make that kind of cut on himself. It's too deep and clean and thorough. He certainly couldn't have disposed of the instrument."

Pope went back to the head again, squatted, and studied it intently. Finally he shook his head and stood up.

"It's like Burns, all right. Nothing holding it but the bone and a little skin and muscle. He glanced at Milly. "Just like Fielder and Switzer."

Milly's eyes widened. "Four? You think we have another mass murderer, Ham?"

Pope barked a laugh. "If four is a mass we do." He

watched her, a faintly wolfish grin on his square face. "Does four constitute a mass, Milly?"

Her lips tightened. "It's a good start," she said tersely.

Pope grunted and turned away. "Let's take a look at that other bedroom."

CHAPTER
SIX

Big flat feet slapped resoundingly on the tiled corridor; Hamilton Pope looked up from his desk at Hack Wind, slouched morosely in his visitor's chair.

"Here comes the big fella," Pope said, smiling a little at the thought of his superior's expected agitation. He leaned back in his chair and locked his hands behind his head and waited.

"Ham, dammit!" Roscoe Tanner loomed in the doorway. "What's this—hello, Hack—what's this shit you're giving me?" He slapped the four manila folders on Pope's desktop and towered over him, glowering.

"What kinda shit does it look like, Roscoe?" Pope asked mildly.

"Man, are you trying to tell me we got another asshole psycho on our hands?"

"No, I'm not trying to tell you that. All I'm telling you is that we've got some asshole in the area slicing throats. Whether he's a psycho asshole is an entirely different matter."

"A mass killer, then?"

"I'll ask you what I asked Milly. Does four constitute a mass?"

"It does in my book," Hack said. He got up and rolled the chair toward Tanner. "Sit down, Captain."

"Thanks, Hack," Tanner said gratefully. He lowered himself into the chair. "Okay, I want to know exactly what we have here, Ham."

Pope picked up the folders. "Didn't you read these?"

"Hell yes, I read them. Most of it, anyway . . . well, I read your report. That was enough. Too damn much. Man, we've had that mass killing shit. I don't want no more of it."

"Why don't you take out an ad in the paper, Roscoe. Tell him, don't tell me."

"All right now," Tanner said soothingly, "ain't no use in us getting edgy with each other."

Pope looked at him curiously. "I'm not edgy. Are you?"

"Hell yes, I'm edgy!" He looked from Pope to Hack Wind. "You know what's gonna happen," he said ominously. "The goddamn media's gonna pick up on this thing. They're gonna go wild just like they done before, and my ass is gonna be mud around here. His honor the fucking mayor and—" He broke off at the disgusted look on Pope's face. "Well, it's the damn truth and you know it."

"You want to trade places, Roscoe? You want to get out and slog through the shit and let me play administrator? I'll be glad to handle the media. Come on, Roscoe, let's trade."

"Hell, no," Tanner said, grinning. "I put in my time. It's up to you young bucks now."

Pope snorted. "Young, my ass. You're only four or five years—"

Tanner spread his hands and made shushing motions.

"Okay, okay. Now that we got all the hot air out of the way, what have you guys got? Anything?"

Pope looked at Hack and threw up his arms. "I wonder why we bother making reports? Nobody reads the damn things. If they do, they evidently don't understand English."

"I read it kinda in a hurry. Why don't you just tell me?" Tanner's tone was wheedling, but he was watching the stocky detective intently, his gray eyes curious. "What's wrong with you lately? You been acting like a she-wolf with six pups and only one tit." He cocked his head, his eyes becoming shrewd. "I know what it is. You ain't been getting enough lately."

Pope glared at him, his eyes snapping to narrow slits.

Tanner flinched and raised his platter-sized hands in front of his face. He glanced at Hack Wind and grinned.

"By God, I think I've got it."

"Kiss it, Roscoe, just kiss it." Pope took out a cigarette and tapped the filter tip on his desk. He lit up and picked up the folders, his face suddenly expressionless.

"They have a couple of things in common: they all had their throats cut with the same type of instrument. I say 'instrument,' because we don't know yet what it is. Our best guess would be a utility knife. A very sharp utility knife. Another thing: They're all approximately the same age. Within a few months of each other. That may or may not mean anything. We're checking backgrounds to see if there's a link. Whatever their backgrounds or pasts, they are all very different now, or were at the time of their deaths. Clinton Fielder was a successful businessman, very wealthy. Clyde Burns was on the other end of the stick. He had to work two jobs to make it from payday to payday. Clarence Switzer was a down-and-out derelict, a panhandler, well on his way to being a wino. And Jesse Bond.

He was a criminal, a burglar. He had six arrests and two convictions. He served a total of four years behind bars. Two divorces, two kids by his first wife, who now resides in California." He stubbed out his cigarette and looked from Tanner to Hack, who was doodling on a pad.

"Physical evidence. Zilch. Nobody's come up with anything. Our man is very careful. No prints, no hairs, no dirt from his garden on his shoes. And nobody saw or heard anything. Not only is our man the neatest asshole in the country, he's invisible and soundless too."

"Thank God only two of them are in Merriweather," Tanner said fervently.

"A small favor. Two are bad enough when you've got zilch."

"And maybe there'll be more," Hack said, his eyes intent on the pad in his hand.

Tanner's eyes rolled toward the ceiling. "Heaven forbid."

Hack cleared his throat and regarded Pope, an odd look on his handsome face.

"What is it?"

Hack shook his head. "Nothing. Not anything really."

"Come on, Hack, we're not so rich in ideas we can afford to discard one, no matter how farfetched."

Hack shook his head again. He tore off the page and tossed the pad back on Pope's desk. He crumpled the page and put it into his pocket. "Nothing, Ham, just doodling."

"How about your big three: friends, relatives, and lovers? Anything turn up there?" Tanner leaned back, crossed his tree-trunk legs, and began unwrapping a cigar.

"We're still working the Bond list. Nothing on Burns to speak of. Outside of his family, he was pretty much a cipher. Only one friend and he's clean. No lovers that we could find, but a guy like that couldn't afford a lover, prices being what they are today. Bond could be a different story. He was something of a chaser, liked to tipple a bit. We'll see what develops.'' He glanced at Hack. ''Anything turn up on Fielder at all?'' He knew the answer, but it was Hack's case.

Hack shook his head. ''No . . . just the one . . . lady.'' He looked slightly bewildered.

Pope nodded. ''Globe drew a big fat zero on Switzer. How many derelicts have lovers or friends? Relatives? He's hasn't located any of those, either.''

Tanner's shoes slapped the tile floor. He pushed himself to his feet, grunting. ''Well, it's in capable hands. I'll leave it with you boys.'' He came around the desk and squeezed Pope's shoulder until he winced.

''Get laid, buddy,'' he said seriously. He turned without another word and clumped out.

Hack laughed. ''Son of a bitch! I can't help but like him.''

''He's a likable feller,'' Pope said sourly. ''He gives good advice, though.''

''Yeah,'' Hack said, his face suddenly somber, his dark eyes staring into nothing.

Pope picked up the folders and stacked them on edge. He put them down and picked them up again, his eyes on his companion. He slapped them down a second time and lit a cigarette. He cleared his throat and tapped a letter opener on the edge of his desk. He leaned back in his chair, then came forward with a clunk. He cleared his throat again.

''Okay. You brought this up, and if you don't want to talk about it, tell me. But . . . have you talked it out with her? Are you sure, Hack?''

The younger man inclined his head slowly, his breath

hissing between his teeth in a long sigh. "I'm sure—pretty damn sure, Ham."

"But you haven't talked about it?"

Hack stared at him, aghast. "Talked about it? Hell, no! I can't talk to her about it. If I do that, she'll know I know. If she knows I know, then I'll have to . . . do something . . . leave her . . . something!"

"You're not thinking straight, boy," Pope said gently. "It's not written down anywhere that you'd have to do anything. Sure you can talk about it. You're not even sure she is fuc—doing whatever you think she'd doing. The thing to do . . ."

Hack was shaking his head doggedly. "She'd think I was some kind of sniveling coward . . . some kind of weak jerk-off if I let her get away with it. I can't discuss it with her, Ham!"

"That's a lot of macho bullshit! If you were screwing around, you'd expect her to at least talk to you about it. A little talk, Hack. A little talk never hurt anyone."

"Man, I can't do that. Jesus! I don't want her to know I know. But . . . but I can't just go on living with her . . . I can't do that, either, man!"

Pope rocked back in his chair, the anguish on the younger man's face stroking a chord somewhere deep inside him. He could feel the deputy's pain across the space between them, a dry, tingling chill. He flinched and grew silent under a flood of memories. Another time and another place. The pain had been just as real, the anguish his own.

He examined the blunt ends of his fingertips and let the silence build around them. Not once but twice it had happened to him. He had loved and lost. And nobody had proved it was better than never having loved at all. Not to him, not to his satisfaction. It had been pure, unadulterated hell, and how could you miss something if you'd never had it?

"Talk it out, Hack. I couldn't talk and I lost. I lost both times because my pride or my ego or my some-damn-thing wouldn't let me ask why. Why. One simple damn little word. All I wanted to know was when and how many times. And the biggest question I wanted to ask and wouldn't let myself was if he was better than me. Macho bullshit, buddy. We strut around and flex our muscles and make manly noises, but we're still kids underneath. And kids can be the cruelest kind of people, man. Our bodies grow, and maybe our minds, and we get this adult outlook and polish and even a little sophistication. But something happens and we're right back to kids again, jealous, possessive, bullheaded . . . it's like we haven't learned a damn thing. And maybe we haven't. We want to own the people we love but we want to stay free. The first thing we learn as kids is to take, and for the rest of our lives we try to unlearn it. If we ever do. But maybe that was nature's plan. Procreation is nature's thing, and taking is a good part of that. If she hadn't made it so damn good and so available, none of us would be here. We get this fix at about eleven or twelve or thirteen, this fix on that thing between our legs, and our lives revolve around it as long as we're around. Freud had it right, man. Sex makes it go around and up and down and sideways. A lot of us admit that and go after it like they were going to quit making it tomorrow. But some of us, the frugal ones, we hoard it, cherish it, even try to store it up—and then we're surprised and shocked when some poor sap comes along and tries to—" He broke off and leaned back, a rueful look on his face. "I think I forgot my point."

Hack folded his arms across his chest, a faint, quizzical

smile on his lips. "I don't know, but would you repeat it? I didn't get it all down."

Pope laughed and reached for another cigarette, pleased to see that some of the pain had gone out of the handsome face, the haunted look out of the dark eyes.

"I talk too much," he said mildly. "On some subjects I can't find a stopping place."

Hack pushed to his feet. He ambled to the doorway, one balled fist slapping against the palm of his other hand.

"I'll see you in the morning, okay?"

"Sure," Pope said, wondering if he should push a little more, deciding against it.

Hack walked out into the corridor, then turned and looked back. "Thanks, Ham."

Pope spread his hands in a self-deprecating gesture. "For what?"

Hack smiled and shrugged and walked off down the corridor.

Pope listened until his footsteps faded, staring fitfully at the empty doorway. Then he sighed and leaned back in his chair and wondered what he would do in the young deputy's shoes.

No question, he told himself dryly. *You'd do exactly what you did with Alice. You'd force the issue, call for a showdown, and lose her. Hard heads never change, they just get older and harder.* Nancy Lessor was ample proof of that. Two nights of jangled nerves and thrumming tension and his core of resolve was still alive and well, sustaining him, but just barely, in constant vigilance against her artless war of emotional attrition, the ever-present danger of total, abject surrender. Two nights of fitful slumber: a gnawing discontent that he refused to recognize for what it was. For what Roscoe Tanner had so aptly said it was: He wasn't getting laid enough.

He grunted with disdain. He stood up and paced around the office. He came back and sat down and mashed out his cigarette. He rummaged in the center drawer and found a pencil. He reached across and dragged Hack's doodling pad toward him. He began brushing the pencil lead back and forth across the paper.

Circles and swirls and angles, a recognizable cat with a pointed tail: a five-pointed star, a crude hexagon, and, on the bottom portion of the sheet, a series of names.

Clinton Fielder	—rich
Clyde Burns	—poor
Clarence Switzer	—beggar
Jesse Bond	—thief

And then below:

Rich man, poor man, beggarman, thief?

A grin spread across Pope's face, escalated into a chuckle, became a laugh. He threw back his head and roared, his laughter filling the small room, spilling out into the corridor, causing a passing patrolman to stop and stare at him in astonishment, shake his head, and walk away smiling.

CHAPTER
SEVEN

She had everything ready when he got home. Everything except the spareribs marinating in a pan awaiting the white-hot charcoal in the brazier on the patio. His favorite meal: barbecued spareribs, potato salad, and no-sex-tonight green onions. The spareribs had been precooked in the pressure cooker for ten minutes, removing excess fat and tenderizing the meat, and fifteen minutes over the coals was more than enough to allow for browning and to absorb the tantalizing flavor of the sauce.

She was witty and gay, popping a pan of his favorite rolls into the oven, bringing him a beer, staying to chatter aimlessly while he watched the meat, dodging the swirling smoke with her usual joke about smoke following beauty. Nervous talk: a lot of movement and quick-flashing smiles, bright glances that bounced off his cheekbones, forehead, chin.

He answered in monosyllables, smiling mechanically at appropriate places, making chuckling sounds when the small silences became awkward. She asked him about his day and he briefly considered telling her his theory about the slasher murders, then decided against it when she immediately launched into a spirited discourse regarding a brilliant discussion in class the night before by the erudite Al Judson.

Listening to her glib fabrications, blatant lying, his last faint hope that he was wrong began to wither and die. He felt a listless kind of helpless rage, a smoldering anger that warred with the desperate need not to lose her. His reaction filled him with dismay, and deep down, around the edge of his consciousness, he felt a stirring of self-disgust.

"Meat's ready," he said harshly, catching her quick look and covering immediately by coughing and waving a hand at the swirling smoke. "This stuff'll kill you," he muttered.

She laughed and turned toward the door. "Everything else is ready. Mmm, the ribs smell delicious, Hack." She wiggled her eyebrows and smacked her lips.

He watched her cross the patio, slim and lithe and full-breasted, ivory skin faintly flushed from the stress of her perfidy, eyes moist from the smoke and sparkling, heartbreakingly lovely, the last rays of the sun burnishing her honey hair with gold.

And he felt the impotent rage wash out of him, his mind darken with the black misery of sorrow. His soul shrank from the inevitable, and his brain searched frantically for reasons, excuses, for some way he could forgive her.

"Ham, I can't possibly eat all of this." Nancy surveyed the plate of pork chow mein and grimaced. "Why did you get so much?"

"I like Chinese food," he said complacently. "And besides, you don't have to eat it all."

She picked up her fork and pierced a morsel of pork.

"Yes, I do," she said glumly. "I have this obsession. I have to clean up my plate. We didn't have food to waste in my family. My daddy's cardinal rule was take all you want but eat all you take. If I leave anything, I feel guilty."

"We had the same rule in basic training, but it never left me with any kind of guilt complex."

She giggled around a forkful of noodles. "I would think by then you had all your basic quirks in place and working."

He shook his head. "Not me. I was a very uncomplicated guy—still am, as a matter of fact."

She looked up from her plate, her eyebrows arched. "Uh-huh, I've noticed. About as uncomplicated as an idiot savant." She cocked her head and wrinkled her nose.

"How so?"

She shook her head quickly. "No, I don't want to make you mad."

"Bad as all that, huh?"

"No, it's not bad. I simply don't understand you, is all."

"What don't you understand?"

"Well . . ." She hesitated, the line of freckles across her nose slowly fading as color moved higher in her cheeks. "Well, I just don't see why you don't want to . . . to make love to me anymore."

He laughed, surprised that he could, more surprised that it sounded genuine. "What makes you think I don't want to?"

"Because you haven't, dammit! And quit answering my questions with more questions." Her lips parted sulkily, and gleaming blue eyes zeroed in on him.

He laid down his fork. "It's not that. I don't take things as lightly as you do."

"Lightly. I don't take it lightly. I happen to enjoy sex, but I don't jump into bed with every man I meet."

"I didn't think you did."

"But it's not the be-all and end-all, either. It's just sex." She leaned forward, her face earnest. "Haven't you ever made it with someone just for fun? Just for that time? Because it felt right?" She leaned back, her face incredulous. "Don't tell me you and . . . and Milly the Muppet aren't making it?"

"I'm not going to tell you anything," he said stiffly. "It's none of your business whether we are or not."

She jabbed a finger at him. "See! You're all uptight. Why are people from your generation so uptight about sex?"

"You mean from the olden times?"

"See," she said sagely, smiling. "You're uptight about the difference in our ages too."

"You're right," he said, willing to concede defeat just to shut her up. "I'm uptight about everything. Now eat your dinner."

She smothered a laugh. "Yes, Daddy. Do I have to eat it all?" Her silky tone and emphasis on the last word left no doubt as to her meaning, and Pope felt heat slowly creeping into his face. He began eating rapidly, acutely aware of her eyes, the amusement she made no effort to hide. He ignored her.

"Any luck today?" he asked when the silence had become oppressive, unendurable.

She shook her head solemnly. "Not much. Things are bad. People are laying off, not hiring. But don't worry, I'll find something soon."

He looked up quickly. "I'm not worried about that, Nancy. You're welcome to stay as long as it takes."

"What will Milly the Muppet think about that?" She sounded flippant, derisive.

He shrugged and finished the last of his noodles.

"You haven't told her, have you?" Her voice was accusing, almost hostile.

"No reason to. We're not engaged or anything like that."

"Engaged? Do people still do that?" Disdain this time, a hint of scorn.

He looked at her quizzically. "You're trying to irritate me, Nancy. Why?"

"Because, dammit," she almost yelled, "I'm tired of you ignoring me."

"Ignoring you? I'm sitting right here talking—"

"Don't talk to me, dammit!" she yelled. "I want you to fuck me!"

"I thought you'd quit talking dirty," he said coolly, a lot more coolly than he felt.

"All right! I'm sorry! Make love to me. Whatever you want to call it, do something!" She reached across the table and dug her fingernails into his wrist.

"Must be all this rich food," he said, more to stall for time than anything.

"Oh, shit, Ham!" She released his arm and slapped her hands together in a flurry of despair. "Don't you understand anything? I want you to. I treated you like . . . like crap, and I've felt bad ever since."

"You want to make it up to me, huh?"

"Yes!" She blinked slowly, on the verge of a smile. "And I happen to be horny as hell too." She leaped up and yanked his chair away from the table. She plopped into his lap and pushed her face into his neck. "What do I have to do?" she said plaintively. "I can't rape you, you're too damn big."

"We just ate," he said around the thickness in his throat. "You have to wait thirty minutes after you eat." He could feel the warmth through the two layers of clothing.

"That's swimming, dummy." She lifted his dangling arm and placed his hand on her breast. Her lips trailed across his cheek to his mouth, gently worked his lips apart.

She broke away, her cheeks rosy. "Don't you like me anymore?"

"A little," he said huskily.

She stretched and pressed against him, warm and soft and yielding. "Then show me, you big brute, prove it to me."

"All right," he said with a sigh. "I guess I give up."

"Well, think about it this way," she said, bouncing on the bed and coming to rest in the crook of his arm, her hair, damp and cool from the shower, splashing across his cheek. "You held out three whole days. I think that shows outstanding willpower."

He tightened his arm. "You mean, considering the fact that you're such a delicate, luscious morsel?"

"Right," she said musingly. "No, most of the men—all the men—I've known would have banged me, out of revenge if nothing else. Rushed to take advantage of the situation." She rubbed her hand across his chest. "But you didn't." She tilted her head to see his face. "Maybe that was your way of paying me back."

"No," he said soberly. "Revenge was the farthest thing from my mind."

"What was the closest?" she asked teasingly.

"You. What we just did. All the time." *Stupid, stupid, stupid. Won't you ever learn?*

"You certainly hid it well." She paused, then added dramatically, "I won't hurt you, Ham. Ever again."

He chuckled. "Sure you will. But don't worry, I have it all in perspective now." *Rah, rah, rah, you lying bastard,* he thought morosely. *You're crazy about this little-girl woman, and losing her again won't be any easier than the first time.*

She wiggled for a better position, stretched out against his side. Her hand strayed, cupped him loosely, gently.

"You gave me so much pleasure," she said solemnly. "I don't deserve it."

"Old good-hearted me."

"I'm grateful, I really am. I'm serious now."

"So am I, and you're very welcome."

"I can feel you laughing down inside. You think I'm a silly kid."

"No way. Not a silly kid—no, ma'am."

"You're laughing," she said. "I can feel the tremor all the way down here." She removed her hand.

"I'm not laughing," he protested. He put her hand back where it was. "I promise you I'm not."

"Then why is it quivering?"

"I don't know. It's got a mind of its own. Ask it."

She chuckled throatily. "It's certainly moving oddly."

"It's like a puppy dog. It responds to affection."

"So it does." She moved fluidly across him, slowly impaled herself. "Well," she said apologetically, a lascivious gleam in her blue eyes, "as long as it was just standing there doing nothing."

Long after Wendy had gone to bed pleading exhaustion, Hack Wind sat staring vacantly at the blaring TV, a cable movie that was a remake of a 1940s sizzler starring Lana Turner. But it failed to sizzle, barely penetrated the murky fog inside his head. He gave up finally and went out onto the patio with a beer.

Never before had the night sounds seemed so melancholic, the soughing of the wind through the trees so mournful. Ominous April thunderheads loomed high over Fort Worth to the southwest, and he sat watching the jagged hairs of lightning, wondering what life was going to be like without her. It was a harrowing thought, a concept his mind refused to entertain for long.

Maybe Ham's right, he thought. *Maybe I should talk to her. What if I'm wrong? What if there's a perfectly logical explanation for her being in Al Judson's van at a time she professed to be in class? What if there's a perfectly logical reason for her to lie to me about the class hours? What if there's a sane, plausible excuse for avoiding intimacy with me, avoiding sex, avoiding everything except the most casual physical contact? What if—my God—what if there's a sane, logical plausible reason why she's going to bed with another man? And what if that sane logical plausible reason turns out to be that she no longer loves a black Indian honkie named Hackmore Ryder Windinniquitta? Or, even worse, that she never did?*

CHAPTER

EIGHT

Perhaps it was indolence, or chance, or possibly the balmy spring weather that prevented the Dallas/Forth Worth news media from making a connection between the throat slashings. Each was reported in its own time, the Clinton Fielder killing receiving by far the most coverage. Only three among many—a poor man, a derelict, and a thief—rated no more than two minutes on the prime-time evening news.

But then something happened. A fifth victim. A lady obstetrician named Muriel Haygood. She was found in her home in Arlington, Texas, Merriweather's southern neighbor, at approximately eight o'clock in the morning, and by the time the six o'clock news rolled around, somebody had put it all together. Channel 5 devoted fifteen minutes of their news time to the slasher murders. Solid, comprehensive coverage that closed by posing the question: Was the Dallas/Fort Worth Metroplex being stalked by a random psycho murderer reminiscent of the Merriweather Trashman?

Hamilton Pope opened his eyes, finished his beer, and

wondered about that himself. A fifth victim. A doctor. Jesus Christ! A doctor! *Rich man, poor man, beggarman, thief, doctor—*

The phone rang. He struggled out of his chair and beat Nancy by two paces. He winked at her and picked it up.

"Hello, Hack."

"How the hell did you know . . . ?"

"An educated guess." He sighed. "I laughed my fool head off when I read your doodling. But this one is a doctor and I'm not sure any longer."

"Five, Ham! Five, and the damn riddle or poem or whatever the hell it was is still holding."

"What comes next?"

"Let's see . . . doctor, lawyer, Indian chief. Is that Indian chief or Indian and chief?"

"Beats me."

"Coincidence? Or some nut using it as a guide?"

"Coincidence kinda sticks in my craw along about now. So until we know different, I think we ought to figure him as a random nut." Pope paused and lit a cigarette. "For all the damn good that'll do."

"I'll buy that. Particularly since he's killing them in the right order. If they were all mixed up, I'd say maybe a coincidence—" He broke off, his breath rasping faintly over the sizzling line. "I wonder if there could be a connection somewhere."

"First thing I looked for. Haven't turned up anything. No common denominator of any description except . . . did they say on the broadcast how old she was?"

"Mid-thirties was all I heard."

"That's about right, then. The other four were either thirty-seven or thirty-eight. Just a few months apart. Looks like she may fit the pattern."

"What pattern?"

"Age. What do people of the same age have in common?"

"Well, hell . . . they coulda been in the Army together—I guess not with the lady doctor, though. Let's see . . . school. They coulda been classmates . . ."

"Very good, Hack. Where did your man go to school?"

"Damn, I don't . . . yeah, I do. He went to the old Merriweather Junior High School. That was back before they built the new school."

"How about high school?"

"I don't know. Do you?"

Pope chuckled. "No, it never occurred to me to check."

Hack laughed. "And you had me feeling guilty because I hadn't, either. The only reason I know about the junior high is because his wife went through school with him and she happened to mention it."

"Okay. Why don't you hang up and call your Mrs. Fielder, and I'll see if I can't raise Mrs. Burns. If these two went to the same school, maybe we have something. If they didn't, it'll probably mean the whole idea is a bust."

"Okay. You want me to call you back?"

"Whatever. If I get through first, I'll call you."

"Good enough." For the first time in days Wind's voice contained a thread of excitement.

Pope hung up the receiver, stared at the phone for a moment, then lifted it and dialed the operator.

"Hello."

"Wendy? This is Ham Pope?"

"Oh, hi, Ham. How're you doing?"

"Just fine, and you?"

"Oh, I'm doing fine."

"Is that matinee-idol husband of yours around there somewhere?"

"Oh, my, don't call him that to his face. He's got a big head as it is. Just one second, Ham. He had to step into the bathroom."

He heard a low murmur of voices and something that sounded like a giggle.

"Ham. Fielder went to Merriweather High. Graduated in '68."

"Bingo. So did my man."

"Really? Hey, that's great."

"Maybe not so great for them." Pope took a deep breath. "We may have something, Hack. I called Milly while I was off the phone. She handled the inventory at Jesse Bond's place. She remembers a Merriweather High School yearbook and she's almost sure it was '68."

"Terrific. But how's it gonna help us, Ham? They had three or four hundred students graduating in those classes. Jesus, don't tell me we may have to talk to all of them."

"We may," Pope said grimly. "We'll have to find out about the others first. Unless they all went to Merriweather High . . . well, we'll find out first thing tomorrow. That yearbook of Bond's is in the property room down at the shop." He paused. "Keep your fingers crossed. This may be the connection we've been looking for."

"You think maybe we ought to go down there tonight?"

Pope looked at his watch. "Not much use. Nobody working in there at night, and Lodack keeps his location records locked up. We could rummage around for a week and not find it. We need another man in there at night." He expelled his breath in a sound that was half snort, half laugh. "Good night, Hack," he said gently, and hung up the receiver.

Nancy looked up from the magazine she was reading.

"Was that the good-looking hunk I talked to at Clint Fielder's place?"

Pope went to his recliner and sat down. "That's him."

"He's the prettiest man I've ever seen. Too bad he's a—"

"He's not," Pope said curtly. "He's black, Mexican, Indian, and white in about equal parts."

Nancy stared at him reflectively. "If that's the case, he's more Indian than anything."

"How do you figure that?"

"A Mexican is half Indian and half Spaniard. So if he's already got a quarter of Indian in him . . . wouldn't that be right?"

"I guess so, I never thought about it. I don't see that it matters."

"Maybe not to you. You're not a duke's mixture like he is. It might be important to him."

He scowled at her with mock ferocity, then pushed to his feet and crossed to the couch. He picked her up and settled her in his arms.

"I've got something that might be important to you. Wanna see?"

She threw back her head and let her arms dangle limply. "Oh, my God, I've created a Frankenstein monster."

"Not yet," he said darkly. "But it will be by the time we get to the bedroom."

She slipped her arms around his neck and nuzzled his cheek. "Braggart."

When Hackmore Wind arrived at Hamilton Pope's office the next morning, the burly detective was already there. Face somber, his forehead wrinkled, he was hunched motionless over his desk, his hands clasped loosely on the pages of a large white book spread open in front of him, a dangling cigarette trailing smoke across his narrowed eyes.

Hack came to a halt in front of the desk, stared at the sphinxlike figure for a moment, then cleared his throat loudly. He yanked the visitor's chair around and sat down.

"Hey, are you meditating, asleep, or what?"

Pope stirred sluggishly, widened his eyes, and took the cigarette out of his mouth.

"Four hundred and two," he said.

"Four hundred and two what?"

"That's how many kids there were in the graduating class of '68."

Hack sat up straight, his dark eyes glittering. "They were all in there."

Pope nodded slowly. "Yep. All five of them. Class of '68."

"Well." Hack crossed his long legs and stared at the toes of his gleaming boots. "Well, what the hell does that mean to us now that we know?"

Pope leaned back and blew a ragged circle of smoke at the ceiling fixture. "It's too much to be coincidence. That means there's a link, some kind of connection, between the victims and the killer—or killers."

"You think there could be more than one?"

Pope shrugged. "Who knows? We don't know enough to even guess. It's just that the killings seem to have been so easy for him. No fuss. He gets close to them, cuts their throats; and disappears. That could suggest one person to restrain, another to do the deed." He rubbed his chin. "Or it could suggest a friend or close acquaintance."

"That would rule out random psycho killings, then?"

"Random, yes. Not necessarily the psycho part. The way I see it, anyone who deliberately takes a human life is a bit deranged. No matter what the motivation."

"I won't argue that. But where do we go from here? Surely twenty years is a little long for some classmate to be holding a grudge."

Pope's eyes twinkled. "Haven't you been going to movies lately? Or read a book? Revenge is the most popular current motive there is—except big money, of course."

But Hack refused to be sidetracked. "Okay, so we have to talk to classmates?"

"It's the only link we have. We'll start there and work forward. Maybe something will show up . . . political affiliations, a social club, a subversive organization, the KKK, religion, something."

"The only thing Fielder belonged to was the Jaycees."

"Burns didn't belong to anything. He couldn't afford it. I seriously doubt if Switzer or Bond did, either."

Hack reached for a cigarette and then remembered he had decided to quit again. His hand ended up raking through tousled black hair. "We're gonna need some help."

Pope nodded. "I've talked to Sergeant Globe in Fort Worth. He agrees this is the right way to go. He can bring in a couple of men. I have Milly, and I'll badger Roscoe into giving us a couple of men out of Robbery. If we can get a couple from Arlington, we'll be in pretty fair shape. At least half of the four hundred students are bound to be scattered around the country or even the state. If they're not in the Metroplex area, we won't worry about them. At least for now."

Hack gave him a gloomy look. "Locating the ones left is going to be a hell of a job. The women will be married, the men probably moved a half dozen times."

Pope closed the book and stood up. "That's a good reason to start humping. I'll get a list compiled." He stopped, his fingers tracing the embossed lettering on the front of the book, an odd look on his face.

"Would you believe Clarence Switzer was voted the student most likely to succeed?"

"Was that the beggar?"

"Yeah, the one in Fort Worth."

Hack unfolded his long frame from the chair. "Who knows? Maybe he did. Panhandling is a big business up north. Some of those suckers make forty, fifty thousand a year."

Pope came around the desk carrying the yearbook. "If Switzer made any money, he must have lived it up. They didn't find a cent on him, or in his room at that flophouse he lived in."

"That's the trouble with people nowadays," Hack said solemnly, falling into step with Pope as he headed down the corridor toward Roscoe Tanner's office. "Nobody wants to save money. That's why everything's so screwed up. That's just what the president was saying the other night—" He broke off, looking at Pope expectantly, his dark eyes gleaming.

But Hamilton Pope just snorted softly.

CHAPTER

NINE

Roscoe Tanner's long, thick fingers stacked the last of the manila folders on the pile at his elbow. He picked up a thin sheaf of papers and looked at the faces arrayed on each side of the conference table. He cleared his throat, took the cigar stub from the corner of his mouth, and dropped it into a large metal ashtray in front of him.

"Well, there you have it, gents. All we have to date. Our lab is positive—and the Fort Worth lab backs them up—that the same, or a very similar, instrument was used in all five murders. Namely an extremely sharp, curved instrument commonly referred to as a utility knife. They say they are positive, but they won't get on a witness stand and swear that's what it was, either. Another of their educated guesses. But it does give us one relatively safe assumption: All five murders were committed by the same person or persons." He paused and glanced around warily, as if expecting rebuttal. When none came, he shrugged thick shoulders and went on.

"Assuming that to be true, I believe our decision to create a task force and pool our information is the smartest thing we could do. Not that any of us have any information to speak of. Not yet. But we will have, and the quicker that information is correlated and passed out among the troops, the quicker we'll get this asshole behind bars. If none of you have any objections, we can establish our base headquarters here in this room. Merriweather is pretty well centrally located. Besides, we have two murders instead of one, like the rest of you.'' He stopped and looked down the table, smiling faintly.

''A dubious honor at best,'' Milly Singer said dryly.

Hack Wind stirred and moved his long frame to a more comfortable position. He grinned across the table at Hamilton Pope. ''You can have mine, that'll give you three.''

''And mine.'' Detective Sergeant Jack Kilgarten tugged at the end of a sharp, predatory nose and winked across at Milly Singer. ''Us Arlington folk are right generous about things like that.'' He was a small, slender man with carefully styled brown hair and bright gray eyes that had not strayed far from Milly Singer since the meeting began. He followed the wink with a dazzling smile that revealed two rows of perfect white teeth with the silky glaze of artificiality.

You pompous little ass, Milly thought, returning the smile sweetly.

''What was this about the class of '68?'' Sergeant Jonas Globe, a short, burly, red-faced man with almost no hair and even less patience, leaned forward on his elbows in an effort to see Hamilton Pope, seated at Roscoe Tanner's right. ''You telling me all these people went to school together?''

Pope nodded. ''That's right. All graduates of the class of '68, Merriweather High.''

Globe sat back and ran a beefy hand across his balding

head. He leaned forward again. "What the hell do you make of that?"

"That's obvious," Kilgarten put in. "Somebody didn't get invited to join the club. Either that or nobody came to his birthday party." He paused, grinning at Milly. "Or maybe they gang-banged his squeeze, turned her into the class punching bag."

Pope gave him an annoyed glance. "As ridiculous as that sounds," he said crisply, "it could be something as simple as that—or as complex. One man's crumbs are another man's feast. It may not mean anything to us right now, but in my opinion it takes it out of the realm of random killings. There's a purpose behind this guy's madness. All we have to do is find it. Out of all the reasons we humans find for killing each other, I believe the circumstances here narrow it down to only two." He stopped and lit a cigarette, his blue eyes narrowing reflectively. "Revenge. Payback for some wrong—real or fancied. And if that's the case, that would suggest derangement of some sort. I'm not a doctor, but common sense tells me a guy would have to be pretty well flipped out to start slicing throats twenty years after the fact, whatever the reason was."

"Maybe not," said Kilgarten. "Maybe something happened recently. Something they were all involved in."

Pope shrugged. "We considered that. Nothing has come to light so far. But that doesn't rule out the possibility."

"A class reunion," Milly said. "That could have brought them all together again."

"That won't be hard to check." Tanner handed Pope the thin sheaf of papers. "You want to hand these out?"

"Wait a minute," Hack said. "You said two reasons. What's the second one?"

"Gain," Pope said succinctly. "Old reliable: the profit motive."

Sergeant Globe frowned. "I don't see how. These people were about as far apart as you can get on the financial ladder. My man was a beggar, for chrissake."

"And Fielder was a multimillionaire," Hack said slowly. "How about the last one, the doctor?" He looked down the table at Kilgarten.

Kilgarten shrugged. "Judging from her residence and her office setup, I'd say she wasn't hurting for bucks. I'll dig a little deeper and find out."

Hamilton Pope and Hack Wind exchanged glances. Pope shrugged and smiled faintly. "It was your brainstorm. You tell them." His eyes gleamed at the younger man.

Hack fidgeted, feeling the concerted shift of attention in his direction.

"Tell us what, Hack?" Milly asked, watching curiously as the young deputy's face darkened perceptibly with an invasion of blood.

Wind shot Pope a baleful glance. "All right. Starting with the first one, Clinton Fielder. What was he?"

"A businessman, a tycoon," Tanner said.

"A multimillionaire. You said it yourself." Milly was watching him intently, her gray eyes bright.

"A rich man," Hack said. "Okay, the second one, Clyde Burns. What was he?"

"What the hell is this, twenty questions?" Sergeant Globe moved in his chair, impatient as usual.

"A workingman," Milly said thoughtfully. "Okay, a poor man. Right?"

"Right. And Clarence Switzer?"

Milly's eyes ignited, gave off sparks. "A panhandler . . . beggarman, right?" She looked at Pope, then back to Wind, her lips moving on the verge of a smile. "Rich man, poor man, beggarman . . . and Jesse Bond was a thief." The smile died unborn. "Damn. The next one was a doctor!" She stared at Hack, her eyes rounded in disbelief. "My God!"

"That's right," Wind said laconically. "It may sound stupid, but it damn well fits."

"What the hell are we talking about here? Globe looked around the table, his heavy brow wrinkled in a scowl. "What's this rich-man, poor-man crap?"

"A poem," Kilgarten said musingly, his pale eyebrows arched.

"Bullshit," Tanner said emphatically, slapping the table with huge splayed hands.

"Maybe not, Roscoe," Pope said quietly. "Think about it. I laughed my ass off when he first . . . when I first discovered Hack's theory. But that was before the Haygood woman was killed. I don't feel so much like laughing anymore. I have a funny feeling this guy is playing with us, or at the very least taking us on a nice stroll down the garden path. It could be a coincidence, but the mathematical probabilities of that staggers me a little."

"I don't know, Ham," Milly said. "Out of four hundred odd students, it shouldn't be too hard to find the elements to fit the poem." She paused reflectively. "*Indian Chief* might be a problem, though."

Kilgarten's eyebrows arched again and he allowed himself a meager smile. "Perhaps someone has been reading too much Ellery Queen."

Milly bristled. "Perhaps someone should learn to read," she said briskly.

Kilgarten's eyebrows dropped, and he gave Milly an ingratiating smile. "Hey, I didn't mean you. I was talking about our killer. Maybe he has a thing about poems. . . ."

"Okay," Pope said. "Maybe it means something,

maybe it doesn't. It obviously means something to him."
He held up the sheaf of papers Tanner had given him. "So
far we've located forty-two people out of the class of '68.
Broken down by cities, it works out fairly well. Fort Worth
has eleven. Arlington nine. Merriweather only has six, but
there are eight in Dallas that we'll have to cover. Hack,
there are three in county territory, and the other five are
in the mid-cities area. Hurst has three, and Bedford and
Haltom City have one each. We'll handle those also. But
keep in mind that this is only the beginning. More names
will be coming in all the time. So the more help you can
cadge out of your various departments, the better. We already have three people working full-time, and Milly and
I make five for Merriweather. That's a lot of personnel for
us. Both Fort Worth and Arlington should be able to field
a few more than we can. What do you think?"

Sergeant Globe studied the list of names. He looked up
and grunted, his face noncommittal. "We'll give it a try.
But we're always shorthanded."

Kilgarten shrugged thin shoulders and looked down the
table at Tanner. "It might help if you'd give Captain Fer-
guson another call."

Tanner pushed himself up from the head of the table on
splayed fingers. "I'll do it." He turned to Pope. "Anything else, Ham?"

Pope nodded, his square face expressionless. "A couple
of things. So far as we know, only one of these forty-two
people is a lawyer. And he lives in Merriweather, so he'll
be ours. But our system is not foolproof. All we've really
done so far is confirm that these people live at the addresses noted. If you do run into an attorney . . . call it
in." He paused and waited for comment. None came. He
went on: "We're all experienced investigators, and I'm
not presuming to tell you how to conduct your interroga-

tions, but sometimes it helps to have another viewpoint. I've jotted down a few things it would be helpful to find out. They're on the backs of your address sheets . . . if you want to use them.'' He nodded perfunctorily and stood up. ''That does it for me. Anyone have anything?'' He glanced down the table as he closed and latched his brief- case.

Hack said something that was lost in the noise of scrap- ing chairs and shuffling feet as the small group left the table and moved toward the door.

Pope looked at him and lifted his eyebrows inquiringly. ''You say something, Hack?''

''I was just curious. Who's the lawyer?''

Pope grinned. ''His name's Malcolm Carlyle.'' He looked past Hack, and the grin died as he saw Kilgarten drape a casual arm across Milly's shoulders as they reached the door. It was reborn when she firmly knocked Kilgar- ten's hand away and stepped back from the dapper detec- tive. He said something, shrugged eloquently, adjusted his carefully knotted tie, and disappeared through the door- way. Milly glanced over her shoulder and caught Pope watching. She smiled faintly and winked, then wrinkled her nose in a grimace of distaste and followed the slender man down the corridor.

Everything about the Malcolm Carlyle estate spoke elo- quently of money. The house itself, not as large as many in the Mayfair district, was nonetheless richly appointed with gingerbread balconies, gables, a rust-colored tile roof, dormer windows, and sparkling white colonnades that supported a screened second-story porch. The grounds were meticulously kept, manicured shrubbery and a fair- way lawn spreading beneath oak and elm and lofty pecan. A concrete driveway curved a hundred and fifty feet from the street and ended before a six-car garage that Pope estimated would hold his small, three-bedroom house without cracking a seam. Long accustomed to the trappings of the wealthy, more or less content with his lot in life, he liked to think of himself as being impervious to the siren peal of big money and power and prestige. He was, nevertheless, impressed, and perhaps, if asked, would have admitted to a small tug of envy.

He parked his battered Dodge on the apron in front of the garage. He mashed out his cigarette and, despite the dulling effects of years of nicotine on his olfactory nerves, caught the rich aromas of spring and growing things as he climbed out. A flock of small brown birds swooped down on a nearby bush studded with small red berries. They caught sight of him and bombed away again, frightening a feeding squirrel that scampered up a tree and onto a limb and chattered at him angrily, tail whipping in small, excited jerks. Pope grinned up at him.

"Hey, don't blame me, partner. I don't want your berries."

The squirrel sat up and stopped barking, watching him with tiny beady eyes, the bushy tail curved in a graceful arc along its back. Then, obviously contemptuous of this strange, earthbound, two-legged creature, it scampered leisurely along the limb to the tree trunk and disappeared.

He chuckled and left the parking apron for a wide, curving sidewalk that led to the front door. He punched the bell and rocked on his heels, fully expecting a reasonable wait while the maid or butler broke away from whatever maids and butlers did and traversed the obviously considerable distances inside the house, depending, of course, on where they happened to be when the doorbell—

The door swung open immediately; not a maid, he thought distractedly, staring at the woman who towered over him, bulky and shapeless in a bright blue dress that hung without constriction to her ankles. Formless, gross, she had a round moon face, a pretty smile, and amazingly clear green eyes that gazed out at him almost timidly.

"Yes, sir, may I help you?"

Pope ducked his head and smiled. "Yes, ma'am. I'm Sergeant Pope. I have an appointment with Mr. Carlyle."

"Oh, yes, of course." She stepped back daintily. "I'm Mrs. Carlyle. My husband's expecting you, Sergeant Pope." She extended a surprisingly small, plump hand.

Pope swallowed the tiny hand in his, almost startled at its pleasing warmth. "I'm a few minutes early. If I'm interrupting your dinner or anything . . ."

"Oh, no. We never eat until seven. My husband's waiting for you in his study." She smiled her hesitant smile again and preceded him down a tiled hallway.

He watched her broad back, and broader buttocks, and wondered how a woman, how anyone, could allow themselves to burgeon to such proportions. His hand strayed unconsciously to the region of his belt, the beginnings of a paunch. *Only one beer a day from now on,* he told himself firmly. *No more pizza or ice cream or pasta . . . and maybe I'll take up jogging again.*

"Here we are," she said. She rapped lightly on a closed door, then opened it and went in. She stepped lightly to one side. "Mal, honey, the policeman is here to see you."

If the immensity of Mrs. Carlyle had been a surprise, Malcolm Carlyle's appearance was a shock. From the woman Pope had formed an instantaneous opinion of what the husband would look like: either short and fat and balding, or short and thin and balding. Years of subliminal conditioning by movies and TV would allow for nothing else: if the woman was fat, the husband invariably had to be short and thin, or fat and balding.

So much for stereotyping, he thought amusedly, shaking the hand of the compact, handsome man who leapt agilely out of a deep leather chair and gripped his hand with a firm, dry clasp. Bushy brown hair and quiet, penetrating hazel eyes combined to shatter Pope's preconceived image totally.

"Sergeant Pope. I'm very glad to meet you." He had a dry, husky voice and a quick flashing smile. His hand pumped Pope's one beyond the obligatory three before he released it. He bounded to one side and waved at the chair he had just vacated. "Please have a seat, Mr. Pope . . . or should I call you Sergeant?"

"Just Pope would be fine," Pope said. "I can sit over here. I don't want to take your chair."

"Oh, no . . . please. Sit here." He turned toward his wife, who was waiting hesitantly by the door. "Darling. Come in, come in. This may very well concern you as well." He whirled back to Pope. "I understood from your secretary that your visit has something to do with the class of '68 at Merriweather High." Without waiting for an answer he bounded across to meet his wife. He ushered her to a seat on a couch facing the leather chair, as if she were visiting royalty. "Matilda graduated in that class, also, didn't you, my love?"

The fat woman nodded shyly. She melted into the couch and clasped her hands across her abdomen. "It seems so long ago. Twenty years."

Carlyle came to rest beside his wife, stiffly erect on the edge of the cushion, his eyes bright and intent, a half smile on his well-shaped lips. He was up again immediately, standing in front of Pope, literally wringing his hands, his expression contrite.

"What a terrible host I am! What can I get you to drink, Sergeant Pope?"

"Nothing, thanks. But you and your wife go right ahead."

"No, no." He abruptly sat down again, then absently reached for his wife's plump hand and held it in both of his. "Now, Sergeant Pope, how can we help you?"

"The Merriweather class of '68. I'm sure you're aware that five members of that graduating class have recently been killed . . . murdered."

Carlyle's head bobbed, a woeful expression on his face. "Yes, isn't it terrible? One of them, Clinton Fielder, was a very good friend of mine. I remember the others vaguely, but there were so many in our class. I saw Clinton Fielder around town all the time. Matilda and I went to his funeral, didn't we, dear?"

Matilda nodded, her clear green eyes on her husband. "I remember the others. I'm sure you would, too, dear, if you stopped and thought about it. They were all in our school band, remember?"

Carlyle nodded uncertainly. "Yes. If they were all in the band, I'm sure I would remember." He scowled fiercely, as if to frighten a recalcitrant memory into action.

"The school band? All of them? You're sure of that?" Pope looked from the pale moon face to the thin, angular one and back again.

Matilda nodded her head firmly. "I can even tell you what instruments they played."

"And you? Both of you? Were you in the band also?"

"Yes. I played the clarinet and Mal played the trombone." She gazed fondly at her husband. "He was very good, even if I do say so."

"No better than you, my love," Malcolm said gallantly.

Pope found and lit a cigarette, his mind working furiously. The school band. All five of them playing in the school band! Another coincidence? Not damn likely, not this year. He felt a prickle on the back of his neck. Maybe a connection, a more cohesive, more closely knit connection than just being members of the class of '68.

"The school band," he said. "It was made up of more than just seniors, I take it."

Their heads bobbed in unison, but it was Matilda who answered. "Oh, yes. We had kids from all four classes. If I remember correctly, there were only twenty-two or twenty-three seniors in the band. The rest, about seventy more, were made up of the other three grades."

"Have any of you ever met since—to play together, I mean?"

"Not to my knowledge," Carlyle said. "I know Matilda and I haven't."

"Then Clinton Fielder was the only one of the five that either of you ever saw socially?"

"Yes. At parties and various functions around the area." Carlyle frowned thoughtfully. "I don't believe he ever attended one of our parties, did he, dear?"

"No. We sent him several invitations, but he was usually out of town." She hesitated, then gave her husband an indulgent smile. "Not that we have all that many parties." She looked back at Pope. "My husband is a game freak. If he had his way, we'd never leave the house. We simply have hundreds of games. Give him a game, a puzzle, and he's set for the night."

Carlyle shrugged eloquently and smiled. "It stimulates the mind. Better that than boozing it up every night, like some of our friends."

"I'll buy that," Matilda said fervently.

Pope stubbed out his cigarette slowly and methodically. Matilda seemed to have the sharpest memory, and he directed his next question at her.

"Can you remember anyone who may have had a grievance against the people who have been murdered?"

The two heads wagged in unison again.

"Maybe not a big thing. Someone who didn't make the band. Someone who may have felt they were being discriminated against for some reason. Someone unduly upset."

"Oh, there were a lot of people upset about not making band," Matilda said. "Almost all of the girls cried, as well as some of the boys. Some of them were very upset."

"But not one in particular? Someone who may have made threats of some kind—reacted violently, perhaps?"

"No, I can't remember anyone like that. Can you, Mal?"

Carlyle pursed his lips and shook his head soundlessly.

His hopes dwindling, Pope struck out in a new direction. "All right. How about something that happened? Something that involved all of you as a group?"

"I can't think of anything," Carlyle said. He nibbled at his lower lip. "Maybe some of the other band members . . . have you talked to anyone else?"

"Not many," Pope admitted. "But we will in time." He smiled ruefully. "There're a lot of you."

Carlyle nodded absently, then suddenly sat up straight, his eyes widening. He turned to look at his wife and picked up her chubby hand again. She was watching him intently, the customary half smile on her round face, her green eyes burning almost blue.

He turned back to Pope. "Something that happened, you said. There *was* something that happened. Not long before graduation . . ." His voice faltered, then picked up. "That Bull Henderson thing."

"Bull Henderson thing?"

"Bull Henderson. He was lead sax player in the band.

He was killed. They . . . the sheriff—well, I guess it was a deputy sheriff—thought he was murdered.'' He stopped and wet his lips. ''And a bunch of us saw—well, almost saw—it happen.'' He stopped and watched Pope intently, his hazel eyes bright, a tiny crescent of small brown moles dipping downward on his cheek as his face bunched into an expectant smile.

CHAPTER
TEN

"Tell me about it," Pope said, the prickly feeling on the back of his neck growing stronger, a faint fluttering in his stomach.

"Oh, I don't see how it could really matter," Matilda said. "We didn't really see anything . . . not about the murder. Only what . . . went on before." She made a deprecating gesture, her lips tightening in disapproval. "And that was just gross." She glanced at Pope, then back at her husband. "And anyhow, they were never certain that he was killed. He could have fallen."

"That Deputy Stringer didn't think so," Carlyle said almost sullenly, as if his wife's words had taken the edge off his story.

"Tell me about it," Pope said again.

"Well," Carlyle said, dropping his wife's hand and leaning forward. "We were all on an outing—this is the band I'm talking about, not the whole class. Our bandleader, Mr. Stearns, had promised that if we reached the finals in the state band competition, he would give us a barbecue picnic at whatever location we chose. Well, we came out in third place and we chose Gooseneck Park on Possum Kingdom Lake.''

"We really should have won," Matilda said firmly. "Everybody said we were the best band in the finals, but . . ." She trailed off and shrugged plump shoulders, allowing Pope to deduce from her cynical expression her low opinion of band contest judges in general, *those* band contest judges in particular.

"It was really pretty much of a dud," Carlyle went on as if his wife hadn't interrupted. "Dull. Especially for us seniors. I suppose we considered ourselves above the silly games they were playing, and even the music Mr. Stearns's wife picked to play on their portable phonograph was mawkishly sentimental stuff from the forties and fifties.''

"Now I, for one, disagreed with that. I thought the music was just fine. I still like it." Matilda cocked a defiant eye at her patiently waiting husband.

"Yes, she does," Carlyle told Pope, his tone faintly apologetic, as if explaining the slightly aberrant behavior of an unruly child. "I've never been much of a nostalgia buff, I'm afraid." He gazed fondly at his huge wife. "We agree on most things, but when it comes to music—"

"Not all music," Matilda put in quickly. "I like some of the contemporary—"

Carlyle picked up her hand again and patted it. "Now, my dear, you must admit you find rock music—"

"This Gooseneck Park," Pope said. "Was that where it happened? The Bull Henderson thing?"

Carlyle nodded solemnly. "Yes. A bunch of us, about a dozen seniors, had wandered away from the picnic area of the park. We ended up down at the water's edge, a narrow, rocky beach between the trees and the lake. We were pretty much bored with the whole thing—"

"Not everybody was bored," Matilda said darkly. "A

lot of them were smoking pot and acting like idiots. It was way too cold to swim, but some of the boys jumped in, anyway." She looked at her husband. "At least you had better sense than that."

Carlyle acknowledged the left-handed compliment with a smile. "Well, to make it shorter, we all decided to climb up the gooseneck—that's a long neck of land that extended out into the lake about fifty or sixty yards. It wasn't a terribly hard climb, but it was about forty feet high and difficult enough to make you huff and puff a little by the time you reached the top."

"I only weighed a hundred and eighteen pounds then," Matilda said musingly. She sighed heavily. "I was the skinniest thing."

Carlyle gave her a sympathetic smile and another pat on the hand. "At the top we all flopped down on the rocks to catch our breath. We were resting and talking—I remember the wind was blowing rather strongly and we were almost cold."

Matilda laughed. "Especially the idiots who got wet."

"We had a lovely view," Carlyle said. "Possum Kingdom Lake is the prettiest lake in Texas, wild and rough with beautiful, clear blue water."

"Yes," Pope said, "I've been there. What happened next?" He shifted in the confines of the glove-soft leather chair and lit another cigarette, his face stoic despite his growing exasperation.

"Oh, yes, well . . ." He paused and knitted his brow. "Someone, I'm not certain who, crossed the top of the cliff—"

"Stacy Crump," Matilda put in firmly. "It was Stacy Crump who saw them first."

Carlyle nodded. "Yes, I do believe you're right. Stacy Crump. I remember now. She was holding her hand over her mouth and waving at us to come and see. She motioned for us to be quiet and . . . and to hurry." He stopped and cleared his throat. He glanced sideways at his wife, his face slowly gaining color. "My dear, if you'd care to leave the room while I tell Mr. Pope what we saw . . . ?" He let it trail away.

She shook her head firmly. "No, of course not, Malcolm. Don't be such a fuddy-duddy. My goodness, they talk about things like that on TV talk shows all the time." She turned to Pope. "Don't they, Mr. Pope?"

"I'm not exactly sure what you're talking about," Pope said apologetically.

"Oh, well . . . well, of course you aren't." Her head lifted, her lips crimped in expressive disapproval, she went on. "They were having sex. Right there on the little beach at the end of the gooseneck." She paused, avoiding her husband's flaming face. "Oral sex, it was." She cocked her head, eyes a burning blue again, and waited for Pope's reaction.

"Hmm," he said, and cleared his throat. "Well, that doesn't sound . . . I mean, after all, that's not—" He stopped and stubbed out his cigarette. "And that's all you saw?"

Matilda bobbed her head. "Yes, pretty much." She sniffed. "That Bull Henderson. He was an animal from the word *go*."

"It was the Henderson boy with the girl?"

"Oh, yes, we could see him plainly. He was leaning against a tree, and the girl was kneeling . . . in front of him." She glanced at her husband as he stirred restively, his face slowly returning to normal. Her face softened and she smiled.

"Who was the girl?"

Matilda wagged her head. "We never knew . . . not for

sure. We all made guesses, but we never found out for sure. We only got a glimpse of her face, the side of her face, when someone knocked a rock off the edge of the cliff, and she glanced up and saw us.'' She halted, the half smile back on her face. "Boy, howdy, did she ever take off!''

"You mean she ran?''

"Did she! She took off like a rocket. Old dumbo Bull Henderson just stood there with a stupid look on his face like he didn't know what hit him.'' She chuckled roguishly and glanced again at her squirming husband. "Honey, don't be embarrassed. Mr. Pope isn't.''

"I'm not,'' he said stiffly.

"What did that have to do with Henderson's death?''

"I don't know if it had anything to do with it,'' Matilda said. "There was this deputy . . . Deputy Stringer. He asked a lot of questions, seemed to think maybe Bull's fall wasn't an accident. At least that's the impression I got.''

"Yes,'' Carlyle agreed. "I definitely got that impression too.'' After the rosiness of his fierce blushing, his face seemed inordinately pale, strained. "I think he believed someone had struck Bull with a stick, or a rock, or something that caused him to fall.''

"Fall from where?''

"Well, after the girl ran away, Bull finally came out of his daze. He shook his fist at us and pulled up his pants and took off after her.'' Matilda's green eyes sparkled. "I don't think it bothered Bull a bit that we were watching. That boy had absolutely no morals and very little sense.'' She paused, her eyes narrowing reflectively. "One thing was funny, though. When he ran off, he was calling out her name. It was hard to hear with the wind blowing and everything, but we finally decided he was saying Ginger Belle.''

"The thing that was funny," Carlyle said, "was that there wasn't anyone by that name in our band, not even in our school that we knew about."

Pope shrugged. "Maybe she wasn't from your school."

Matilda moved her head slowly up and down. "Yes, I think so. She was wearing one of our band sweaters, and she wasn't wearing Bull's, because he was wearing his own. And, too, someone would have noticed a strange girl at the barbecue. It was for band members only." She lapsed into silence, studying her stubby, immaculately manicured fingers.

"Where did Bull fall from?" Pope prompted gently.

"On the other side, the south side of the gooseneck, there were wooden stairs built up a bluff, very much like the ones we climbed. There was a wide trail from there, back to the picnic area. They found Bull near the bottom of the stairs. His neck was broken. A piece of the guardrail had fallen with him." Carlyle shook his head. "I didn't get to see it, of course, but I overheard Deputy Stringer telling the sheriff that he believed someone had struck Bull with a rock or something, causing him to fall."

"And the twelve of you? Did you go back the way you came?"

Carlyle nodded. "Yes. Some of us fellows looked for Bull, but we couldn't find him. We wanted to razz him a little, see if we could find out who the girl was. We just figured he was hiding out, but when he didn't show up for roll call before we left on the buses, Mr. Stearns got worried and went somewhere and called the sheriff."

Pope leaned back in the chair and lit another cigarette. "And you're positive that all five of your murdered classmates were among the twelve on top of the bluff?"

"Yes," Carlyle said emphatically. "I'm certain of that."

"Okay. With the two of you, that leaves five more. I'll

need their names . . . and their addresses if you should happen to know them.''

Carlyle squinted his eyes, hesitated. ''I'm not sure I remember all—''

''I do,'' said Matilda. ''I don't know their addresses, though.''

''Names will be fine, then.'' Pope dug his notebook and a ballpoint pen from his jacket pocket. He flipped to an empty page and handed the notebook to Carlyle, who passed it to his wife. ''If you'd just write the names in there, please, Mrs. Carlyle.''

Carlyle looked at Pope uneasily. ''You think all this may have some bearing on the killings, Sergeant Pope?''

''I don't know. Doesn't seem likely on the face of it, but you never know.'' He stroked his chin. ''I have to tell you, though, if it has . . .'' He paused, acutely aware of Carlyle's eyes boring into his. ''It's quite possible,'' he went on quietly, ''that you and your wife . . . and the others . . . well, it's possible that you may be in danger also.''

Matilda's sleek head popped up from the notebook. ''You really think so?'' She sounded more curious than frightened.

''It's a possibility,'' Pope repeated, ''considering what you've told me here today. Five people murdered, all of whom were in a certain group on a certain day at a certain location. Coincidence? I don't believe in coincidence, Mrs. Carlyle. Not that kind of coincidence.''

She regarded him blankly, her round face slowly contorting into a grimace of disbelief. ''It all . . . all sounds so . . . melodramatic.'' Her eyes moved to her husband for support. ''Don't you think so, honey?''

Carlyle shook his head, his face confused. ''My wife is

right, Sergeant Pope. All this . . . it does sound . . . so . . . so . . .''

Pope shrugged. ''I can only tell you what I think.'' He accepted the notebook and pen from Carlyle and scanned the list of names. None of them matched his Merriweather list that he could remember. He looked at the two worried faces across from him. ''I think you should be very careful. Particularly around any stray member of the class of '68 you may come across.'' He took a deep breath. ''And in your case, Mr. Carlyle, since you're an attorney, I'd advise you to be especially careful.''

Matilda looked at her husband, her face filled with confusion. ''What on earth does that have to do with it?'' She ran one hand across her smooth hair to the bun at the nape of her neck.

Pope stood up. ''I can't explain . . . not fully. It's just that we have reason to believe his next victim may be an attorney.''

Carlyle rose automatically, helped his wife to her feet. ''Are . . . are you certain of that?''

''No, we're not,'' Pope said heavily. ''Not certain. We're not certain there will be another victim. But if there is, it appears likely it will be an attorney.'' He crossed to the door and went out into the hall, the two Carlyles following closely on his heels like a couple of nervous puppies. He walked swiftly, taking refuge from a sudden feeling of guilt behind a thin veneer of irritation.

''In that case, Sergeant Pope, do you think we should request police protection?'' Malcolm Carlyle darted in front of him to open the front door.

Pope stopped just outside and turned to face them. ''You could ask, Mr. Carlyle, but to be honest with you, I don't think you'll get it. Mainly because we don't have the manpower to spare. But there's also another reason. Our supporting evidence is pretty thin, to say the least.''

Matilda crowded in beside her husband, filling the doorway, her green eyes clouded. ''What do you suggest we do, Sergeant Pope?''

Pope sighed. ''You could hire someone. Maybe a private detective. I can arrange for additional patrol coverage, but that's not much help in something like this. Other than that, all I can advise you to do is be careful.'' He looked away from their silently anxious faces, then looked back, his expression apologetic. ''It isn't much help. I wish we could do more. One other thing, if you believe in it. You could pray that we catch him.''

CHAPTER

ELEVEN

Feeling oddly out of sync in a neat brown business suit instead of his familiar, comfortable uniform, Hackmore Wind climbed the Sycamore Arms' single flight of stairs and walked along a carpeted corridor toward the rear of the building and Apartment 16B.

Bareheaded for a change, his carefully combed black hair in total disarray from the gusty April wind, wide shoulders unnaturally constricted by the crisp new polyester cloth, he was already regretting his decision to conform to his Department's uniform dress code for investigative staff members. Even the small-caliber gun under his arm chafed, seemed bulky and conspicuous; also, his right hip, where the .357 usually hung, felt strangely naked and gave him an eerie feeling of vulnerability.

He came to a halt before Apartment 16B. He tugged at the gun and brushed, irritably and ineffectually, at his hair before pressing the bell.

Karen Michele Fields. While he waited, he mentally reviewed the scanty information provided by Roscoe Tanier's intelligence-gathering team: flight attendant, American Airlines; divorced; childless; valedictorian of the class of '68; two years at Tarrant County Junior College; and winner of the Miss Merriweather Beauty Pageant, which had led to the second runner-up position for the crown of Miss Texas.

She must have been something at twenty, he thought musingly. *I wonder how she looks at thirty-eight?*

Seconds later he was finding out, staring dumbly down into an unbelievably lovely face that glared up at him in extreme annoyance—firm, full lips puckered on the verge of scathing indictment; sleep-swollen eyes sparking green fire, dazzling in their brilliance, mesmerizing in their intensity.

"Dammit, can't you read?" Her voice slid down the scale from scorching indignation to mild reproach in the space of the four words. Her eyes blinked slowly, belatedly registering his dark, manly beauty. She swallowed and moistened sleep-dry lips, a halfhearted, apologetic smile appearing as if by magic. "The sign says daysleeper," she said matter-of-factly. "I guess you didn't see it."

He managed a smile of his own, wondering if it looked as odd as it felt. "Yes, ma'am, I . . . no, ma'am, I didn't see it. I'm sorry if I got you up." He looked at her tousled hair, the rumpled nylon pajamas. His face began to heat up. "I mean, I'm sorry I got you up."

She ran her fingers through her hair and smothered a yawn. "I sure hope it's something important." A caustic edge had come back into her voice, the smile acquiring a frosty curve. She pulled the door closed another inch. "If you're a salesman, forget it."

"No, ma'am, I'm not a salesman." He handed her the leather case containing his badge and identification card.

"I'm Deputy Hackmore Wind. I'd like to talk to you a few minutes if I could."

"Hackmore?" A slow smile spread across her face. She handed him the case and raised sparkling eyes to his. "I'm not making fun of your name. It's just that my granddaddy was named Hackmore, Hackmore Winthrop. Isn't that a coincidence?"

"Yes, it is," Hack said seriously. "Do you think you could spare me a few minutes, Mrs. Fields?"

She stepped back and swung the door wide. "Sure, why not? I'm already wide awake." She made an exaggerated gesture of welcome. "But only if you'll promise me there's no law against a messy apartment."

Hack looked around the room and smiled. "It looks great to me."

"A blind deputy sheriff. Now I've seen everything." She flitted around, picking up stray articles of clothing and rolling them into a ball under her arm. She crossed to a door he assumed to be the bathroom and tossed the bundle inside. Then she closed the door and came back smiling. "There, that's better. Not much, but better." She had found a blue nylon robe. She slipped into it and knotted the belt. She ran cupped hands through her hair and motioned toward the couch. "Have a seat, Deputy Hackmore Wind."

"Thank you, Mrs. Fields," he said gravely. He sat down and enviously watched her light a cigarette, his hand automatically straying to his empty pocket.

She expelled a cloud of smoke and pointed the cigarette at him. "I'm not Mrs. Fields. I was Ms. Fields for twenty-two years, then Mrs. Schnell for five. I am Ms. Fields again. I refused to be burdened with a name like Mickey Schnell for the rest of my life." She smiled, dimples popping into cheeks the color of new honey. "Actually, I answer to Mickey better than anything else. Mickey is from Michele, I guess. That's what they've always called me.'' The smile slipped a little, became lopsided. ''I'm rambling. When I'm nervous, I ramble. I can't imagine why a deputy sheriff would visit me. So that makes me nervous. Have I forgotten to pay a ticket or something?'' She cocked her head entreatingly, a thick tangle of strawberry-blond hair tumbling forward across her shoulder. ''I don't remember getting a ticket.''

''No, it isn't a ticket.'' Hack smiled reassuringly, convinced suddenly that he could feel the slow, throbbing pulse of blood through his veins. ''It's a routine matter, Ms. Fields.''

''I told you, Mickey,'' she said chidingly, dusting the ash from her cigarette and wondering fleetingly why her fingers were trembling. She left the cigarette in the ashtray and brought her hands together on top of her thighs, clasping them together tightly, going on to wonder how old this dark, young god might be, whether there was a goddess somewhere. . . .

''All right, Mickey,'' Hack said. ''It's a routine . . . no, it's not routine, as a matter of fact. It's a very serious matter. Several people have been violently killed . . . murdered. I'm sure you must have heard or read about it. Here in the Metroplex area. Five people, to be exact.'' He hesitated. ''All of them from the Merriweather High School graduating class of 1968.''

Her eyebrows arched, rounding her eyes. ''That's . . . 1968, that's my class!'' One slim hand disentangled itself long enough to fly to her mouth. ''My God!''

Hack studied her stricken, bewildered face. ''You hadn't heard or—''

''No—yes. I—I knew about Clint Fielder, and I heard

about Muriel Haygood on TV, but, my God, I didn't know
. . . *five* of them?''

Hack nodded unhappily. ''Yes. Five. I'm sorry.''

Her hand dropped back to her lap. ''Who were . . .
were the other ones?''

''Clyde Burns, Clarence Switzer, and Jesse Bond,''
Hack recited mechanically. ''Did you know them?''

Her blond head bobbed slowly. ''Yes, I knew them. They
were all . . . we were all in the band together . . . the school
marching band.'' The hand had found its way back to her
mouth, pressed against her lips. ''How awful!'' Her hand
moved downward to clutch the robe above her breasts.
''I—I used to . . . to date Jesse Bond. That is, I dated him
for a while in my senior year.'' She suppressed a shiver. Her
troubled green eyes raised to meet his quiet, dark ones.
''Have they . . . have you any idea . . . ?'' She let it trail
away, her voice filled with dismay.

''We're working on it,'' he said gently. ''A lot of us.
We have some ideas, theories. We'll get there. It's just a
matter of time.''

''But why would anyone *do* that?''

''That's why I'm here. That's the thing we hope someone in your class can tell us. And now, with what you've
just told me, maybe we've narrowed it down some. Maybe
someone in the band has some answers. How many seniors were in the band?''

''I'm not sure. I think maybe twenty-five or so. Quite a
few. Some of us played all four years.'' She reached for
the cigarette and discovered it had burned to the filter. She
lit another, puffed greedily.

''Do you think you could remember all their names?''

She shook her head. ''No, I don't think so. Most of
them but not all. It's been too long.''

"We can find out easily enough. The school will have some kind of records."

"Or Mr. Stearns," Mickey said around small jets of smoke. "I'll bet he'd remember."

"You think so? Is he still around, do you know?" The smoke drifted tantalizingly in front of him.

"He's around. I saw him at the Northeast Mall not long ago. I don't know if he's still teaching, though." She picked at her lower lip with a thumb and forefinger. "My God," she said suddenly.

Hack looked at her inquiringly.

"This means," she said slowly, incredulously, "that out of twenty-five seniors in the band in 1968, only about fifteen of us are still alive."

"Fifteen? That would mean ten dead?"

"Only twenty years. My God!"

"Are you sure of that?"

"Yes, I'm sure. We lost three boys in Vietnam, and Jenny Perkins was killed in a car crash in 1975 . . . and then there was Bull Henderson." She paused. "But Bull didn't graduate. He was killed a month or so before graduation."

"How killed?"

She made a face and shrugged slender shoulders. "No one was ever sure, exactly. He was either pushed or fell from a cliff in Gooseneck Park on Possum Kingdom Lake."

"What made you think he was pushed?"

"I'm not sure—not really. There was this deputy sheriff who asked a lot of questions. We sort of thought he suspected Bull may have been pushed, but I don't think any of us kids really thought so. That's the way I remember it, at any rate." She combed slender fingers through her hair, one hand picking absently at the dark blue piping on her nightgown. She glanced up with a small, humorless smile. "Everything considered, it was a bad day for Bull Henderson."

He nodded in agreement. "Dying is about as bad as it gets."

"Not just that. Even before . . . earlier in the afternoon . . . we—a bunch of us—sort of spoiled his fun for him." Her voice faded, the smile changing somehow, becoming enigmatic. "Not intentionally. It was an accident. We were watching them . . . someone knocked a rock off the cliff, and they heard us . . ." Her voice faded again, eyes bright on his, daring him to pursue it, daring him not to.

"Watching what?" he asked, unable to resist.

Her hands ceased their aimless wandering, came to rest in her lap. She sighed. "They were making love, and when they heard us up on the cliff above them, his lover split."

"Boy or girl?" he asked calmly, his voice as even as her own.

"What?" She looked at him, startled. "Why . . . girl, of course. Oh, I see what you mean. No, it never occurred to me that it wasn't . . ."

"And how long after this experience was it before he fell?"

"I don't really know. Bull chased off after his Tinker Bell and . . ."

"His what?"

"Tinker Bell. That's what he called her. He was yelling 'Tinker Bell, come here, dammit,' or something like that. Obviously that was his nickname for her."

"If you could recognize Bull, why couldn't you recognize Tinker Bell?"

Mickey wrinkled her face in a grimace, shrugged. "She had her back to us. We only caught a glimpse of her face, not enough to tell who she was. It was a high cliff, maybe thirty-five feet or so, and she was out of sight so quickly . . .''

"You couldn't tell by her hair, her clothing?"

She shook her head. "No. Almost everyone, boys and girls both, wore band sweaters and jeans. And a lot of the boys had longer hair than we girls." She frowned thoughtfully. "She just *looked* like a girl, Hack." She stopped, her face coloring. "I'm sorry, Mr. Wind."

"Hack is fine. This group on the cliff. How many were there?"

"Oh, I don't know, ten or eleven maybe."

"You think you could give me their names?"

"I—well, most of them, I guess. I'm not sure I remember them all."

Hack nodded and took out his notebook. "Just give me what you can."

"Well . . . there was me, of course, and Jesse Bond— we were dating then. Then there was Muriel Lindstrom— oh, Muriel Haygood was her married name." She stopped and frowned again, then went on slowly. "Clint Fielder, Clyde Burns . . . my God, Hack! They're all—" She broke off, her face blanching. "They're all dead! Clarence Switzer, he was up there with us too!"

Hack felt a tingle along his spine, a cool prickling across the back of his head. He stared at her stricken face, his brain racing.

"Are you sure, Mickey?"

"Yes . . . yes, I'm sure."

Hack wrote furiously in his notebook. "With you, that makes six. Who were the others?"

"I'm—let me think. Teri, Teri Smith . . . she's a librarian in Dallas. She never did get married. Matilda Boyce. Matilda and Clyde Burns were going together . . . and, let's see . . . Johnny Ringley. I heard he's a fireman in

Fort Worth." She stopped and lit another cigarette, her eyes squinting at the ceiling. She shook her head. "I don't think I can . . . oh, wait, Stacy Crump." She nodded emphatically, her hair spilling across her shoulders. "I think that was all. If there was anyone else, I can't remember."

Hack nodded absently, studying what he had written on the pad, a fine edge of excitement building inside him. A common thread. That all-important common denominator that Hamilton Pope was looking for. A specific happening that linked all the victims in an unbroken chain of circumstances. Illicit sex and violent death. It *had* to mean something, however senseless or irrational it seemed after twenty years. A smoldering, festering malevolence spawned in the dark recesses of a madman's brain? Gain? Fear? Something! Nobody killed without a reason, *some* reason, be it so amorphous as to defy definition by so-called rational minds. Even Sirhan Sirhan and David Hinckley had had their reasons.

Hack closed the notebook and looked at the quiet, introspective woman across from him, her fulgent eyes half shuttered in silent, sorrowful reverie, her lovely face solemnly composed. He felt a sudden rush of warmth that had nothing to do with the force field of magnetic sensuality—well, almost nothing, he told himself—that emanated from her in almost palpable waves.

She absently wrapped a tendril of hair around a finger and let it spring free. The color had returned to her face, the emerald sparkle of her eyes almost startling against the restored honey tones of her skin. Bereft of makeup, she had pale pink lips; the vital, rosy glow of a young girl; the tantalizing allure of a vibrant, mature woman—and Hackmore Wind was finding it increasingly difficult to keep his thoughts centered on murder and murderers.

Again and again he found his eyes drawn back to her downcast face, to incredibly long, sandy lashes so pale as to appear almost translucent, to upturned lips that forever damned her to the appearance of a budding smile; a face that could never express rancor no matter how hard it tried. He found himself wondering if the honey-hued skin would feel as smooth as it looked, as soft and warm as . . . He heard the quiet amused sound, the throaty chuckle that she tried to stifle, and discovered that he had been caught: smoky-green eyes gleaming at him from under half-raised lids. Their eyes met, locked, ripped free, only to return and collide once again—the palpable, magnetic force at work again across the empty space between them.

She spoke without moving, except to moisten dry, parted lips.

"It *would* be interesting, wouldn't it?"

He nodded without speaking, unable to tear his eyes away from hers, wide open now and on full candlepower.

"You're beautiful," she went on softly, "but I guess you know that." She drew a deep, shuddering breath. "They tell me I'm beautiful also. Am I beautiful to you?"

He nodded silently.

"Beautiful enough?"

"More than enough." He found his voice finally, went on hoarsely, feeling foolish. "But I'm married."

Her lips quirked, worked closer to a smile. "I never doubted it for a moment. That doesn't matter to me. I'm not looking for till-death-do-us-part."

He tried to laugh, turn it into a joke, but the laugh got stuck somewhere in his diaphragm, and all that came through was a small croak of dismay.

"I wish I could, Mickey. I feel . . . I really wish I could, but I can't."

She sighed regretfully, unleashed a dazzling smile. She

shook her head and got to her feet, her smile intact, beaming down at him. "It's your loss, too, old buddy. I'm really something when I put my mind to it." She laughed softly. "I have this funny feeling that you are too." She leaned forward and touched the tip of her index finger to the corner of his mouth and drew it lightly along his lower lip. "We'll never know, will we?" She whirled and strode to the door, opened it, and stood leaning against its edge, her face placid, smiling.

"And now, Mr. Deputy Hackmore Wind, if you're finished grilling me, you can get your fanny out of here, and maybe, just maybe, I can get back to sleep." Her bantering tone broke the mesmerizing spell; he lunged to his feet, nodding mechanically, jerkily, a puppet with tangled strings.

He crossed in front of her, turned outside the door. "If there's . . . there may be something else later on . . . sometimes things develop like that . . . I may have to come back . . . you see, we don't always know what's . . . should I call first?"

She eased the door forward until there was only a crack, peered out at him with one gleaming eye. "It appears I'm not the only one who rambles when they're rattled," she said crisply, and closed the door.

CHAPTER

TWELVE

"Hey!"

Nancy shook him gently, ran a warm, wet tongue over his ear. "Don't go to sleep on me, old man."

He stretched, yawned before he could stifle it, grinned sheepishly. "I wasn't going to sleep. I was deep in thought."

"Deep in thought, my ass, you were about to slip into deep sleep." She pressed a splayed hand on his chest and let it drift downward. "Seriously, though, Ham, if you're too tired, we don't have to do anything." Her fingers explored his body tentatively. "I'm serious now. I don't want to wear you out."

"Never happen," he said heartily, tightening his arm and pulling her hard against his wide body, searching for willing lips and marveling as always at the sericeous feel of firm, cool skin that could blossom into swollen incandescence during the course of one brief kiss.

"Well, in that case," she murmured, flowing across him like liquid velvet, her eyes darkly glowing, absorbing him into the innermost folds of her secret flesh. She tugged his broad hand to the juncture of their joined bodies, arced forward, and pressed herself tightly against his chest, her warm breath bursting against his chin in small ragged puffs.

"Lie still," she whispered. "Let me do the work. Mmm . . . that's it right there." She pressed her palms flat against his cheeks and tilted his head downward to meet voracious lips, clamped his hips between her thighs as she felt his burgeoning response. He lay tense, motionless, the pressure building. He could feel the vibration of muted sounds deep inside her chest, the familiar, convulsive roll of her body as her time neared. She began to melt, dissolve around him, the heat unbearable, the pressure expanding to impossible limits.

She parted their fused lips long enough to whisper, "Now!"

He stifled a groan, tossed aside the rigid restraints, joined her pulsing cadence, collapsed shudderingly, his twinkling blue eyes as blank and empty as his mind.

She adjusted the rumpled covers before slipping back into bed. She sighed deeply and let an arm fall across his chest. "Before you go to sleep . . . I found a job today."

He stirred, moved his lethargic body minutely, then rolled his head to look at her, heavy-lidded eyes opening slowly. "Well," he said, intending to add "good" but deciding she might misinterpret that. "Well, how about that," he said. "Something good, you think?"

"A secretarial job," she said, watching his face intently. "I'll bet you didn't think I could do that kind of work. I'll bet you thought waitressing was all I was good for."

"No, I didn't think that. I'm sure you have a lot of talents I don't know about."

"How could you?" she said, a tart edge to her voice.
"You never ask me anything about myself."

"I didn't want to pry. You say I always sound like a cop
when I ask questions."

"Well, you do, but being interested is not prying. Being
interested is . . . I'll bet you don't even know how old I
am . . . exactly."

"Not exactly, no." He sighed. "Too damned young."

"Not so damned young. I'm almost thirty."

He studied her round, delicate features, a sudden grin
breaking across his face, a boyish grin that relieved the
sternness. "You sure age fast," he drawled. "A year ago
you were only twenty-five."

"I never told you that!" Her face was coloring rapidly,
blue eyes flashing.

"You didn't have to. It was in your file."

She flounced away from him, rolled over, and clicked
off her bedside light. She yanked at the covers, settled on
her side of the king-size bed, a yawning two-foot gulf
between them.

"I'm sorry, Nan," he said, already regretting the per-
versity in his nature that made him call her on her small
lie. Particularly since he was certain why she had told it.
"It doesn't really matter, you know. Not to me."

"You're lying," she said, her voice small and tight in
the darkness. "It does matter to you. You act like it
doesn't, but it does. You joke about it too much, and I
know you think about it all the time. That's . . . that's
why you don't want to know anything about me . . . why
you never ask me any questions, why you keep everything
inside, why you keep our . . . relationship on such a . . .
a sexual level."

"I wasn't aware of that," he said, genuinely puzzled.
"It's not intentional. I'm just not much of a talker and

. . . well, if you want to know the truth, I don't want to hear about you and the other men. Maybe I don't show it, but I'm jealous as hell.''

"There weren't all that many damned other men," she said, the crisp tartness back in her voice. "There's only been my husband, you, Clint Fielder, Jerry Longston, and Murphy—"

"I don't want a list."

"—Allen in high school. See! See there! You don't want to know about me. You want to think the worst. I'm just someone you relate to in bed. A sweet little piece, a hot ass to warm you on cold nights, a—" Her voice choked off and he reached up and turned on his lamp, stared in surprise at wet cheeks and tightly closed eyes, a clenched face abraded by misery.

"What's the matter?" he asked gently, moving across the bed toward her.

"I'm miserable!" she wailed brokenly, huddling into his reaching arms. "I—I want you to . . . to take me seriously."

He wiped her face with a fold of sheet, kissed each leaking eye. "I do take you seriously. Very seriously. Too much for my own good, my own peace of mind. But whatever else I am, I'm a realist. Nancy, you're so young and vibrant and lovely, and I'm a stodgy middle-aged man set in his ways. Opinionated, not so lively anymore, aches and pains you don't even know exist. I've got bunions and a varicose vein or two if you look close enough. I'm hardheaded, cantankerous, and I snore. I smoke too much, eat too much, and it'll probably be a toss-up whether I'll die from a heart attack or cancer. I have a failed marriage, a lousy job, and no future to speak of." He stopped and sighed. "Don't you think I know that someday you'll look at me and see what's there instead of what you think is there . . . whatever that is? If that happened at fifty-five or sixty, I might not be able to handle it like . . . like now.''

She stirred in his arms, looked up at him with damp, reproachful eyes. ''Are you telling me you want me to leave?''

He sighed again, heavily, resignedly. ''No. No, I'm not telling you that. I don't have the guts.''

She snuggled deeper into his embrace. ''Good. I wouldn't, anyhow. Now turn out that damn light and let's get some sleep around here. I have to start work tomorrow.''

By the time Hamilton Pope turned off U.S. Highway 180 onto the state highway that would lead him to Gooseneck Park on Possum Kingdom Lake and his appointment with Sheriff Marvin Stringer, he estimated he was running ten minutes behind schedule. And that worried him. Sheriff Stringer had not sounded particularly interested in discussing the twenty-year-old case and was even less enthused at having to meet him at the site. He had the uncomfortable feeling that he may have made the ninety-mile drive for nothing, that the irascible sheriff likely as not wouldn't show up at all and, if he did, would undoubtedly depart for parts unknown one minute past the appointed hour.

He eased forward on the accelerator, winced at the old Dodge's quiver of indignation as the needle passed beyond seventy-five. He leveled off at eighty, then grimaced again and goosed it up to ninety and tried not to think about the mangled and bloody wreckage he had worked as a patrolman, the hundred thousand odd miles that were already a part of the old car's history. He tried to remember when he had last bought new tires, and failed dismally, tried to recall the last time he had checked the air pressure in the ones he had; he failed again. He whistled bravely through his teeth, lit a cigarette, and stared dumbly as the gravel road that led to Gooseneck Park blurred by outside his window. He braked gingerly, unable to remember when he had last checked his brakes, either.

Air resistance and the drag of the heavy motor rapidly slowed the big station wagon. A half mile past the turnoff he swung onto the shoulder, made a looping turn, and came back.

A mile of dusty gravel road across a wide, flat field liberally studded with cactus, sage, and the ubiquitous mesquite, and he was entering the gates of Gooseneck Park, a narrow strip of rocky soil shaded by stunted oak and cedar and an occasional elm. A large sign announced that heavy fines would be levied against vandals and users of alcoholic beverages, along with excessive boisterousness, disorderly, and/or lewd conduct. Another smaller sign warned that no running water was available and that loitering was prohibited.

How do you not loiter in a park? Pope wondered. Was that not the purpose of parks? To loiter? To linger? To commune with nature, a time for introspection, mayhap a sip or two of the brewer's art, a bit of slap and tickle in some secluded nook? Take away your loitering, your sipping, your lewdness—what the hell was left?

He grinned a little and followed the hard-packed gravel to where the blue-on-blue Dodge was parked at the rear of the park, Detroit glitter sparkling in the sun, whip antennas and a multicolored light bar, a door decal in the shape of a Texas Ranger star, and a pregnant hood that screamed supercharger and was designed to chill the blood of any would-be highway cowboy.

Pope braked and spotted a khaki-clad, big-hatted figure

seated at a picnic table, his arm upraised, a dim gray outline against the shimmering blue waters of Possum Kingdom Lake.

Pope waved back. He lit a cigarette with the dashboard lighter, settled his Stetson squarely on his head, and got out. Feeling slightly foolish in his Western getup, faded Levi's, gleaming boots, and a tan, four-button shit-kicker shirt with dark brown stitching around the pockets and along the edge of the collar, he walked across to meet the lanky man unfolding from the picnic table bench.

"It's always kinda stuck in my craw." Sheriff Marvin Stringer spat a stream of amber-colored fluid over the painted two-by-three railing. Both men leaned forward to watch the glob of spittle land on the flat granite rock thirty feet below. "Right about there is where he was. Landed flat on his back, headfirst probably, because his neck was broke in three places. Had about as much chance as an armadillo on a freeway. That there rock looks flat from up here, but she's got some jagged edges sticking up. A couple of them went right into his skull." He laid a long-fingered, brown hand on the railing. "This here whole section was down there with him. The way he felt when we lifted him out, I allus figured his back was broke too. But old Doc Lindner never went past the head wound, which is what killed him, I reckon."

"I understand you thought at the time that he may have been helped along his way?"

"Still do," Stringer said emphatically. "Ain't had no reason to change my mind in twenty years. If I'da been sheriff then . . ." He let it fade away and turned dark brown, deeply socketed eyes on Pope. "I was just a deputy back then. I been sheriff near about six years now. Clifford M. Blythe was sheriff back then. Not much of one at that. Too damn old, first thing. Never wanted to muddy up the water, stir up the ashes. That there Henderson boy wasn't one of our'n. But the biggest reason was that he was coming up for re-election. Didn't want no unsolved murders on his hands.'' He looked across the cove toward the twisting blue snake that was Possum Kingdom Lake. ''We put it down as an accident.''

''What made you think it wasn't?''

Stringer removed his sweat-stained, battered Resistol hat and ran a hand through sparse gray hair. ''Like I said before, he was flat on his back. There's nothing between here and there but air, and he had cuts and a bruise on his forehead.''

''Maybe he hit his face here on the landing while he was falling?''

Stringer wagged the hat impatiently, ''There were bits of dirt in some of the cuts. And some tiny pieces of shale. I could see that for myself, but Doc Lindner confirmed that much. It was the same kind of rock you see laying here on these steps. It keeps peeling away from this old, crumbling cliff. Sometimes pretty big chunks too. Big enough to addle a man's brains if you hit him hard enough to make him stagger backward and fall through this flimsy railing.'' He massaged the hat-band groove across his forehead, fingered the flowing silver mustache above his thin upper lip. He replaced his hat, the sun wrinkles deepening at the edge of his eyes as he squinted at Pope. ''Somebody hit that young feller. Maybe more'n once.'' He turned and spat over the railing again.

''Ginger Belle?''

He gave Pope a quick, sharp look, then turned his eyes back to the lake and nodded. ''I reckon it musta been. It don't make much sense any other way. But there's some difference of opinion about that name. A couple of the kids said Tinker Bell, not Ginger Belle. Take your pick.

Wasn't nobody with either one of them names in that bunch of kids, anyhow."

"Tinker Bell? Like in *Peter Pan*?"

Stringer smiled wryly. "Yeah. I looked her up in the county library. She was a mean little dickens. Jealous. Wanted that boy Peter Pan all to herself, I reckon. Seems like she killed this little kid named Wendy out of pure damn meanness."

Pope nodded, smiling. "I saw the play. By the way, you do know what happened out on the point below the cliff? The perverted sexual act between . . . ?"

"You mean the head job?" Stringer said, his face amused. "And the kids watching? Yeah, they told me about that."

"Maybe there's a parallel here between the Peter Pan story and real life. If the Henderson boy had a girlfriend who saw . . . ?"

Stringer shook his head. "Picture I got from the other kids was that nobody much liked Bull Henderson. None of the girls, anyhow. First thing, he was a purty ugly kid, as far as I could see. Second thing was they said he didn't know how to act with a nice girl. Too horny, I reckon. Too nasty-talking. I got the same story from everyone. Creep, nerd, . . . them was just some of the things they called him. And here the poor sucker laid dead." His head wagged again. "I reckon I just don't understand kids anymore."

"They're no longer kids," Pope reminded him. "They're in their late thirties, and somebody's killing the hell out of them . . . limited, so far, to the kids on the cliff."

"That's sure passing strange, all right enough. You think there might be some connection to this thing that happened here?'' His dark eyes ambushed Pope from under shaggy brows, gleaming with interest.

"I don't know what to think yet. I was hoping you could shed some light on a possible motive."

Sheriff Stringer squinted ruefully. "I ain't been much help. I done what I could back then in the time that old fart gave me, but I came up empty. Only chance we had was to grill them kids one at a time, but it was late and everybody put up such a stink, the sheriff said let them go. All I could do was talk to them a busload at a time. We never got a peep out of one of them that meant anything.'' He scratched the back of his neck reflectively. "I did get a chance to talk to them kids on the cliff, but they wasn't much help, either. They never got a good look at this Tinker Bell."

"Must have been a pet name, a nickname," mused Pope.

"Kinda what I figgered."

"Odd choice, though," said Pope. He sighed. "Well, is there anything in your file that could be of possible use, do you think?"

"I doubt it, but I'll run you some copies all the same. Won't hurt nothing." He turned and clumped back up the last section of stairs, the entire structure vibrating under the thud of his run-over boots.

Pope followed him more slowly, a sour taste in his mouth. Ninety miles for nothing, after all, and ninety more still ahead. But not entirely an absolute waste, he told himself. He was taking back the makings of a possible motive and the knowledge that long dead Bull Henderson obviously considered his paramour a mean little bitch of a witch.

CHAPTER

THIRTEEN

Hamilton Pope was three blocks away from his house when the squad car pulled out of a side street and eased up beside him. The grinning patrolman lifted a hand in greeting, then motioned for him to pull over. He automatically glanced down to check his speed before turning into the curb and braking to a stop. Five miles per hour over the limit . . . surely not even a rookie would try to give him a ticket for that. He watched the patrolman get out, ticket pad in hand, and swore under his breath. He rolled down his window and lit a cigarette and waited, storm clouds building.

"Hi, Sarge." The young rookie was still grinning like an idiot. Pope scowled up at him silently. The freckled face was familiar, but he couldn't put a name to it. At least the gung-ho asshole knew who he was, he thought sourly.

"Radio not working?" the young cop asked genially.

Pope's scowl changed to a perplexed frown. "No, as a matter of fact, it isn't. Why?"

The patrolman nodded. "Captain Tanner said it probably wasn't. We've had three calls on you in the last hour. They want you over at the Mayfair district.'' He looked on the back of his ticket pad, a scribbled note. ''Malcolm Carlyle residence. They said you knew where it was.''

Pope felt a fluttering tingle in his stomach. ''Any idea what's going on?''

''No, sir. Detective Singer answered the call, if that's any help.''

Pope nodded and switched on the engine. ''Thanks.''

''You bet, Sarge.''

Pope drove away from the curb with a familiar tightness building along the back of his neck and down across his shoulders. Death. He could almost smell it already. If Milly Singer had caught the squeal and they were looking for him, it couldn't be anything else. Death at the Malcolm Carlyle residence. The lawyer? It had to be. But maybe not. Matilda Carlyle had been on that bluff also, had been a witness to . . . to what? To what, dammit? An aberrant sex act. The opening scene of a two-act play that ended in murder? If so, why was the whole thing being resurrected twenty years after the final curtain had been brought down by an ambitious old sheriff? The case had been closed officially and for all time an accident. But what if Sheriff Stringer was right? What if horny Bull Henderson had caught up with his Tinker Bell on the cliffside stairway, insisted on resuming their interrupted lovemaking—if it could be labeled that—and had met with strenuous objections, violent rejection in the form of a rock in the middle of his sweating face, undoubtedly an unexpected reaction from someone who had only moments before been caught up in an ultimate act of sexual obsequiousness?

Okay, he thought. Accepting the Bull Henderson death as a brutal murder, albeit unintentional, accepting the events of that dark, portentous day as the evil seed that had lain dormant for twenty years before bursting forth in a riotous bloom of bloody deaths—accepting that as the gospel according to deductive genius Hamilton Pope—where did that lead him? What had the motive been? There had to be reasons, no matter how irrational, how senseless they appeared when exposed to the cold, penetrating light of logic, when analyzed by reasoning minds. Nobody selected a specific group of people and began systematically killing them without reason—even Hitler thought he had good reasons.

He remembered his pompous declaration at the task-force meeting: revenge or gain. No margin for error, no room for doubt. During the short span of one day his certainty had been shaken for no readily discernible reason, his deductive reasoning cloudy and vague, amorphous.

What about fear? Jealousy? Lust? Rage? Traditionally good, solid emotional motivations for murder; but would they sustain the prolonged state of remorseless dedication necessary to effect the deliberate and difficult murder of half a dozen people? Common sense and logic said no, but history and experience cast doubts on such unequivocal conclusions, and forced consideration of more nebulous reasons like the command of a righteous God; the contempt of an uncaring society; the savage, scathing scorn of a lover lost; the acid bath of a ruptured ego. And finally there was pain: emotional pain as real and as piercing as a hammer-smashed thumb.

He had seen the incredibly corrosive effects of pain sustained over a long period of time, and he wondered briefly as he turned into the Carlyle driveway if it was perhaps déjà-vu time, if history, as they were fond of saying, was repeating itself.

• • •

Roscoe Tanner broke away from the small group of people and strode toward him down the hallway.

•"Where the hell you been all day?" His tone was halfway between a gruff demand for an explanation and a querulous request for information.

"Fishing." Pope replied succinctly, spying Milly's honey hair inside the group that Tanner had just left and heading directly for her. "On Possum Kingdom Lake."

He ignored Tanner's surprised grunt, reached between the shoulders of a uniformed patrolman and a white-frocked ambulance attendant, and tugged at Milly's shoulder. She turned, annoyed, then grimaced sheepishly and broke through to follow him down the hall.

"I didn't know you were here," she said. "I was just—"

"Holding court," he said crisply. "What are they doing in here? Who was killed and where's the body?"

She flipped open her notebook. "Malcolm Carlyle, aged thirty-eight."

"Okay, I have background on him. The same as the rest?"

She shook her head. "No, not like the others. He was shot in the head at close range. Looks like a small-caliber . . . maybe a .32. Could be even smaller—"

"Shot?" Pope stared at her, stunned. "Shot? Are you—" He stopped and shook his head. "Of course you're sure." He rocked on his heels and reached for a cigarette, then let his hand come away empty. "Shot. Why shot, for chrissake?"

Milly tapped a pen against her notebook and smiled faintly. "I don't know that, Ham—not yet."

"Where's the body?"

"In the study." She indicated the door Pope had gone through the day before. "Dr. Paris has been here and gone.

He estimated two o'clock this afternoon, give or take two hours. Since we happen to know he had lunch at twelve-thirty, he promises to give us a tighter estimate after the autopsy.''

"How do you know when he had lunch?''

"His wife and his mother. They had lunch with him downtown. He left them at about a quarter to one to go back to his office, and they went out for an afternoon's shopping. I've already checked his office. He never showed up. His wife and mother came home around four o'clock and found him. They—'' She broke off as two men came out of the study. One carried a vacuum cleaner and a black satchel, and the other—a tall, skinny redhead wearing a baseball cap—carried camera equipment.

"All finished,'' the redhead said cheerfully. "How're you doin, Ham?''

"Just fair, Otto. Anything?''

Otto shrugged. "Nothing that jumped out at me. Looks like somebody just put a gun to his head and went bang. Still in there somewhere. Mighta been a hollow-point. Entry hole seems a little larger than normal, and the bullet's still in there.''

"No gun?''

"No gun, but we have the casing. That makes it an automatic, .32-caliber.''

"No chance of suicide?''

Otto cocked an almost lashless eye. "Not unless the gun sprouted wings. We bagged his hands for a gunpowder residue test, but my guess is it's a waste of time.'' He formed his right hand into the shape of a gun and pointed to a spot above and slightly behind his right ear. "Right about there. Close, angled down, and back. An awkward spot for a suicide.''

"Okay,'' Pope said. "Thanks.'' He turned to Milly.

"Give me a couple of minutes, then come on in." He brushed past her and went in the study door.

It was the same room: Nothing had changed that he could see. The same and yet vastly different. The difference not so much the presence of death as the absence of life in the shapeless form sprawled facedown across the mahogany desk, its vital juices spread in an irregular red pattern around the leached, contorted face. One hand was outflung on the gleaming desktop, a shining plastic bag taped securely to its wrist. The other, hanging out of sight behind the desk, would be similarly bagged.

Pope felt a tremor pass through his body, a fleeting surge of rage. He closed his eyes and breathed deeply. Then he opened them again and crossed deliberately to the body.

Otto Terkin had been right; it was an awkward spot for a self-inflicted wound. But not impossible, Pope told himself. The matted hair had been pulled back from the small, ugly hole that was covered almost entirely by a viscid film of dark blood. He closed his eyes and leaned over and sniffed, caught a faint odor of cordite, and something else he decided was singed hair.

Close, hell, he thought, the damned gun was pressed against his head. He was still sniffing when the door opened and Milly came in. She crossed to him, an odd look on her face. "What are you doing?"

"Come here. Tell me what you smell."

Milly leaned forward gingerly, took a cautious sniff. "I don't smell anything."

"Closer," Pope said impatiently, pressing on the back of her head. "Now try it."

"Shit, Ham, don't get my nose in it!" She bunched her hair into a rope and held it behind her neck with one hand, eased her head forward, eyes squinted.

Milly sniffed again. "Gunpowder, I think, maybe burned hair. Is that it?"

"That's what I got, but my sense of smell is so screwed up from smoking, I wasn't sure."

"What do you want to do about the wife and mother? Do we take them together, take them one at a time, each take one . . . or what?"

"I'll take them both tonight, separately. You can do the same tomorrow for a follow-up. What kind of condition is the mother in?"

"Holding up admirably. Much better than the wife. Much better than I would, I think." She grimaced wryly. "But then I'm not a blue blood, either." She followed up with an apologetic smile. "Seriously, I think she's doing real well."

Pope grunted and glanced toward the body on the desk. "If her blood's blue, she sure didn't pass any along to her son. Looks like plain old red to me."

Milly wrinkled her nose. "You're gross, Pope," she said.

He reached for the cigarette he'd been wanting for the last half hour. "I'm damned tired too," he said, lighting two and giving her one. "I just drove two hundred miles to find out a kid named Bull Henderson took a fatal thirty-foot free-fall because his girl, whom he called Tinker Bell, didn't want to go down on him again."

Milly's eyebrows lifted. "Again?"

Pope told her about it while they finished their cigarettes. He looked around for an ashtray, found none, and stubbed the butts carefully on his boot heel. "It seems to me there has to be a connection, Milly. I'm as sure of that as Sheriff Stringer was that Bull Henderson was cold-cocked. But I'll be damned if I can find a thread that runs back twenty years."

"Patience, Ham. We have a lot of people to talk to yet." She glanced at Malcolm Carlyle, then back at Pope. "A lawyer," she said softly.

"Yeah, I know. That's another damn thing that's bugging me."

Milly pursed her lips thoughtfully and looked toward the dead man. "Maybe it stops here."

"How so?"

She shrugged. "He's out of rhyme. No Indians. Specifically, no Indian chiefs."

He gave her an annoyed glance, then chuckled wryly. "You've checked, huh?"

"If there's Indian blood in any of the others, it's well hidden. I thought for a moment when I saw Teri Smith . . . but she's Italian and Irish."

Pope nodded wearily and rubbed his face with both hands, feeling suddenly old and tired.

Milly scrutinized his face, a mocking look in her eyes. "Maybe you're not getting enough sleep these days." She tilted her head, her hands stuffed inside the pockets of the quilted windbreaker he had bought her on her last birthday. A typically practical gift from a practical man.

"Yeah," he said vaguely, "this damn case." His eyes moved around the room. She knows, he thought. Well, it had to happen sooner or later, but he couldn't help wondering if a real man wouldn't have told her, faced her with it, pointed out their relationship's lack of commitment, permanency, pointed out that it was a now-and-then thing, that a guy liked a little stability in his life, a little continuity.

His eyes came back to hers. "You know, huh?"

She made the wry grimace again. "I'm just easy, Ham. I'm not dumb."

He bristled. "You're not easy, Milly. Hell, as I remember it, I had to take you out half a dozen times before I could get you in the sack.''

She made a brittle, rueful sound meant to be a laugh. ''Maybe that reveals more about you than it does about me, Ham. You ever think of that? They're waiting to pick him up.'' She turned toward the door without waiting for an answer, walking stiffly erect, her face expressionless. She opened the door and stopped with her back toward him. ''If you're going to take the Carlyle women yourself, I won't wait. They're in the game room.''

''All right, Milly,'' he said meekly. ''Go home. Have a nice night.''

She turned and looked at him coldly. ''What a shitty thing to say, Ham,'' she said hotly. ''Under the circumstances, a really crappy thing to say.''

''Hey, I wasn't being facetious—'' he began, then broke off, suddenly mute with dismay, reading the pain in her face and wondering if he should try to explain that a whimsical fate had dealt him new cards in an old game: a flush of hearts, a sometimes winning hand, and that the hope that springs eternal had decreed that he must play it out until the bitter losing end. He wondered if he could make her understand, without hurting, that what they had had was warm and good and comfortable, but that the fire in his brain, the fever in his blood, came from a vivacious slip of a woman three fourths her size and probably less than half her intrinsic worth.

But the doorway was empty; she was gone and he had explained nothing. He listened to the babble of angry voices in the hall and watched stoically as they came to take the body, sullen young men who gave him reproachful glances, stacked the body on their carrier like so much useless garbage, tarped it, belted it, and wheeled it out of the room without a word.

Silence descended and he sat on the arm of a leather chair and smoked quietly, utterly weary. His eyes surveyed the room leisurely, noting for the first time its lack of masculinity: the pastel walls a faint blush of pink, the gaily colored draperies, blood-red roses against a field of white. Even the paintings, he guessed, had been selected to soothe the feminine psyche, flowers and sunsets and women tending their young, woodland nymphs frolicking amid big-eyed creatures of the forest. Globe lamps hung suspended at each end of the huge free-form desk that was carved from a single slab of wood, glossy and dark, slanted across one corner to form a neat, triangular alcove accessible from one side only. Overflowing bric-a-brac shelves abounded, and as a final assault on the male ego, a two-foot statuette of Adonis, muscular and bronzed, adorned a small round table directly across from the desk.

Not my kind of room, Pope thought, crushing his cigarette against his heel, pawing absently with the toe of his boot at fallen ashes and sparks. He pushed erect, reluctantly crossed to the desk. He glanced briefly at the smear of blood on the dark, smooth surface, the chalked outline, then dropped laboriously to his knees on the thick beige carpet and slowly began to crawl.

CHAPTER

FOURTEEN

She was tall and willowy and graceful: taller than her son; taller, even, than Matilda. Under the simple brown dress, belted tightly at her slender waist, she looked as supple and resilient as a hickory branch. She had a pale, handsome face that time had almost forgotten, that had seldom, if ever, seen the sun; a wide, unfurrowed forehead above cool gray eyes that sized him up intently as she rose lithely to her feet and stood waiting for him to cross the large well-lit room.

"I'm Detective Pope," he said, not really expecting the slim hand she held out to be shaken, pleasantly surprised at the warm dry palm, the strength of the slender fingers that gripped his own. How grotesque she must make Matilda feel, he thought musingly, so slim and poised, so meticulously groomed. He found himself wondering about her age, common sense allowing no less than fifty-two or fifty-three years, and that assuming her a mother at the tender age of twenty or twenty-one. She looked forty.

"Detective Pope. I'm Marsha Carlyle. I'm terribly sorry, but Matilda just this minute went to her room. She's terribly distraught, poor dear. I hope this doesn't inconvenience you, doesn't interfere with your investigation."

"Not at all. I understand fully. We can speak with her later. For the time being, I'm sure you can give me what I need for my report."

She nodded quietly and moved back to her seat. "Of course. I'll do anything I can. This terrible thing . . . my darling son . . . why would anyone want to do such a terrible thing?" Her voice rose, a hint of anguish breaking through her iron-like control. She dropped her head, one hand fluttering briefly before returning to her lap. "I'm sorry. You couldn't know that, of course." She raised her head, lips quivering in a meager, courteous smile. "Please go ahead with your question, Mr. Pope."

He nodded, glanced around furtively for an ashtray, saw none, and pushed the thought from his mind. He cleared his throat.

"You and your daughter-in-law. I understand the two of you had lunch with your son."

"Yes, we lunched at Dion's."

"And you finished about what time?"

"About twelve-thirty. My son stayed and talked for a few minutes, then left to go to his office. Matilda and I left a few minutes later . . . one o'clock, perhaps."

"Do you have any idea why he came home instead of going to his office?"

She shook her head slowly, one hand absently testing the swirls and loops of her silver hair for springiness. "No. I have no idea."

"Did he actually say he was going to his office?"

"Yes, he commented on the amount of work ahead of him for the afternoon. That was the reason he cut short our luncheon engagement."

"Did he often come home during the working day?"

"No. Not to my knowledge. I'm certain Matilda could tell you more about that."

"How did you and Matilda get downtown? Did one of you drive?"

"No. We took a taxi both ways. Parking downtown can be such a nuisance."

"Do you recall what cab company you used?"

"Yes, of course. Sunshine Cab Company."

"How did . . . would you mind telling me exactly how you found him?"

She nodded, her face pale, composed, her tightly clenched hands the only indication of internal agitation. Watching her, Pope felt a rising surge of admiration.

"I—I discovered his . . . body. Matilda had gone into the . . . this room to make a drink. I was walking down the hallway to the bathroom. The door to Malcolm's study was standing open. I glanced in . . . and saw him." She moistened her lips, went on in a low, dry voice. "I tried to stop . . . to keep Matilda out . . . but she came looking for me too quickly. I was certain he was dead, but I called an ambulance, anyway . . . and then I called the police. Matilda came in while I was on the phone. . . ." Her voice died away.

"You didn't move him . . . touch anything, move anything?"

She gave him a perplexed look. "I—I touched . . . I felt for a pulse in his wrist. No, other than that, I didn't move anything." A tremor rippled through her. "He was already . . . already cold."

"No one else entered the room except you and Matilda before the police arrived?"

She shook her head slowly. "No. The police were here

before the ambulance. The men from the ambulance never came in. The police sent them away after they discovered that Malcolm was dead.''

"And Matilda? Was she in the room alone with her husband at any time?''

Her eyes came up and locked on his face. "No. She was near collapse. After the police arrived, I brought her in here. I gave her a Valium and made her lie down here on the couch. She wouldn't go to her room." She blinked her eyes slowly, her face subtly changing, her voice suddenly cool and flat. "Why, Detective Pope? What are you implying?''

"I'm not implying anything, Mrs. Carlyle. I just need all the facts. To be honest with you, except for one thing, your son's death has all the earmarks of a suicide.''

The change was no longer subtle; her face had become a cold, unreadable mask. "What thing?" she asked tonelessly.

"The gun." He hesitated, plunged on. "Has your son been depressed, Mrs. Carlyle? Is there any reason you can think of—''

"Absolutely none!" Her voice was a whiplash. "My son did not kill himself! He was murdered! I must warn you, Mr. Pope. Neither my husband nor myself will allow the police to pass over his death lightly, try to clear their books by calling it anything other than what it is!" She breathed deeply, her bosom heaving, the gray eyes igniting with anger. "I want my son's murderer found and punished, Mr. Pope.''

Pope endured the blazing eyes as long as he could, then dropped his gaze to his notebook. He made a meaningless mark. "We have to consider everything, Mrs. Carlyle. I said your son's death bore the earmarks of suicide. I didn't say it *was* one. The wound itself, the position of the body, the—'' He broke off at the shadow of pain that passed across her face. He cast around in his mind and grasped the first thought that came winging by.

"Did your son ever mention the name Bull Henderson to you, Mrs. Carlyle?"

She bit her lip, tiny wrinkles appearing at the corners of her eyes as she considered it. She nodded slowly. "Yes, I believe so . . . a long time . . . if I remember correctly, he was one of Malcolm's classmates, a fellow band member in the school band . . . yes, the year they graduated . . . an accident or something." Her brow cleared. "Yes, he was fatally injured on a band excursion on Possum Kingdom Lake. It was a terrible accident. We had taken all the kids on a picnic to celebrate their winning third place in the state band competition."

"We?"

"Yes. I was a band sponsor. I attended all their functions. So did my husband when he could. We believe young people need all the encouragement they can get from parents." She hesitated, her forehead wrinkling. "I seem to recall some question about the young man's death. Something one of the deputies said, I believe."

Pope nodded admiringly. "You have a good memory, Mrs. Carlyle. Did Malcolm ever mention the name Tinker Bell?"

"Tinker Bell?" Her face moved in the beginnings of amusement, then abruptly sobered as she shook her head from side to side. "I assume you mean other than in connection with the play *Peter Pan*. We saw that when he was a youngster."

"No, it has nothing to do with *Peter Pan*. How about Ginger Belle?"

"No, I don't believe so."

"Did he ever discuss with you the circumstances surrounding Bull Henderson's death?"

"No. Other than the fact that the boy fell from a staircase of some sort."

"But he hasn't mentioned the name recently, even obliquely?"

She smiled faintly. "No."

He returned her meager smile. "Did I say something amusing?"

The smile became sheepish. "I'm sorry. I'm not being patronizing, and I don't wish to insult you, but I'm afraid my conception of policemen has been unduly influenced by movies and television."

"So?"

Her eyes crinkled with amusement. "So I've just never heard one use a word like *obliquely*." She laughed self-consciously, uncertainly, watching his face, her own face changing color.

He closed his notebook and stood up, chuckling with her, not at all unhappy to see color and laughter in a face that had been pinched and frozen with pain and grief a short time before.

"Believe it or not," he said lightly, "some of us even read a book occasionally."

"Oh, I'm sure you do," she said warmly. She lifted gracefully to her feet and held out her hand, her face already working its way back to solemnity. "I'm afraid I haven't been of much assistance, Detective Pope."

He gripped her hand, gave it a reassuring pat. "You never know." He smiled his most confident smile. "Don't worry, Mrs. Carlyle, we'll find out who killed your son."

She smiled wanly and nodded. "Thank you, Mr. Pope."

He moved to the door. "If you would, please tell your

daughter-in-law that I, or a detective named Milly Singer, will be by tomorrow to talk to her.''

"Would that be the lady detective I talked to this afternoon?"

Pope opened the door and smiled. "Yes. Milly's one of our very best men."

She walked a few feet toward him, the amused crinkle back around her eyes. "I think you must have lied to me, Mr. Pope. If your eyes are all that bad, you couldn't possibly read a book."

"Please forget what I said. She doesn't work at it, but she can be as mean and ornery as any of them Yankee bra burners anytime she sets her mind to it.''

A glint came into her eyes. "Not all bra burners are Yankees, Mr. Pope."

"Oops," he said. "Deeper and deeper. Good night, Mrs. Carlyle."

"Good night, Mr. Pope."

He drove directly to his office from the Carlyle residence. He rummaged in his large desk drawer and produced a manila mailing envelope. He typed a short note on Milly's typewriter, then inserted the note and the six-inch square of beige carpeting he had cut from the Carlyle study floor into the envelope. He sealed it securely, addressed it, then trudged down the corridor to the duty sergeant's desk. He spent five minutes discussing with the sergeant the fastest and most reliable method of transmitting the envelope to the Rossacher Institute in Houston. He drove home slumped behind the wheel of his Dodge, his eyes burning, his back quivering from fatigue.

The house was dark and silent, the driveway empty. He felt a thrill of apprehension when he saw the note taped to the refrigerator, another thrill of relief when he read it.

Old Stud,

I waited and waited! I have some work to clean up
so I'm going back to the office for a couple of hours.
Should be home by eight-thirty. Nothing interesting
in the fridge, so why don't we go out to eat? Eating
out makes me horny!

                              Your willing concubine

Pope grunted and scowled, the next moment grinning
at the salutation and signature on the note. He rummaged
in the freezer and found two Hungry Man TV dinners. So
much for eating out. He uncapped a beer and was settling
into his favorite chair before a flickering, muted TV when
the phone began to ring.

He ignored it for five jarring cycles, then, prodded by
belated compulsion, scrambled to answer it before it
stopped.

"Hello."

"Jesus H. Christ, Ham! Do you know what we've got
here?"

Pope sighed. "No, Roscoe, tell me, what have we got?"

"Do you have any idea who Malcolm Carlyle is?"

"Some. He was a hell of a good lawyer, judging by his
estate. A wealthy one, at any rate."

"Not so much him," Tanner said, his voice an octave
or two higher than normal. "It's his daddy."

"What's his daddy?"

"I just got off the phone with His Honor the fucking
Mayor, and I'm standing up right now if that tells you
anything."

"In your cute way you're trying to say you got your ass
chewed on. Okay. So what's new? What about Carlyle's
daddy?"

"Lawrence Peal Carlyle," Tanner said ponderously.

"Hmm. I seem to remember that name—wasn't he an ambassador a few years back? To Brazil or Costa Rica, or one of them coffee-bean countries?"

"Not only that, he's a personal friend of the president's, on his Council of Economic Advisers or some damn thing. And not only that, he owns about half of Houston. You ever hear of Carlco? Or Peal Electronics? Or Majesty Freight Lines? Or Carlyle Oil Company?"

"Okay," Pope said irritably, "so he's a wheel. I'll take your word for it. What am I supposed to do, Roscoe? Piss my pants? Or maybe work a little harder? I'm putting in sixteen hours a day now. You want me to try for twenty-four?"

"No, no," Tanner said hurriedly, his voice lowering, soothing. "No, I just think you should concentrate on this one for the next few days and let Milly and Sheldon—"

"It's all the same," Pope said wearily. "You haven't been reading your damn reports again, Roscoe. Didn't Milly turn in a report this afternoon?"

"Yeah," he said uncomfortably, "but I didn't get a chance . . . the same, you say? But Carlyle was shot!"

"The result's the same. Maybe he lost his utility knife. Maybe Carlyle wouldn't hold still—the thing is, Roscoe, Carlyle was one of the group of kids who figured in the Bull Henderson killing somehow. You did read about Bull Henderson in the reports?"

"Yeah," Tanner said, his voice vague. "I read about that. I just don't see how you can tie that into this."

"I can't. Not yet. Not positively beyond a shadow of a doubt. But I damn well will, because there's a connection somewhere. This guy is not killing for fun. He has reasons. And sooner or later—"

"We ain't got no later," Tanner said heavily. "Carlyle's flying up from Houston in the morning."

"It's not the end of the world, Roscoe. Whatever happened to equality under the law? I'm a lot more disturbed by Clyde Burns's death. He left six kids and not enough insurance to bury him. So this guy Carlyle's a hot-dog Mr. Big. So goddamned what?"

"You ain't gettin the heat," Tanner grumbled. "His Honor the fu—"

Pope hung up on him. He stood waiting patiently for the phone to ring again, and when it didn't, he shrugged and took his bottle of beer back to his recliner.

Roscoe's getting old, he thought. He's letting old age and the grubby little politicians suck the spine out of him. He took a drink of warm beer and made a face. Maybe it happens to all of us, he ruminated sourly. Old age, for sure. The blood cools and ambitions shrivel along with a lot of other things. The ass sinks and its a toss-up whether your hair or your teeth falls out first. He shifted in the chair and tongued a neglected cavity in one of his molars. He ran questing fingers across graying hair and was gratified at the wiry fullness that met his hand. Not yet. Not for a while.

He was dozing to the sounds of tinned TV laughter when he heard Nancy's key in the door. He roused sluggishly, blinked at her bright, cheerful face in the doorway.

"Ready, tiger?" She stood poised expectantly, eyes shining, the heavy mass of blond hair framing her face, diminishing her small features to even more childlike proportions.

"Ready? For what?"

Her face fell, lips pouting, forehead crumbling in a frown. "Didn't you find my note?"

"Oh, yeah. Yeah, I found your note." He washed his

face with his hands. "Old Stud also found a couple of TV dinners in the freezer."

"Oh, pooh," she said. She tripped across the room and fell into his lap. She seized his jaws with tiny hands and kissed him warmly. She leaned back, face flushed, beaming.

"We haven't celebrated my new job yet. I thought a nice dinner would be just the thing." She tilted her head to one side, her face puckered appealingly. "Whatta ya think?"

"I'd have to shower and shave and change clothes. It's pretty late."

"Late? It's only eight-twenty. Quality folks never eat before nine." She ran a finger into his ear, wiggled it. "Unless, of course," she said artlessly, "you're too tired."

He sighed, pulled the hand away from his ear and raked it across the stubble on his chin. "Well, quit pestering me. Let me up so I can get to the bathroom."

"Great!" She leapt to her feet and tugged on his hand. "I'll get the water started while you shave chop-chop. Maybe I'll just slip out of these things and take mine with you, now instead of later."

"Uh-uh," he said emphatically. "We've been there before. You do that and it's a cinch you won't be eating restaurant food tonight."

She glanced over her shoulder and wiggled her eyebrows. "What'll I be eating?"

"Hungry Man TV dinners," he said, and grinned.

She passed the bathroom and continued down the hall laughing. "Okay, chicken. I'll lay out your blue suit."

"Suit?" He muttered under his breath, wondering where she was planning on going.

He finished in record time, padded down the hall in a

towel, and dressed in the clothing she had laid out, grumbling with dismay when he saw the tie and glossy loafers.

She tightened the knot in his tie, adjusted his collar, and stepped back. "My, don't you look handsome." She walked around him, her eyes squinted critically. "You could use a haircut, though."

"I could use a new head, letting you dress me up like a store-window dummy just to go eat. By the way, where're we going, anyway?"

"There's a new restaurant out by Northeast Mall I've been wanting to try. It's called La Muchacho."

"Muchacho? That sounds like pepper-belly food. My God, you mean you made me shower and shave, dressed me like a dummy to go eat Mexican food? What's wrong with Taco Bell or El Fenix?"

She ran a comb through her hair, fluffing it, ignoring him.

"I'll bet they won't even have any beer," he groused, watching her face wrinkle with exasperation.

"Oh, don't be so . . . so damned plebian."

He grinned, then smothered it as he caught her warning look in the mirror.

"Don't say it," she said crisply, her lips on the verge of a smile.

"Pepper-belly food gives me the trots."

She patted his stomach and ushered him down the hall to the front door. "A little trotting might do you some good." She swayed toward him, lips puckered. "Just keep your mind on the dessert and all the fun times between trots."

"I'll try," he said, following her through the door, admiring the fine sway of a neatly rounded bottom. "But it'd be a hell of a lot easier if these damn shoes didn't hurt my corns so bad."

CHAPTER

FIFTEEN

Milly Singer was alone in the conference room when Hackmore Wind stopped in to leave the last of his interrogation report.

She looked up from a stack of paperwork, leaned back, and smiled. "Hi, Hack." She stretched and reached for a cigarette pack on one corner of the table. "More damned reports, I guess?"

"My last two," Hack said cheerfully. "Jean McCormick and Stacy Crump."

"Stacy Crump?" Milly checked a list at her elbow. "I thought her married name was Crock?"

Hack nodded. "Divorced. She took back her maiden name." He grinned boyishly. "I can't think why."

Milly made a check mark beside the name. "Did either of them have anything new or different on that thing at Gooseneck Park?" She made a wry face and then smiled faintly. "Ham has a fixation on Gooseneck Park."

"Nothing new. McCormick came up with eleven names. I believe that's more than anyone else has remembered."

He handed her the report. "Here, they're listed on the bottom."

Milly ran down the list. "No new name, though. All of them are on one or the other of the lists."

Hack nodded. He looked at her package of cigarettes wistfully and resolutely turned his eyes away. "One thing might be new," he said. "At least I don't remember reading it in any of the other reports. She mentioned that one of the other girls was carrying a camera, a small one, that fit into her jeans pocket. She remembers it was sticking out of the pocket, and she warned the girl she might lose it." He shrugged. "I don't see that it makes any difference."

"You never know," Milly mused. She ran a pencil down the list. "Well, that leaves John Ringley." She leaned back and sighed. "So far we don't have much, Hack. I look for Ham to start hitting them again anytime now."

Hack surrendered: He reached across and shook loose one of her cigarettes. "Again?"

"Follow-up. Nobody ever tells something the same way twice. Standard operating procedure. Two or three follow-up interrogations are not uncommon in something like this. It's just that there's so many damned people involved and we don't have the manpower."

"Ham in his office?" He drew smoke deep into his lungs and covered his mouth and coughed.

Milly shook her head. "He's meeting with Malcolm Carlyle's father this afternoon." She wriggled a limp-wristed hand and made a face. "Big mucky-muck from Houston. Rich as Bob Hope, adviser to the president, that sort of thing. Bringing a ton of pressure with him, I suppose. Roscoe walks around like he's got a prickly pear stuck in his bottom."

Hack laughed and sucked on the cigarette, his eyes

thoughtful. "A second interrogation, huh? That sounds like a damned good idea. I've run out of names; maybe I'll just start over again."

Milly eyed him dubiously. "I think the idea is to switch subjects. No two people ask questions alike, either. You might come up with a question that I didn't. Like that."

"Oh!" Hack's face fell.

Milly stared at him intently, her eyes bright. "What? What did you have in mind?"

"Nothing," Hack said quickly. "Nothing important."

Milly worried a yellow pencil between her fingers. "Well, since we haven't started over yet, I suppose it wouldn't hurt to go around again . . . that is, if you want to." She lowered her eyes to the list. "Let's see, you had Michele Fields and the two you brought in a while ago."

"Yeah," Hack said. He cleared his throat. "Mick— Michele Fields. Maybe I ought to drop by and talk to her again. You never can tell." He shoved to his feet and headed for the door, the cigarette forgotten in the ashtray.

"Right," Milly said, her eyes suddenly twinkling. "You never can tell."

But Mickey Fields wasn't at home, and Hack walked back to his pickup glumly, the flush of anticipation slowly draining out of him.

He glanced at his watch and wondered if Wendy would be home from her art class. Probably not, he decided. He had been scheduled for an afternoon run to Austin to deliver a prisoner, an eight-hour trip that would have kept him away well into the evening. She had decided she would eat out and catch a movie at one of the mall theaters.

But the prisoner delivery had been canceled; he had finished his scheduled interrogations, and offhand, he couldn't think of a thing to do until the movie ended at eight-thirty. He leaned against the fender of his truck and pondered it, decided finally on a quick dash home to change clothes, a quicker hamburger and a malt, and meet Wendy at the theater box office. It would be a nice surprise for her since she hated going to the movies alone.

Lawrence Peal Carlyle was not at all what Pope had expected, neither physically nor in demeanor. A relatively small man, slightly under average height, he had rounded shoulders, a small potbelly, and watery blue eyes so pale that they appeared almost translucent. He was wearing a dark blue blazer with elbow patches, baggy gray pants, and blue-and-white running shoes. He looked, Pope thought, more like a bartender fallen on hard times than a multimillionaire economic adviser who had the ear of the most important elected official in the world. Unlike his wife, his face plainly revealed the ravages of grief; his handshake was limp and damp.

"How do you do, Sergeant Pope." He smiled meagerly without showing teeth, stepped backward, his clammy hand sliding out of the detective's. "I believe you've met my wife."

"Mrs. Carlyle." Pope inclined his head toward the unsmiling woman who towered over her husband a good five inches.

"Good afternoon, Mr. Pope." She reclaimed her seat in an uncomfortable-looking chair near a sliding glass door that overlooked Malcolm Carlyle's patio and pool. She watched quietly as Pope and her husband found seats, her face cool and remote, her incredibly unlined skin glowing faintly with the rosy blush of artfully applied makeup.

"Very pleasant weather we're having," Lawrence Carlyle said, surprising Pope, who had expected no less than an immediate barrage of harsh, impatient questions regarding his progress in finding the killer of his son. "Could I get you something to drink, Sergeant Pope?" His voice was low and soft, almost apologetic.

"No thank you, Mr. Carlyle." Pope sat back and crossed his legs, uncomfortable suddenly with the uncharacteristic animosity he had brought into the room, an edge of belligerence initiated during an earlier meeting with Roscoe Tanner and strident Brad Durkin, Merriweather's chief of police, a sycophantic political appointee, a nervous nellie with ulcers and an uncertain future. He had first implored, then, inflamed by Pope's stoicism, commanded him to be the soul of discretion during the interview with the great man. Pope had come away smarting, a razor's edge of resentment building. But Lawrence Carlyle's kindly, almost meek behavior was disarming, to say the least.

"I realize this is an imposition," Lawrence Carlyle was saying. "I'm taking you away from your investigation, time that could be spent more profitably elsewhere, I'm afraid."

"Not at all." Pope found himself lying glibly, responding in kind to the old man's courtesy. "I had intended coming to speak with your daughter-in-law, at any rate."

"She is totally devastated, I'm afraid," Carlyle said sadly. "My son was her entire life." He breathed deeply, his already sunken eyes seeming to shrink farther inside dark-colored sockets. "But then he was everyone's—mine, my wife's . . ." His voice trailed away, then resumed, stronger, more vibrant. "He was all a man could ask for in a son, Sergeant Pope. Intelligent, resourceful . . . a loving son, a loving husband." He shook his head. "The great disappointment of his life was that he had no children. He would have made a fine father." He tilted his head, the light from the patio doorway washing across his coppery, weather-beaten skin. "Do you know," he said, his voice filled with a quiet pride, "that from the day he graduated law school he would accept no further help from me? He was determined to make his way on his own, make his fortune or fail on his own. I probably never told him, Sergeant Pope, but I was inordinately proud of my son." He looked quickly away, his pale watery eyes glistening, thin callused hands knotting in his lap. He blinked rapidly, looked back at Pope. "I asked you here to tell you, Sergeant Pope, that if you will find the man who murdered my son, we—my wife and I—will make you a very rich—"

"Whoa," Pope said, his tone harsher than he had intended. "You don't seem to understand, sir. I'm a police officer. It's my job to find the man responsible for your son's death. I'm attempting to do that now. No amount of money . . . I understand your feelings, Mr. Carlyle, but I couldn't take your money for doing my job. And no amount of money can make me do it any faster or any better."

Carlyle nodded jerkily, cast a quick glance at his motionless wife. The apologetic, hesitant smile came back. "I did not intend to insult you, Sergeant Pope. Please forgive me if I did. Sometimes in a world motivated by money you tend to lose sight of principle."

"You didn't insult me. What you did was . . . ill advised." He returned the smile. "Immoral, maybe, but not illegal. What you can do, Mr. Carlyle, is help me by telling me what you know about your son's financial dealings, if, to your knowledge, he had enemies sufficiently—" He broke off as the old man began shaking his head firmly.

"I can tell you nothing about my son's financial affairs, Sergeant. As I said before, he was adamant, almost fanatical, about doing everything on his own. I respected his wishes. I happen to know that he was primarily involved in real estate but only because he occasionally mentioned as much when we were together for a family visit. I never pried. Perhaps it would have been better if I had. I'm sure at times he must have thought I was simply disinterested, but that wasn't the case at all. I was bending over backward in an effort to fulfill his wishes.'' He moved his arm in a sweeping, expansive gesture. ''As you can see, he was doing rather well.'' He closed his eyes suddenly and seemed to sway, his face crumpling, pain emanating from his huddled figure to palpable waves.

''Are you all right, Larry?'' Marsha Carlyle's soft voice was filled with concern.

''Yes,'' he said quickly. ''Yes, I'm fine.'' He got up and paced the long room, turned and came back and sat down. In control again, he sighed and resurrected his small, lopsided smile. ''Mal was a fine athlete. A gymnast. I always thought he would have made a fine quarterback, but he didn't care for contact sports. I tried never to interfere. It was his life. I had mine. I did what I wanted to do, I could do no less than allow him the same prerogative. He was a fine musician, an excellent student. He was interested in everything that had to do with the human spirit, the human mind. He loved to read—good literature, poetry, and art excited him. He saw things I could never see in paintings.'' His voice dwindled and the apologetic smile came back. ''I'm bragging, I know. Please forgive me. I didn't intend to turn this into an eulogy, but I suppose that's what one does at a time like this.''

Pope nodded, his small smile understanding. ''Did he ever mention anything about . . . oh, let's say his senior year in school? Anything about the band, perhaps, a band outing on Possum Kingdom Lake?''

Carlyle shook his head slowly, his brow furrowed. ''No,

not that I recall." He turned inquisitive eyes on his wife. "Perhaps Marsha . . . ?"

"Did he ever mention the name Bull Henderson or Tinker Bell?"

His head tilted, the frown deepening. "No. I don't see . . ."

Pope bobbed his head, smiling genially. "Just background, Mr. Carlyle, if—" He broke off as the phone began ringing.

Marsha Carlyle swept lithely to her feet, crossed the floor in long, graceful strides, her slender figure encased in a form-fitting beige-and-brown dress, a chocolate-brown velvet choker encircling her neck. Pope was struck again by her vibrant, youthful appearance, struck, too, with a startling thought: Could she be Lawrence Carlyle's second wife, not the mother of Malcolm Carlyle? There had been no mention of divorce or death in the brief dossier he had read on the elder Carlyle, but that didn't mean a whole hell of a lot.

"Were you married before, Mr. Carlyle?" He asked it bluntly, the only way that came to mind.

Carlyle glanced around, startled. His eyes blinked slowly, his lips pursed. And then he smiled and shook his head. "I understand why you asked, Sergeant Pope. The years have been exceedingly kind to my wife."

Pope sighed, his face sheepish. "That's the truth. Either that or she's discovered the fountain of youth and is keeping it all to herself."

Carlyle's moist eyes moved to where his wife murmured into the phone. "Is it any wonder that my son was such a handsome boy with such a lovely mother?" His eyes came back to Pope. "I have always been a prideful man, Sergeant Pope. Too much pride in acquisition, perhaps. But nothing I have done can begin to equal the pride I felt for my beautiful wife and wonderful son." He spoke gently, painfully, unashamedly sentimental, his eyes seeping again.

Pope nodded wordlessly, feeling an unaccountable tightening in his throat.

"Darling, it's Alan. I hate to interrupt, but he says it won't wait." She winced apologetically, her hand over the mouthpiece. "Shall I tell him . . . ?"

Carlyle stood up. "No, I'll talk to him. Excuse me please, Sergeant Pope."

"Certainly." Pope looked around for an ashtray, spotted one finally on an end table next to a long, low couch. He crossed to get it, wondering how he had missed it the day before.

Marsha Carlyle had returned to a seat next to her husband's on the couch. She smiled when she saw the cigarette in his hand. "Why didn't you say something, Mr. Pope? I used to be a chain smoker. I know how you feel."

Pope lit the small cylinder gratefully. "It's getting to be a touchy thing. It's the reformed smokers mostly, I think. They look at you like you're a willful nitwit out to destroy the ozone layer or something."

She laughed, a low, husky chuckle, a pleasant sound that he enjoyed listening to. "I still suffer tortures of the damned sometimes. Particularly after meals and in the wee hours of the morning when life is at its lowest ebb and a cigarette is worth at least as much as a life preserver to a drowning person."

"Aptly put. I smoke because I enjoy it. I wonder why it is that the moment someone quits, they seem to forget that little fact."

She laughed again, her gray eyes warm and sparkling, and he suddenly felt awkward, foolishly inept, but somehow inordinately witty.

"Well." Lawrence Carlyle was coming back from the phone. "As usual they seem to have a catastrophe brewing at Malcolm Field. I'm terribly sorry, Sergeant Pope, I'm afraid I have to leave." He frowned and shook his head. "I had intended asking you to dine with us. You still can, of course; my wife and daughter-in-law would be more than pleased to have you." His watery eyes blinked expectantly down at Pope.

"Thank you, sir, but I wouldn't be able to stay, anyway. My . . . fiancée and I have previous plans."

His head bobbed agreeably. "Very well, but you're more than welcome." He bent and kissed his wife on the cheek. "I'll call you from Houston, my dear."

He whirled around, tugged briefly at Pope's hand, then waved and bustled out the door.

"Does he always move like that?" Pope asked wonderingly, a little stunned by the old man's sudden departure.

Marsha Carlyle smiled wryly. "When it's business, he does. Much too much, as a matter of fact." She sighed. "He's had one rather bad heart attack, and the doctors have warned him . . ." Her voice trailed off and she moved her hands in a gesture of resignation. "But he won't listen to them—or me." She took a deep breath. "Well, I suppose if that's what makes him happy . . ." Her voice faded again, her eyes drifting around the room, coming back to meet his, calmly and confidently and, it seemed, frankly appraising.

"Are you sure you won't have dinner with me, Mr. Pope?" Her eyes held his steadily.

He noticed the pronoun, wondering what the invitation meant, if anything. He decided he didn't want to know, preferred not to know whether this suddenly warm-eyed woman was quietly coming on to him, or perhaps simply perpetuating the courtesy of her husband.

He took a last drag on the cigarette and stubbed it out. He pushed to his feet. "Thank you, no." To give his eyes something to do, he glanced at his watch and frowned. He cleared his throat and coughed lightly behind his hand. "Since Milly—Detective Singer—talked to you and your daughter-in-law this morning, I don't believe I'll disturb her again so soon. I'd like to talk to you both again . . . tomorrow, if it's convenient."

"Yes, of course, if you think we can be of help. I'm not sure there's any more we can tell you, Mr. Pope." Her head moved, a stray of light sparkling on diamond earrings.

He nodded and smiled lightly. "Probably not. But sometimes people forget small, insignificant things . . . one thing leads to another . . . it happens all the time." He brought his gaze back to her finally, caught a fading crinkle around her eyes, as if she had been watching him with amusement. The ghost of a smile still lingered around her mouth.

She ducked her head in acquiescence, the impeccably coiffured, silver-blonde hair holding diligently. "I'm certain you know what's best, Mr. Pope," she said quietly.

He walked to the door, searching her voice for irony, found none.

"Until then, Mrs. Carlyle," he said without looking back.

"Good day, Mr. Pope."

Hackmore Wind was halfway up his fifty-yard-long driveway before he spotted Wendy's small red Plymouth parked beneath the spreading limbs of the giant oak that shaded their small frame house.

Hey, he thought, no movie after all? Or maybe she had dashed home for a quick tuna salad rather than eat another sawdust hamburger drenched with catsup that invariably gave her heartburn.

He glanced at his watch; still time to make the movie if she really wanted to see it. What the hell? It *might* be worth watching. And if it wasn't, he could always take a couple of smoke breaks in the lobby. That is, he could have taken a couple of smoke breaks if he hadn't quit smoking. He made a note to pick up a pack of cigarettes on the way to the movie.

Another fifteen yards and the psychedelic Ford van came into view.

He braked automatically, stunned. He let the pickup coast to a halt, his brain reeling, flinching, a feeling akin to terror sweeping over him as awareness insinuated itself into his consciousness.

He stared at the van, disoriented, the pickup bucking unheeded to a halt, lurching, dying. He clamped his long arms across his rumbling stomach, leaned his forehead against the cool, hard curve of the wheel.

"Jesus, Wendy," he whispered. "Not in my own house. Jesus God, not in my own bed."

CHAPTER
SIXTEEN

He angled across the yard, walking stiffly erect, holding himself in check. He paused at the steps and removed his boots, then crossed the porch in a swift, silent rush. The door was unlocked; a gesture of supreme complacency or of total innocence, he thought, and he was going to look damn silly carrying his boots if they were huddled over one of her manuscripts on the kitchen table.

There was music on the stereo, low, throbbing, a mellow resonant voice he had heard hundreds of times and couldn't put a name to. . . . Late-afternoon sunlight slanted through a window, speared his dark smoldering eyes, and turned the faded ocher carpet to burnished gold; dust motes danced and shimmered. He discovered that he was trembling, breathing through his mouth, the membranes dry and harsh, his throat raw. He closed his mouth and swallowed and moved across the living room toward a rhythmic murmuring that came from the bedroom and wasn't part of the music.

He moved slowly, awkwardly, an old man with fragile, worrisome joints, a part of him holding back, shrinking away from the fount of that insidious sound, a vague en-nui warring with cold determination, a destructive turmoil that was steadily pushing him toward helpless rage.

He halted just outside the bedroom door. He threw back his head and closed his eyes and breathed deeply. *I can still leave,* he thought, suddenly panic-stricken at the familiar measured cadence of the sounds. *I can leave right now and she'll never know I've been here.*

He opened his eyes and stepped into the room, the gun leaving the holster of its own volition, leaping upward into his reaching hand.

Wendy saw him first; a second or a minute, he was never sure. Dilated eyes over a hairy white shoulder, a nightmare sound, and thrusting arms sent Al Judson rolling away from her, his features trapped in mindless contortion, a dead zone between ecstasy and shock. His heels kicked at slick sheets for traction, backpedaled frantically in an effort to push himself through the headboard.

"Sweet Jesus!" he whispered hoarsely, features crumpling as he read his fate in the glittering eyes above the gun. He tried desperately to shrink into himself, to disappear, to never have been.

"Hack! Please! Don't!" Wendy's muffled voice came from behind her hands.

Hack could feel the gun, heavy and rough in his hand, the energy coursing up along his arm into his body. It was an extension of himself, held waist-high, his mind's eye sighting along the barrel, the picture in the sight a palsied head on a cringing body, popping eyes in a fish-belly face. Reason tugged at him and he lowered the barrel toward the floor, holding them transfixed with his eyes.

Then Al Judson moved again and broke the spell; Hack tilted the barrel upward, and Judson screamed, and Hack found himself roaring his rage and pain and humiliation and pulling the trigger.

Beside the bed, a hanging globe lamp exploded, a thousand bits of pebbled glass showering naked bodies like hail. Again, and its mate on Wendy's side of the bed disappeared. He smashed their wedding picture and the dresser mirror with one bullet. Another and the small TV imploded silently beneath the roar of the gun. He stopped, crouching, panting, his blood bubbling with fever, an icy band around his heart. One last bullet. His eyes skimmed the room restlessly, came back to two stricken faces staring at him in horrified fascination.

He made an anguished sound and sent the remaining bullet into the headboard between them.

Hack straightened and holstered the empty weapon, swaying a little, his knees trembling as erratic signals impulsed from an overcharged brain. He breathed heavily and faced them, his face as smooth and hard as polished oak, eyes as dark and quiet as rust.

"Five minutes," he said loudly above the ringing in his ears. "I'm having a beer and a cigarette out on the patio. Five minutes is about what that'll take. If you're here when I come back, I'll kill you." He walked out of the room and down the hall with his ears still ringing, wondering if they had heard him, wondering also if they had been as frightened as he.

He found a pack of Wendy's cigarettes and opened a beer. As good as his word, he went out onto the patio and slumped into an aluminum chair with plastic webbing. He lit a cigarette and threw beer at the dry, metallic taste in his mouth and wondered how he was going to get through the rest of the night . . . tomorrow . . . next week. He sat huddled, scared, dreading the moment the numbness would go away and the pain would begin. His throat was tight and hot, his eyes blurred and stinging behind closed lids. He tried not to think about it, tried not to care that he still loved her, tried to remember if this was the way it felt before you cried.

Hamilton Pope was reading his way through the stack of interrogation reports for the third time when the button on the conference-room phone began blinking. He lit a cigarette before answering.

"Pope."

"This is Sally, Ham. We have Mr. Ringley on the phone now."

"Fine. Thanks, Sal."

"Hello."

"Hello, Mr. Ringley? John L. Ringley?"

"Yes, is this Sergeant Pope?"

"Yes, it is, Mr. Ringley. Could you speak up a little? We have a weak connection."

"All right." A small pause. "Is there something wrong back there?"

"Mr. Ringley, I don't have time to explain it all to you, but we are investigating the murder of a Mr. Malcolm Carlyle. I understand he was a classmate of yours in high school."

"Malcolm Carlyle. Yes, he was. Someone killed him, you say?"

"It appears so. If I could get directly to the point, Mr. Ringley, I'd like to ask you about an outing on Possum Kingdom Lake you and the other members of your band—"

"Gooseneck Park. Yes, I remember."

"Bull Henderson. Do you remember him?"

"Yes, of course. He was killed that day in a fall."

"Yes, so I understand. And you were among a group

of students who witnessed something just prior to his death, I believe?''

A hoarse chuckle, cut off abruptly. ''Yes. Old Bull getting his ashes hauled.''

''Did you by any chance recognize the girl?''

''No, not really. We all did some guessing, but . . .''

''Who did you think it was? Do you remember? Who was your guess?''

There was a short silence. Pope heard the click and rasp of a lighter.

''Man, I dunno. I don't even remember her name. Just some broad in the band. A junior, I think. I just don't know anymore. Just a guess, anyhow.''

''You said everybody was guessing. Do you remember any of the other guesses?''

''No, not offhand.''

''How well did you know Bull? Did you ever see him with a girl—or, more to the point, did you see him with anyone that day?''

''Naw. Bull didn't get along too well with the girls. He had a dirty mouth on him, plus he smelled a little.''

''You mean that literally? He smelled?''

''Yeah, well, he had bad breath. He had a lot of bad teeth, I think. And he didn't wash none too regularly, like that.''

''You knew him pretty well, then?''

''Yeah, I guess you could say so. We played sandlot baseball on the same team in the summer, and we played some football together. Yeah, I knew him pretty well. He wasn't a bad guy. I felt a little sorry for him, as a matter of fact. His folks were as poor as church mice. His clothes were . . . well, you know.'' He hesitated. ''What does all this have to do with Malcolm Carlyle? Bull has been dead for . . . hell, it's almost twenty years now.''

"I don't know for sure that it has anything to do with it. Not for certain. But the fact is, Mr. Ringley, it's not just Carlyle. Five other people out of the twelve on that cliff have been killed recently. Murdered. What would you think?"

"Jesus Christ! What are you telling me?"

"I'm telling you that six people who witnessed a sexual act twenty years ago have been killed. My common sense tells me that the other six had better make out wills or go into hiding." He stopped and listened to studded silence for a moment. "How much longer do you have on your vacation, Mr. Ringley?"

"Almost a week. Why?"

"Are you by yourself?"

"No, I have my family. We're camping in the Davis Mountains. The sheriff found us and gave me your message."

"I think I'd consider staying for a while, Mr. Ringley."

"Why, do you think I'm in danger?"

"Yes, I believe you may be."

"Jesus Christ!"

"When you do come back, be sure and check in with the Fort Worth police. If you should happen to think of anything in the meantime, call me collect. You have the number."

"I'll sure do that."

"All right, Mr. Ringley, thanks for calling."

Mickey Fields finished her nightly hair-combing ritual. Meticulously she cleaned the brush and placed it with the others on the pewter tray. She raised her arms and critically watched the gentle sag and tremble of moderately sized breasts as she rolled her hair into a rope the size of her wrist and pinned it at the nape of her neck.

Not bad for thirty-eight, she thought, examining her clear, fine-grained skin closely, poking fretfully at a tiny red spot near the corner of her mouth that had all the evil earmarks of an incipient pimple. *My God, I haven't had a pimple in ages. I must not be getting enough.* She wrinkled her nose at herself in the mirror in what she had decided was her most appealing facial gesture short of a full-blown dazzling smile. It was cute without being coy, she told herself, and should melt the heart of any man . . . particularly the callused heart of Rod Chernecke, who wasn't all that damned handsome when you got right down to it and who had no earthly reason to put on airs just because he was a jet jockey. All the dumb-ass stews hung on his every word, not to mention his broad shoulders, every chance they—

The doorbell chimed the first three notes of "Memory."

She looked at herself again and frowned. Midnight . . . no, closer to one o'clock, actually. A thrill of apprehension trickled through her. She shrugged into a quilted nylon robe and drifted soundlessly to the center of the living room, just as the musical notes sounded again. She jumped, found herself holding her breath. Who in the world could it be? Not one of her friends. They had signals they used ever since the two stews had been raped—not Rod, he knew the signal too. Anyhow, he had been flying.

A heavy hand pounded; a staccato rapping, imperiously demanding, paralyzing in its effect on her. Mesmerized, she stared at the door, her eyes wide, breathing shallowly through her mouth. Who, dammit?

The pounding came again, a little more quietly, more uncertain, and she found herself moving inexorably toward the door, her heart pounding, her adrenaline spurting, making her almost light-headed, insatiable curiosity fighting common sense.

She looked through the peephole. Breath whooshed through parted lips as she recognized him. Relief flooded her, and her voice came almost gaily: "Just a moment!"

She fumbled at the chain with her left hand, while her right ripped the constricting pins from her hair. She shook her heavy mane fiercely, feeling it spread across her shoulders, brush against her flushed cheeks. She patted and poked at it even as she opened the door.

"Deputy Wind." She arched her eyebrows and wrinkled her nose. "How nice to see you. And at such an ungodly hour too." She unleashed her dazzling smile to take the sting out of it.

He blinked at her slowly, his face solemn under a thick mass of windblown, tousled hair. He brushed past her without speaking, more or less in a straight line to the chair he had occupied once before, and sat down. He lit a cigarette and crossed his legs with the slow deliberate movements of a man uncertain of his coordination.

Mickey watched him, perplexed. She closed the door and crossed to the couch.

"Did you forget something the other day, Deputy Wind?"

"No," he said heavily. "I didn't forget anything. I remember every little thing about that visit. Everything including what you said."

Her brows knitted. "What did I say?"

"About—" He stopped and cleared his throat. "About how it would be . . . interesting."

"Oh," she said, so softly that it was almost a whisper, realizing suddenly that the faint odor she had been trying to identify was alcohol, and in that same instant realizing that he was more than a little drunk. "Oh," she said again. "That."

"Yeah, that," he said, his tone almost belligerent, his dark eyes meeting hers for the first time, a small diffident smile spreading slowly. "Or maybe I was wrong."

She wrapped a tendril of hair around a finger and shook her head. "No, you weren't wrong, Hack, but whatever happened to 'I'm married'?"

He spread his hand expressively. "It just went blooey. One minute I was, the next I wasn't—just like that."

"Come on," she coaxed softly. "Things don't happen like that . . . that fast."

He shrugged. "I caught her—" He stopped and moistened his lips. "I found her in bed—our bed—with another man. That's how fast it happened."

She felt a light fluttering stir in her stomach, a faint tickle of resentment in her mind. "So you came to me for a little revenge?"

He shook his head. "It's not like that. I wanted to the other day, but I couldn't . . . wouldn't because of her—Wendy. She's not there anymore, so . . ." He let it fade away, his face suddenly slack and empty, eyes half closed and glazed.

"So," she said, picking it up where he had left it. "So you have all this pain and anger and frustration built up inside you. All this tension. And you figure you can dump it all into little old Mickey." She smiled gently and shook her head. "I'm sorry, friend, but I'm not in the garbage business."

He brought a hand up and rubbed his eyes. "It's not like that, but you're right. This was a stupid thing to do. I'm sorry." He pushed on the arms of the chair, tried to rise to his feet. Halfway up, his arms folded and he crashed back to the cushion, a foolish look on his face.

"I musta had . . . had more vodka than I thought." He rubbed his face vigorously with both hands. "Just one minute and I'll be going."

Mickey sighed. "I didn't say you couldn't stay, Hack. You're in no shape to go anywhere."

He gazed at her blearily. "If I could . . . could just lay on your couch for a . . ."

She giggled. "You'd hang over both ends. Come on, cowboy. You can sleep in my bed."

"Really?" His head lolled, his smile more of a leer than anything else.

She smiled wryly and helped him to his feet. She drew his arm across her shoulders and wound her own around his waist. "Not like this, Hack. Not when you're so drunk, you'd never remember how great I am." The smile blossomed. "Later? We'll see."

CHAPTER

SEVENTEEN

"Sure, I remember." Leo Dardine, part-time cabdriver, full-time engineering student at the University of Texas at Arlington, finished the last of his Big Mac and spread his ebony hands wide in a gesture indicating immensity. "A big fat lady and a tall skinny one. Picked them up at Northeast Mall. In the middle of the afternoon, but you'll have to check in the office to see what time exactly."

Pope nodded. "I already have. You picked them up at approximately three forty-five and dropped them in Mayfair at approximately four o'clock."

The young black man nodded. "That sounds about right." He gave Pope a guarded look. "Why, is there something wrong?"

"Just a routine matter. No problem with your end. I was just wondering, what happened exactly when you arrived at the house?"

Dardine frowned. "Nothing . . . that is, nothing unusual. The tall lady paid me—gave me a nice tip, too—and went on in the house. I offered to help her with some packages, but she said she could manage."

"Did they have a lot of packages?"

"Not a whole lot. It was just that they were bulky—you know, hard to handle."

"You said the tall lady paid you. What was the other woman doing?"

"Oh, she had already gone into the house. She jumped out—well, not jumped, exactly, she was too big for that— but she got out and went on in." He stopped and grinned. "Left the other lady with all the packages. That's why I offered to help."

"How much time between the time the fat lady went in and the other one went in?"

Dardine frowned again. "Damn, I don't know. We had to get the packages out of the trunk. I helped her get them arranged so she could carry them . . . maybe three, four minutes. We talked a little. She made a joke about being left with all the packages to carry. Yeah, I'd say three minutes at least, four at most."

"Then you did what?"

"I don't get you. I let—"

"No, I mean, did you leave immediately? Did the tall lady have time to get in the house before you left?"

"Oh, yeah, probably. I had a little trouble getting the trunk lid to catch hold. Then I called in to the office, which took maybe thirty seconds. Then I left, but I'm pretty sure she had plenty of time to get inside. It's just a little ways from the driveway to the door."

"And you didn't hear anything?"

Dardine tilted his head to one side. "Like what?"

"Anything unusual. A woman's voice, a loud noise— anything?"

Dardine shook his head, his lips pursed. "Not a thing that I recall." He gestured toward the waiting cab. "But that old motor sounds like a thrashing machine. It would drown out most anything.''

Pope thanked him and shook hands. He left the garage wondering if Marsha Carlyle could have been lying about who had found Malcolm dead. And if so, why?

Assistant District Attorney Melvin Johns chased the last two green peas around on his plate with a fork, then finally gave up and took a sip of wine. He tongued a bit of steak from between his teeth, swallowed it, then looked at Pope and smiled blandly.

''Even when you catch this guy—if you catch this guy— I won't be trying the case. It'll probably be Richardson or Powers or one of the fair-haired boys. So why don't you go to them?''

''Because,'' Pope explained patiently, ''Richardson or Powers didn't go to law school with Malcolm Carlyle, they didn't move in the same circles as Malcolm Carlyle. They weren't law partners with Malcolm Carlyle like you were.''

''*Were* is right,'' Johns said. ''I hadn't seen much of Mal in the last five years.''

''I know that. All I want to know is what kind of a lawyer he was. What kind of practice did you have? And why did you split up?''

''Some of it's damn personal and none of your business,'' Johns said bluntly.

''That's not what I want to know, Mel—not unless you want to tell me, that is. Was he a good attorney?''

Johns shifted in his seat, a sour look on his face. ''As a matter of fact, no. I didn't think so, anyhow. He was a pretty good P.R. man. He brought in some good clients, but I had a feeling his dad was responsible for that. When it came to the nuts and bolts of law, he wasn't any great shakes. That was surprising too. He made excellent grades in law school. That's one of the reasons I went in with him. We were both in the top ten in our class and pretty good friends. I thought we had it by the nuts. Just goes to show how wrong you can be.''

''Was your business a success?''

Johns barked a short, harsh laugh. ''Would I be here in this dead-end sinkhole if that was the case? Hell, no. We had a couple of pretty good years. Slow, steady growth. I thought we were on our way, but then everything seemed to start sliding. I finally had to bail out and find a job. I didn't have a rich daddy like he did.''

''His daddy help him a lot, do you think?''

Johns gave him an incredulous look. ''What the hell do you think? Our last year netted maybe thirty thousand between us. He bought a Mercedes and started construction on that mansion of his that same year. That was some trick on his half of our profits.''

''How about the five years since you left the business? Maybe he picked up some rich customers?''

Johns shrugged irritably. ''There's not enough law money in Merriweather each year to support his life-style. Not even if he got every damn dime of it.'' He gazed at Pope curiously. ''Why are you being so hardheaded about this? It can't be naïveté. Hell, everybody knows who his old man is. He's a pretty generous old coot from what I hear—for a rich man. Honorable, old family, and like that. Why wouldn't he help his only son?''

''Yeah, that's so,'' Pope said.

''Don't get me wrong. Mal was a nice guy. Friendly as a puppy and would do anything in the world for you. But he just wasn't cut out for the law. He should've gone into business with his daddy, public relations, sales, something like that.''

''Wasn't he also into real estate?''

''Some, I suppose, but you know how that's been for the last couple of years. Poor boy city. Interest rates too high, buyer resistance, very little commercial development. I wouldn't think he'd be making a killing in real estate. Not in Merriweather.''

''Do you think he could have been in financial trouble lately?''

Johns shrugged again. ''I don't think so. I just happen to know he paid the last two-hundred-grand installment on that estate of his. Three, four months ago.'' He smiled. ''Just something I picked up at one of these little lunches. By the way, you or the city paying for this?''

''Hopefully the city. I can't afford steak lunches on my salary.''

''Tell me about it. If it wasn't for an occasional shyster trying to cut a deal, I'd never get a decent lunch.''

Pope grunted. He picked up the check and pushed to his feet. ''Sounds like bribery to me.''

Johns' dark eyes gleamed up at him. ''Yeah, it is. I hope you got your money's worth.''

Pope laughed and lifted a hand and weaved his way across the crowded restaurant to the cashier's desk.

At Police Headquarters he bypassed his office and went directly to the conference room. Milly was seated at the head of the table, absorbed in interrogation reports, a pencil tucked behind her ear, her honey-colored hair pulled back and bound into a ponytail. Hackmore Wind slouched in a chair by the room's only window, his handsome face morose, a cigarette dangling from one corner of his mouth, another burning in an ashtray beside him. He glanced at Pope's entrance and nodded glumly. Milly muttered something without lifting her head.

Pope glanced from one to the other, then shook his head and sat down. "Who died?"

Milly looked up, her eyes cool. "That's not funny, Ham."

Pope nodded agreeably and held up a defensive hand. "Don't tell me, I know. I'm gross."

Milly shrugged and went back to her reports. "You said it, I didn't."

"What're you high on?" Hack asked sourly.

Pope lit a cigarette and leaned back in his chair, grinning at them. "Life, my boy. The simple joy of being alive. It's spring, the time for renewal, time for new life to spring forth from Mother Earth, time for the sap to rise . . ."

Milly made a disgusted sound and cut cynical eyes toward Hack. "Sounds like his sap's rising a little too fast. It's affecting his tired old brain."

Hack smiled and bobbed his head, regretting it instantly as his hangover headache responded with fiendish glee. He touched his throbbing temple with a tentative finger and sighed, trying to remember for the hundredth time what had happened last night.

He had awakened in a strange bedroom, obviously feminine, alone, a pigpen mouth and a balloon for a head, a throbbing balloon that threatened to explode at any moment. It wasn't until he went into the living room that he realized where he was, that he was alone in Mickey Fields's apartment, fully clothed, hung over, with not the slightest recollection of how or when he had arrived, or, what was much, much worse, what had happened after

he'd gotten there. A note taped to the apartment door had
only increased his anxiety.

Good Morning:

Sorry about last night! More than you can imagine.
I'm off to Houston on an early flight. Returning tonight around seven . . . if it matters???

Mickey

Jesus Christ, he thought, scratching gingerly behind his
ear. What could have happened? And what did *if it matters???* mean? He was relatively sure he hadn't made love
to her—surely not with all his clothes on. A frightening
thought struck him and he winced, his head jerking painfully. My, God, what if I . . . what if I raped her?

"How're you doing this wonderful afternoon, Hack, old
buddy?" Pope, refusing to let his two sullen companions
dampen his high spirits, was delving into his briefcase and
grinning at him across the table.

"Terrific," Hack growled. "Just goddamn terrific."

"My!" Pope clucked. "Aren't we in a vicious tizzy
today?" He cocked his head and peered at the younger
man's eyes. "Hangover," he pronounced pompously.
"Your eyes look like the business end of a double-barreled
shotgun."

"That reminds me," Milly put in, reaching for an envelope on one corner of the table. "We have an answer
from Rossacher. He found traces of gun oil and cordite on
that piece of carpet you sent him." She handed the envelope to Pope, her eyes gleaming mischievously. "We also
had a call from Matilda Carlyle—or Roscoe did. She's
sending the city a bill for a new carpet for her study." She

paused and grinned cheerfully. "Roscoe said it was coming out of your, quote, fucking salary, unquote."

Pope took the envelope silently. He extracted the single thin sheet of paper and studied it, a slow smile breaking across his craggy face.

Milly, watching him intently, sat up a little straighter and moistened her lips. "What is it, Ham?"

Pope grunted and stubbed out his cigarette. "You read it. Traces of cordite and oil similar in composition to that normally used in the lubrication of firearms. Conclusion: The specks of cordite and smudges of oil came from a handgun falling onto said piece of carpet." He leaned back and reached for another cigarette, his narrowed eyes on the ceiling, the tracery of brown stains from recent rain. "That poses a pregnant question, boys and girls. Why would a handgun have been dropped on the carpet beside Malcolm Carlyle's body?"

"An amateur," Hack said slowly, "frightened by what had happened. Threw the gun—"

"It wasn't thrown," Pope said quietly. "Dropped. There's a difference."

"Suicide," breathed Milly, her eyes wide with comprehension. "I thought it looked . . ." She let it trail away, unwilling to advance what could be construed as hindsight deduction.

"Like a suicide," Pope finished for her. "So did I, Milly. It did look like a suicide on the face of it. The only problem was the missing gun. The wound was a little farther back than normal for that particular target area, but not excessively so. But the gun, the damned gun . . . if we're right somebody took the gun."

"One of them," Milly said. "Or maybe both?"

"But why?" Hack moved his head gingerly from one to the other. "Why would they want to do that?"

"If you're murdered," Pope said slowly, "particularly if you're just one of a group, you're considered an unfortunate victim of circumstance. No possible stigma applies. If you take your own life—well, no matter how society commiserates with the poor distressed family, our thoughts are of cowardice, insanity, or of possible escape from guilt over past wrongdoing. The difference lies between the true empathy and understanding accorded the murder victim and the malicious wagging tongues and vicious speculation rampant in the case of a suicide—in other words, blameless tragedy versus probably scandal."

"There could be another reason," Milly said, her eyes sparking with excitement. "What if he was involved in the other killings?"

Pope nodded soberly. "I've thought of that, but you're forgetting he was a spectator that day and not a participant. He couldn't possibly have been the one who killed Bull Henderson. No, I think if Malcolm took his own life, it was for a reason we know nothing about—not yet, anyway."

"It all sounds a little vague to me," Hack said. "You're basing all this on some oil and gunpowder traces on a carpet? Maybe somebody dropped a gun there before that day."

"It's a possibility," Pope admitted. "But Malcolm Carlyle wasn't a gun type of man. I can't see him even owning a gun, let alone playing with it in his study."

"Then where did he get one to shoot himself with?"

Pope smiled faintly. "You've just shoved a foot through the biggest hole in my theory. But nobody's perfect. Give me a little time." He closed his briefcase and snapped the catches. "I think it's time to talk to Matilda and Marsha again." He glanced at Hack. "You want to come?"

Hack stirred feebly. "Yeah, sure, I guess so."

"Milly?"

She sighed regretfully. "No, I can't. I'm supposed to meet Sergeant Globe at two o'clock. We have an appointment to talk to Jean McCormick again."

"Good. How're we coming on the rest of the class?"

"Out of the four hundred a few more than two hundred are either dead or have left the Metroplex area. We're more than halfway through the list of the ones that are left."

"Good work, Milly," Pope said warmly.

She smiled crookedly. "I'm not exactly doing it all myself."

"Yes, but you're doing a hell of a job of ramrodding it."

Milly eyed him quizzically. "I'm not ramrodding anything. I'm just up to my behind in paperwork. You guys in the field are doing the work, I'm just shuffling paperwork." Her eyes gleamed dangerously, daring him to pursue his obvious blandishment any further.

"Well," he said lamely, backing away from the red flag of danger, "paperwork, it's always the hardest part." He smiled tentatively and edged toward the door.

Her eyes turned cool, her smile cynical. "Speaking of hard parts, Ham, how're you and the midget doing?"

He could see Hack's smiling face out of the corner of his eye, could feel the heat creeping up his neck and into his cheeks, a small chill of anger seeping into his mind. Dirty pool, lady, he thought, you've got no right to do this in front of Hack.

"Great," he said softly. "Perfect. I have to be careful, though. She's so little, so young . . . and she's not used to it much."

He turned away and went out the door. But not before he saw the flash of hurt in her eyes, the shadow of pain cross her face. Dammit! She had asked for it.

Hack's boot heels thudded solidly beside him. They crossed the narrow buffer zone of delicate spring grass and went into the parking lot.

"I'll drive," Pope said gruffly.

"Okay," Hack said. "Gas went up another nickel, though." He looked down at his companion and opened his mouth, then thought better of it and began whistling tunelessly. He waited until they were settled in Pope's Dodge wagon.

"That was a pretty shitty thing you did," he said conversationally.

"Shit!" Pope rammed the Dodge into reverse. "Don't you think I know that?"

"Yeah, I guess," Hack said. He delicately probed his aching eyes with thumb and forefinger. "Just thought I'd mention it, is all."

CHAPTER

EIGHTEEN

Matilda Carlyle's pudgy left hand fluttered along the dark cap of her slicked-back hair while her pudgy right held the teapot above Pope's cup. She poured; her arm, hidden beneath the voluminous folds of the caftanlike garment she wore, holding the heavy metal vessel with effortless ease.

"Sugar, Sergeant Pope?" she asked and, without waiting for an answer, moved the teapot to hover over Hack's cup on the handcrafted silver tray. Her arm began to tremble a bit; she filled the cup and raised slowly blinking eyes to Hack.

"And you, Deputy Wind, would you like some sugar?" Her voice had altered somehow, a subtle difference, a breathy resonance that had not been there before, an indefinable change in demeanor that hinted at total obeisance, abject surrender.

Pope watched her with amused cynicism, a twinge of pity, and the undeniable twitch of envy he experienced each time he witnessed Hackmore Wind's first meeting with a woman—any woman. Shock city, he thought, a definite regression to genital-level animal instincts.

Marsha Carlyle coughed delicately behind her hand. "I'll have a bit of tea, Matilda, dear, if you don't mind." Her voice seemed constrained also, Pope thought.

Matilda wordlessly filled her mother-in-law's cup and then her own. She dropped in two lumps of sugar, sat back on the couch, and stirred mechanically, her eyes drawn relentlessly back to Hack, as if she were a dog and he the only tree in a forest of cactus.

Marsha Carlyle, trim and elegant in a pleated skirt and a Nile-green silk blouse dressed up with a ruffled jabot and a single strand of pearls, touched her cup to her lips, then deposited it and her saucer on the table at her side. She touched her mouth with a napkin and gave Pope a meager smile. "And now, Mr. Pope, what can we do for you?"

Pope returned her smile. He removed his small notebook from his inside coat pocket and flipped to a paper-clipped page, pretended to read. "Just a couple of small discrepancies, Mrs. Carlyle. I don't know, maybe I wrote it down wrong, but didn't you tell me you were the first one into the house the day of your son's death, that you came directly down the hall and looked through the study door and saw him?" He closed the notebook and looked up into her calm eyes, the tiny smile still lingering.

"Yes, I told you that," she said quietly. "But that wasn't exactly the truth, Mr. Pope. Obviously you know that already."

"Would you care to tell us the truth now?"

She nodded firmly. "Of course. It was only a small lie. I did it to protect Matilda. I realize now that it was an error in judgment, but during the stress of the moment . . ." Her voice faded.

"That's quite understandable," Pope said easily. "But suppose you tell us now exactly what happened."

Her eyes drifted to her daughter-in-law, the round puffy face, the small berry eyes that had finally left Hack and were riveted on the teacup held in both plump hands.

"Matilda found Malcolm. She came into the house a few moments ahead of me. I was going down the hall and I heard a sound from the study, a terrible sound, not quite a scream . . . an agonized moan, then I ran into the study. She was standing looking down at him . . ."

"Where was she standing?" Pope asked, his eyes on the motionless younger woman.

"Oh, I don't . . . yes, yes, beside him. I remember she reached down to touch him, then jerked back her hand. By then I was there. I saw that . . . that he was dead. But I touched his wrist just to be sure. Matilda started screaming . . . I had to slap her to make her stop. I brought her here into the game room . . . the rest of it was the truth, Mr. Pope. Matilda was terribly upset—as was I, of course—but she was very near collapse. I wanted to spare her what I thought would be a terrible ordeal with the . . . with you, the police. I was wrong. You weren't nearly so . . . so unfeeling as I had imagined you would be."

Pope smiled wryly. "We rarely are." He leaned forward slightly, his eyes narrowing, his voice suddenly crisp and cold. "Matilda. Where was the gun lying?"

The sleek head jerked upward, her wide brow furrowed, her eyes vague with confusion. "What? I don't . . . what gun, Sergeant Pope?"

"The gun," Pope said sharply, "your husband used to kill himself!"

"Wha—Oh, my God!" The cup and saucer chattered, tumbled to the carpet. The big woman covered her face with her hands, a keening wail coming muffled from around cupped fingers. She rocked backward, once, twice, then came to her feet, astonishingly agile for her size. She turned and dashed from the room.

Pope and Hack exchanged glances, Hack's faintly disapproving.

"Mr. Pope, that wasn't at all necessary." Marsha Carlyle's voice was sharply chiding, but Pope was sure he could detect a trace of amusement. "I warned you that Matilda is a very emotional child."

"Hardly a child," Pope said curtly, disgruntled at the unexpected development, feeling slightly foolish and defensive. "Why should what I said upset her like that?"

Marsha Carlyle sighed patiently. "Tomorrow is my son's funeral, Mr. Pope. As the time nears, Matilda grows worse. Facing his interment, facing life without him, is difficult enough for the poor girl without the added, intolerable burden that he deserted her by taking his own life. Even if it were true, I would try to keep it from her until at least after the funeral."

Pope's sky-blue eyes studied her closely. "But it isn't true? There was no gun? You were the only other person there, Mrs. Carlyle. If there was a gun, you would have to know about it, what happened to it. No, wait. Before you answer me, let me tell you what we found on the square of carpet I cut from the study floor. We found traces of gun oil, traces of cordite—gunpowder. That indicates a recently fired gun, and that square of carpet was directly under your son's hanging hand. *Directly* under it. That indicates the gun dropped only a few inches, as if his hand relaxed in death and the gun slipped free." He paused, breathing deeply, her quiet, steady gaze somehow disconcerting. "Let's assume a clumsy killer. Let's say he shot your son, dropped the gun for some reason. From that height the gun would have bounced, left traces at more than one place on the carpet, certainly would not have fallen to the floor directly under your son's hand. There were no other traces that I could find, no other smudges of oil, specks of cordite . . ." He paused again, his voice lowering unconsciously. "And, too, Mrs. Carlyle, the gunpowder residue test was positive. Malcolm Carlyle's hand had recently held and fired a gun."

Her cool eyes were unwavering, her head moved briefly and firmly from side to side. "It doesn't matter, Mr. Pope. What you've said may well be true. All I know, all I can tell you, is that there was no gun. Most definitely not below my son's hand. I know, I—I—he looked so uncomfortable. I know it's stupid, but I tried to place his . . . his hand in his lap, but it wouldn't stay, it kept sliding back out again. I finally gave up and left him . . . but there was no gun. It isn't possible that I wouldn't have seen it."

Pope's breath expelled in a short, gusty sigh. "Matilda, is it possible she—"

"No, Mr. Pope. Matilda is frightened to death of guns. And she was in no condition to think of anything except her dead husband."

"A maid?" Pope said harshly. "A gardener? Someone? There must have been someone else here."

Marsha shook her head slowly. "No. Matilda does her own cooking. She has a maid who comes in two days a week to clean, but that wasn't one of the days. The gardener comes once a week, usually on Friday. No, Mr. Pope, there was no one else here."

"I didn't read the report," Hack said suddenly. "Were there any signs of forced entry?"

Pope shook his head brusquely. "No. Whoever it was walked in through an open door somewhere."

"Or Carlyle let him in," Hack said.

"Someone he knew," Pope said automatically, suddenly irritated that he was back to thinking in terms of murder again, despite the overwhelming evidence to the contrary. He winced inwardly, wondering if his theory could be the result of his sometimes overeager imagination, his desire for quick dramatic solutions to difficult problems. But, dammit, there was the gunpowder-residue test. If it was positive—

"Did your son own any handguns, Mrs. Carlyle?"

"Yes. He owns—owned—several." She smiled wryly. "Gifts from his father. He wasn't particularly interested in them, but he pretended to be for his father's sake. He was a pretty fair shot, actually. He visited the range quite often, I understand. I imagine it was to keep his hand in so he wouldn't disgrace himself in front of his father on their occasional shoots."

"Do you happen to know which gun range he used?"

"I'm not certain, but I believe it was called Trinity something or other. Somewhere in the Trinity River bottoms, I believe."

"Trinity Valley Gun and Archery Club," Hack said. "I'm a member there myself. They'd have a record, Ham. They keep a logbook on each day's activities. You have to sign in."

"Why don't you give them a quick call, see when he was in last." He turned to the quietly watching woman. "Is there another phone besides the one in the study?"

"Yes, in the kitchen and in all the bedrooms."

"I'll use the kitchen," Hack said cheerily. He flashed a smile in Marsha Carlyle's direction and strode out the door. "I'll find it."

She watched him go, her face amused. "Quite a handsome young man, your friend."

"Yeah," Pope said. He fished out a pack of cigarettes,

shook one loose, and lit it. "It's the damnedest thing. I don't think he really knows it. Women zero in on him like a bumblebee on honeysuckle, and he thinks they're just being friendly. He's got this hang-up because he's got Mexican and Indian and black blood mixed in there with the white, and I think it makes him a little skittish around women—and some men. He's a damn good cop and a hell of a nice guy and—" He broke off, a little embarrassed. "Well, you get the idea."

She clicked her tongue softly against the roof of her mouth. "You shouldn't be embarrassed because you like someone, Sergeant Pope. Even another man. You men and your macho image of yourselves. You can pummel and hug and feel each other's butts on the football field, and it's perfectly all right, but come any closer than a hand-shake or a fist in the stomach during normal activity and you get all tied up in knots, red-faced and guilty." Her eyes crinkled at the edges, and the wry, friendly smile came back. "That was always my husband's problem. Showing affection to Malcolm after he reached the age of ten or so."

"That wasn't the impression I got from what he said the other day."

Her face softened. "My husband's words were flavored with a generous dosage of wistful thinking, Mr. Pope. Mal disappointed him in a lot of ways, ways he wouldn't have admitted for the world. Contact sports, for one thing. My husband played football, soccer, hockey—everything he was big enough to play. Malcolm hated it. He tried for his father. But he wasn't very good at it, and pretty soon he stopped trying." Pope mashed out his cigarette, marshaling his thoughts, composing his next words carefully, in the end discarding his carefully constructed question couched in useless verbosity and asked bluntly, "Where did Malcolm get his money, Mrs. Carlyle?"

Her lips twitched, on the verge of a smile. "I knew we would get to that sooner or later. I never underestimated you for a minute, Mr. Pope."

"Where?" he repeated softly.

She shrugged, a gentle movement of slender shoulders. "From me, of course. From the time he left law school. Mal was a dreamer, Mr. Pope, not a doer. Oh, he made some money at his law practice, in real estate, sometimes quite a bit. But there were long, dry spells, and I found it simpler to take over his indebtedness and give him an allowance each year. It worked marvelously well. His father never knew. He thought Mal was doing splendidly on his own. He came to be inordinately proud of Mal, in fact. That was my goal, Mr. Pope. Peace and harmony in my family; my husband, whom I love very much, protected from knowledge that would harm him by destroying his faith in his only son. It was only money, a small price to pay for the security it brought."

"You said a lot of ways."

Her brow furrowed, eyes quizzical. "I don't think I understand."

"A lot of ways that Malcolm disappointed your husband."

She made a disparaging gesture with one slender hand. "Oh, small things, inconsequential things, actually, but . . ." She paused, her expression becoming apologetic. "I shouldn't say this, of course, but I'm afraid he was disappointed in Malcolm's choice of a wife."

"How so?" *Not that I don't know,* Pope thought, *and not that I give a damn, but we have to talk about something until Hack gets back.*

"Oh, well," Marsha Carlyle said. "I know this sounds

so . . . so tacky and uncharitable, but, you know, her size. Poor dear, she has always been so fat. And the worst part is that she doesn't seem to want to do anything about it.''

"We can't all be slim-jims," Pope said curtly. "And maybe your son liked fat women. A lot of men do, you know."

"Of course," she said quickly. "There's nothing . . . basically wrong with it, it's just that it's so . . . unhealthy, don't you think?"

Pope shrugged. "The graveyards are full of bony people—no pun intended."

She smiled nevertheless. "Touché, Mr. Pope."

"I seem to remember Matilda saying she was slim back in her high-school days. Has she ever had herself checked for some kind of glandular condition?"

Marsha Carlyle nodded, one hand straying to poke and pat her meticulous hair. "No, there's nothing glandular, and yes, she was slender in high school. But she was already somewhat overweight when she and Mal married. That was somewhere around four years after high school. I remember we wanted them to wait until Mal finished law school, but they wouldn't hear of it—*she* wouldn't hear of it, I think. At any rate, she began gaining weight rapidly after they were married. She's weighed over three hundred pounds for years." There was a sharp edge of distaste in her tone, and she looked at him quickly and brought back the apologetic smile. "I'm sorry, but I dislike gluttony . . . greediness."

"And Matilda is greedy?"

Her chin lifted, her eyes gleaming. "Yes. I'm afraid I must say she is." She swept her arm in an expansive half circle. "This . . . this estate was for Matilda. My son liked simple living, simple things. He owned a smaller house when they were married, a perfectly adequate home for two people, but she wasn't happy. They ended up with this . . . monstrosity. On my money. Please don't get me wrong, I would have spent twice as much to make my son happy, to keep peace and tranquility in my family. But the galling thing is, I don't believe she made Mal happy, after all. I know the things they bought didn't . . . the fancy foreign cars, the boat that sits rotting at a marina in Port Arthur, this house—'' She broke off suddenly, her chin down to her shoulder, her face adverted. ''I'm sorry, I'm running off at the mouth.'' She laughed a small, shaky laugh. ''A lot of this, most of it, I've never told anyone before.'' She looked up and smiled warmly. ''You inspire confidence, Mr. Pope. You're a good listener. I suppose that must be of great benefit to you in your line of work.''

''Some,'' he admitted. ''But I do a lot of gabbing myself. I understand—'' He stopped and turned as Hack came into the room, his dark eyes gleaming, his face solemnly struggling to suppress a smile.

''You're not gonna believe this, old buddy, but Malcolm Carlyle was at the shooting range from nine to eleven A.M. the day he was killed.''

CHAPTER

NINETEEN

Mickey Fields basked neck-deep in the tub for almost an hour, pampering herself outrageously, increasing the temperature steadily by a slow, continuous infusion of hot water; luxuriating lazily in the turbulent, penetrating warmth. Despite the fluid lassitude of her body, her mind was curiously alert, on edge, thoughts hopscotching, flitting over and around and through her mind's-eye imagery of Hackmore Wind, logic failing, reason faltering before the onslaught of fuzzy-headed fantasy.

She cleansed her body meticulously, opening beneath the water, laving thoroughly those parts already exquisitely tender with the beginnings of tumescence. She dried herself with loving care, patting her breasts, stroking, the soft-napped towel cool and sericeous against heated skin, noting with something like awe the way the tiny buds lifted from their pink nests, erect and tingling and palpitatingly sensitive. She anointed her flesh with the rich aroma of Parisian Love and dusted fragrant powder sparingly in those areas not readily accessible to inquisitive lips.

She examined herself in the bathroom mirror, not entirely pleased with what she saw but not distressed either. She raised on tiptoe to admire the youthful thrust of moderately sized breasts and leaned in to monitor the malignant progress of tiny squint lines at the corners of her eyes. She hummed softly under her breath, unconscious accompaniment to the gentle thrumming along her nerve pathways, a fine edge of excitement building inside. She turned away from the mirror, satisfied that she could give as much as she received.

She squirmed into her nightgown, shivering at the delicious slither of white silk across her breasts and down her thighs. She felt suddenly delectable, voluptuous, incredibly desirable.

"Jesus Christ," she murmured, smiling wryly, shrugging into a nylon robe and knotting the belt almost savagely. "I can't believe me. Old Mickey Fields, nemesis of copilots and captains, frigid maiden of the friendly skies. Old above-it-all Mickey, losing my cool over a shit-kicking cowboy sheriff from Squatsville." She had a sudden vision of hard strong thighs, of big fearsome hands, and smothered a nervous giggle. She glanced at the clock. "And I, by God, don't even know if he's coming or not."

She sat down on the edge of the couch. She pressed her legs together and folded her hands primly in her lap. She stared sightlessly at the dark TV and waited, her mind as empty as she could make it but not totally blank; fragments of what she remembered of his dark, masculine beauty steamed into her awareness, left her dry-mouthed and taut-bodied, with a slow, warm dissolving deep inside.

When it came sometime later, it startled her: the first three notes of "Memory." She stirred and raised her head, automatically fluffing the thick, silky hair that tumbled in deep waves to her shoulders. She rose to her feet and waited for the notes to sound again, her lips curving in irony at the quivering weakness in her thighs, the tingling flutter in the pit of her stomach, the undeniable vibration of her pounding heart.

But seconds dragged into a minute and the sound didn't come again, and, suddenly breathless with fear, she rushed across the room and threw off the chain and twisted the lock and flung open the door.

"Hi," Hack Wind waited quietly, dark and handsome and unsmiling, his expression cautious, uncertain. He was standing at parade rest, hands hidden behind his back, feet slightly apart, braced as if to repel an unexpected assault.

"Hello!" She watched his face brighten at the lilting warmth in her voice.

He smiled tentatively and shifted his feet, bringing his heels closer together, self-consciously ducking his head in a slight movement that resembled a bow.

"I wasn't sure . . . well, I couldn't remember what happened. Here, I brought you these." His right hand swept from behind his back: a large oval of multicolored roses in full bloom, trembling from his death grip around the unwrapped stems.

"Oh, my, aren't they lovely!"

"And this." His left hand came into view, holding a slim paper bag. "I don't know a hell of a lot about wine, but the guy said this was a good year."

"Oh, Hack, you shouldn't have. This is too much."

"Not really," he said candidly, grinning. "I picked the roses from our—my garden, and us cops always get a discount on booze." He held the bouquet away from her reaching hand. "Better let me put these in a vase for you. I couldn't find anything to wrap around the stems. They're a little prickly." His dark eyes gleamed down at her. "Anyhow, I wasn't sure what-all I had to make up for."

"Nothing at all," she said brightly, rushing to get a vase, dumping a clump of faintly yellowing carnations into a wastebasket and trying to ignore a sweep of tingling heat into her cheeks. "All you did, for goodness sake, was spend the night sleeping in my bed." She smiled at him and crinkled her nose. "Alone."

He smiled crookedly and winced. "I was halfway afraid of that."

She laughed and held the vase while he seated the flowers, their hands brushing as he made unnecessary adjustments to the densely packed bouquet, their eyes meeting solidly for the first time over the mound of riotous colors.

"I didn't know they bloomed like this, this early," she said, only vaguely aware that she was talking, her low, soft voice sending an unmistakable message.

"Uh-huh," he said, taking the vase from her hands and placing it on a nearby table. "They've been blooming since the middle of March."

He stepped back to stand in front of her, placed his hands slowly and deliberately on her shoulders, his thumbs lightly brushing along the curve of her neck, dark eyes locking with hers, almost painful in their intensity.

"I'm not drunk tonight," he said softly.

She nodded dumbly, her lips trying to smile, feeling her heart thundering.

"No frustrations, no tension, no anxiety. Only me." He bent and kissed her gently, holding the pressure evenly and steadily, breaking away only when her lips began to move, to open.

"Do I pass muster tonight?" he asked huskily.

"I—I think so," she said faintly, finding her voice and feeling suddenly virginal and girlishly helpless in the rush of passion that clouded her mind and sharpened her senses. "Oh, yes," she breathed, pressing against him, acutely aware of her body, the soft melting core, the slow trickling flow of life forces toward her center in anticipation as she became irrevocably aroused, became conscious of his rapidly expanding male hardness.

He pushed her back, held her at arm's length, and watched her flushed cheeks and radiant eyes. "I have to tell you, I'm part white, part Mexican, part Indian—"

"What?" She was having trouble concentrating on the mellow flow of his voice.

"I said I have to tell you, I'm part—"

"Oh, shut up," she murmured. "You're talking too much." She slammed into him, linked her arms behind his neck, and yanked downward. "I don't care if you're part ape. You're beautiful and I want you. I want you right now, and if you're half the man I think you are, you'll do something about it . . . right now!" She kissed him, lips open, warm and moist and melting under his. She broke free, leaned back, their eyes only inches apart. She smiled tremulously. "If it bothers you, just fuck me with the white part."

He laughed, stooped, and picked her up by locking his hands beneath her buttocks. He carried her into the bedroom, his face hidden between her breasts, navigating from memory, dropping her backward when his shinbone ran into the side of the bed.

Dark eyes smoldering, his hands busy with his own clothing, he watched her squirm gracefully out of the robe, stretch seductively like a great tawny cat, eyes hooded, the narrow slits sparking fire, the sheer white silk of the gown revealing, yet tantalizingly concealing.

"Jesus," he said almost inaudibly, "you're beautiful!"

"Am I?" she asked softly, artlessly, her body moving,

the silk sliding on heated flesh like a million tiny caressing hands. "Am I really?" she repeated, watching his progress intently, catching her breath as he wrenched away the bursting shorts, broke free, jutting toward her arrogantly, demanding attention.

"Jesus!" It was her turn to whisper.

They wanted it to last, this first time together that was so important to each of them. They wanted to savor, to revel in the electrifying sensations of caressing eyes and stroking hands, the heady exhilaration of intumescence, of overheated bodies and supercharged emotions.

She gripped him tightly, urging him on with happy, muted sounds, her body arching, binding him, helpless and enthralled, in the flow of her passion, the compelling flame of velvet loins.

Mesmerized, he watched the play of emotions across her mobile face, watched with fascination as her eyelids drooped, then sprang wide, full lips flattening, thinning, curving upward in a gleaming, grinning rictus of pleasure; her body convulsed and she cried out wordlessly, reached for his mouth with hungry, searching lips.

Too much, too much, he thought wildly, her urgency overwhelming him, feeling the irrepressible tug, the last vestiges of his restraint crumbling. Galvanized, he groaned mightily, abandoned himself to liquid, quicksilver flesh, surrendered to the inconsolable demands of his own crying need, the raging fever in his blood; his senses fragmented, steadied, coalesced; his explosion followed hers like a stentorian echo in a dark and silent cave.

But even when it was over, she refused to let him leave her. She locked her legs around his thighs and pressed downward, covering his face with warm, dry kisses.

"I can still feel you. Can you feel anything?"

"Not a hell of a lot," he admitted. He raised on his elbows and looked longingly at his clothes; he was dying for a cigarette. He kissed her rubefacient cheeks and moved tentatively, but the resilient bands across his buttocks held fast. Then she sighed and let her legs drop to the bed.

"Intermission," she said, kissing him one last time.

"Pit stop," he said. He eased away from her, mildly surprised to find he still had an erection. He found his cigarettes and lighter and went into the bathroom. She followed.

"Hey, are you throwing in the towel? What's the matter, can't you take it?" She watched unabashedly as he relieved himself, then raced back to the bed as he growled and faked a lunge at her.

"Time out," he protested. "Even boxers get time out."

A minute later he was back beside the bed, grinning down at her wolfishly. "Second round coming up," he said. He sat down. "Just as soon as I finish this cigarette."

They lay side by side, the pounding in their chests diminishing, their breathing slowly returning to normal, the feeble light from the bathroom glistening dully on a faint sheen of perspiration coating lethargic bodies.

"Ash," Mickey said suddenly, breaking the lengthy silence, bringing Hack back reluctantly from the threshold of sleep.

"What?" he asked drowsily.

"Ash. Dark ash or maybe pecan." She rolled on her side and came against him, her breasts pressing against his rib cage, warm and soft and passionless. "I've been trying to decide what your coloring is." She placed a hand flat on his stomach and pressed. "Well, whatever it is called, it's a beautiful color."

"Aw, shucks, ma'am." He yawned and stretched, wondering why women never wanted to do the sensible thing and go to sleep after sex. A body's sexual apparatus was like a car battery; everybody knew it needed recharging after extensive overuse—everybody that was, except women.

She trailed her fingers lightly across his chest. "Well, even if you're not high on the color of your body, you have to admit you rate a ten on structure and texture." She moved her lips along the edge of his chest, as if she were tasting him. "You're skin's as smooth as mine."

He cupped her chin in his fingers and tilted her face so he could see it. "Hey, you're overreacting. I'm not all that hung up on what I am."

"Yes, you are," she said solemnly, "or you wouldn't have mentioned it. I'm Irish and Jewish and there's even a little Oriental blood in there somewhere. But I don't feel the need to point that out to everyone I meet."

"I don't, either. Just the ones I plan on going to bed with."

"There must be a lot of those. With your moves, as handsome as—"

"Come on, Mickey, cut it out. You're the first one since . . . well, since I married Wendy." Even as he protested, he found her words absurdly gratifying.

"How long ago was that?"

"A little more than six years. Hey, tell me something. Don't you ever sleep?"

She chuckled throatily. "Okay, I can take a hint." Her hand strayed down across his stomach and patted him gently. She sighed. "Do you think you'll ever recover?"

"You'd be surprised at what a good night's sleep can do."

She chuckled again and fell silent. She snuggled against him and lay listening to the almost instant change in his breathing: slow and deep, an occasional bubbling snore. She watched the rise and fall of his chest, studied the sculptured lines of his face in the dim light. Reluctantly she closed her eyes to aid the stealthy creep of warm lassitude that was slowly overpowering her senses. She sighed and huddled contentedly against his warm body and watched the dark wall-cloud descend to envelope her in velvet darkness.

Hack awakened to the imperious demands of a threatening bladder. He disentangled himself from clinging arms and padded into the bathroom. When he returned, she had moved into his spot, lay curled protectively against the early-morning chill. He covered her and found his discarded clothing, dressing rapidly, silently, casting an occasional glance at her bright, tousled head, tempted to awaken her and prove what a good night's rest could really do for a man. He smiled at the thought, at the gentle stir in his loins. He shook his head regretfully and pulled on his boots. He paused beside the bed, studied her exquisite face, innocently girlish and incredibly vulnerable, decided sadly that a good-bye kiss would undoubtedly awaken the sleeping princess, and the prince would never get to work, what with one thing or another.

He tore a page from his notebook and left a note, promising to call and warning her never, *never*, to open her door again the way she had for him the night before, reminding her that a killer still roamed the streets of Merriweather and that she was one of the chosen dozen.

He made certain her door was securely locked, then

stood for a moment in the hallway, gripped by indefinable feelings of malaise. He hesitated, lingered, almost decided to punch the bell until she awakened and go back inside. But finally he attributed his portentous feelings to a belated, misdirected sense of guilt and after-sex blues and walked slowly and reluctantly to his pickup and drove away.

CHAPTER
TWENTY

Milly leaned back in her chair and brushed absently at a smear of ashes on the front of her V-neck sweater vest, her clear, calm eyes watching Pope critically as he settled into the chair across from her, his stern face more haggard than usual, the merry blue eyes lusterless, couched in walnut-colored pouches.

"Hard night?" she asked solicitously, smoke dribbling past her gleaming eyes from the cigarette in the corner of her mouth. "You look . . . whipped."

"No worse than usual," Pope said tersely, taking a handful of papers out of his briefcase, his voice clearly indicating his disapproval of the implications in her words.

"My, aren't we grouchy," she said lightly, tapping her pen on the table and watching with cynical amusement as he studiously avoided her eyes.

"Sorry," he said, not sounding sorry at all. He selected a single sheet of paper from the stack in front of him and became immediately absorbed.

Annoyance chased amusement, and she watched him

for a full minute, her face gradually tightening, a frosty glint creeping into her eyes.

"Well?" she asked crisply, "what happened with the Carlyles?"

"What?" He still refused to look up.

"The Carlyles," she snapped. "Yesterday afternoon. You and Hack. You went to find out about the gun."

"Oh, yeah. Well, maybe I was wrong. We found out he was at the gun range a few hours before he was killed. That knocks the hell out of our residue test. He used a .308 and a .38 Colt Special. The .308 was back in the rack in his closet and the .38 was in a drawer in their bedroom. Neither one had been cleaned. Could be he had the gun in the study and dropped it . . . or something." He gave her a quizzical glance. "What're you getting so testy about?"

She ignored his question. "Then you don't believe it was suicide, after all?"

"I guess not," he said glumly. "His mother doesn't believe it, and she's a pretty sharp lady. I have a feeling nothing much went on that concerned her son that she didn't know about. She stretched the truth a bit about who found him, but I guess her motives were sound. She also told us her son wasn't much of a lawyer, that she had been subsidizing him ever since he graduated law school— without the old man knowing anything about it. All to protect the old man's image of his only son."

"She must have loved him very much."

"He was her son, why wouldn't she?"

"I don't mean the son. I'm talking about the father. Women love their sons. That's understood, but they don't always love their husbands."

He barked a short humorless laugh. "Yeah, that's the truth."

She glanced at him, her face softening. "Bitterness, Ham? After all this time?"

"No, not bitterness. I guess frustration would be a better word for it. I just don't understand women, the way you can hide everything, cover up your true feelings. I never had the slightest idea that Alice had fallen out of love with me—and that's assuming that she loved me in the first place—until the day she announced it quite grandly during an argument we were having. And even then, swift, perceptive detective that I am, I didn't dream that she was having an affair. I found that out later, by accident, and when I braced her with it, she split. Now to make my point! Right up to the time she left, we had relations. She was sweet and cuddly and loving, just the way she had always been. If she no longer loved me, by God, how in hell could she do that? How could she respond so freely, display such damn powerful emotions? I thought all along she was blowing off steam in a fit of anger. But I found out she was telling the truth when she left me. She didn't love me any longer. She made a believer out of me damn quick. It took—" He broke off, smiled sheepishly, and shrugged. "Hell, you've heard all this before."

Milly was watching him, her chin propped on a fisted hand, her smile faintly enigmatic. "To answer your question, Ham, it's partly the way we are and part artifice. You forget that for centuries the only things women had going for them were their bodies and their cunning. The bodies wore out, aged, wasted. All that was left was cunning. Who do you think thought up the idea of marriage? I doubt very seriously that it was a man."

"I don't know. Men are possessive about their women too. I think most men like the idea of one man, one woman."

Her smile widened. "That's only because we've trained

you well. From little boys on up. But not well enough, unfortunately. How many men do you know who've left an older woman for a younger one?''

His quick glance ricocheted off her cheekbone; color flooded his face. "We never had an . . . an understanding of any kind, Milly."

She winced good-naturedly. "You're right, Ham. I was never any good at artifice, and I suppose good living and women's rights have dulled my survival instincts." She sighed. "God save us from righteous women libbers."

"From the righteous, anyway," he said, smiling tentatively, glad to be away from the quicksand of personal confrontation.

But it was not to be. She stacked the interrogation reports neatly on the corner of the table and picked up her purse, an oddly determined look on her face. "When you see Hack, tell him I'm off to talk to Stacy Crump again. She seems to have a better memory than the others."

"Sure."

She walked around the table and stopped behind him. "I'm probably committing a cardinal sin by telling you this—no, don't turn around, I don't want to see your ugly face—but I've been out with a couple of men since your girlfriend came back. Good men. Young, good-looking. And I've slept with them. And you may or may not be pleased to know, you ugly son of a bitch, that it wasn't worth a good goddamn. And what does that mean, you bastard? It probably means you've spoiled me for anyone else ever, and I hope this ruins your goddamn day because it's sure as hell ruining mine." She sucked in a dry, rasping breath. "What really pisses me off is that I don't know why. You're good in bed but you're damn well past your prime. You're too fat and opinionated and stubborn and

. . . and I hope that sweet little piece of ass breaks your fucking heart . . . again!''

She was gone before he could think of a reply, plaid skirt swirling about trim calves, a ramrod-straight back and bouncing hair, defiance and disdain in every line of her compact body, in the haughty angle of her head atop squared off shoulders.

He stared after her, a little dazed and disoriented by her vehemence, the scorn in her voce, more than a little shocked by her profanity. Cop or not, a heartfelt ''damn'' was for her the ultimate imprecation, and he had more than once watched her wince at the freewheeling vulgarity that cops seemed to adopt along with their badge and gun.

Long after she had gone, he was still pondering her behavior, picking at it like an old scab on a cold sore, repeating in his mind what he could remember of her words, coming to conclude finally, sadly, what he had suspected for a long time.

Milly Singer was undoubtedly in love with him.

An hour later he was on his way out the door when the phone began ringing. He whirled, walked back to the table, and picked it up.

''Pope.''

''Ham. This is Milly.''

''Hey,'' he said quickly, warmly, ''If you're calling to apologize, forget it. We all—''

She barked a small, derisive laugh. ''Fat chance, old man. I'm calling about Stacy Crump. I thought you might be interested in knowing she's dead.''

''Dead?'' he echoed inanely.

''Shot in the head at close range. Probably a .32. The County Coroner says he thinks she was killed about ten last night, give or take an hour. Hack is here. I called the sheriff as soon as we found her.''

"We?"

"Her sister and I. I went by her beauty salon to talk to her and found it locked up tight. I came out here to her house and found the same thing. I was ready to leave when her sister drove up. She'd been trying to call her all morning at work and at home, and she was getting worried. She had a key, so we came in.''

"And?"

"And she was lying on the couch as if she had just slipped sideways to rest for a moment. She obviously knew her killer. There was a coffeepot and two cups and some cookies on a tray on the coffee table in front of her. Both cups were full, it looked like they hadn't been touched. The killer was evidently sitting across from her. He, or she, simply leaned forward and shot her—in the forehead.''

"How's Hack doing?"

"Good. He has their tech squad here and four deputies canvassing the area.'' She paused and cleared her throat, her voice subtly changing. "We may have a witness. An eighteen-year-old girl lives almost directly across the road with her mother. She was sitting in her boyfriend's car with him last night about eight. We haven't talked to the boy yet, but the girl said they saw a woman go into Stacy Crump's house, and she was still in there at nine when the girl had to go in. That puts it pretty close to time of death.''

"Description?"

Pope heard the faint sibilance of an indrawn breath. "Yes. Marilyn—that's the girl's name—said the woman looked like a *very* fat lady.''

"A fat—" Pope broke off, a faint chill coursing through him. "Matilda Carlyle!"

"That's who it sounds like, Ham. Dark hair slicked back in a bun, a dress that looked like an Arab's tent, a dark-colored Mercedes."

"What's Hack planning on doing . . . about Matilda, I mean?"

"He—we were about ready to go talk to her. That's why I called. I thought maybe you wanted to talk . . ."

"Yeah, I sure as hell do. But not at her house. Bring her in, Milly. Ask her nice, and if she won't come, arrest her ass and bring her in, anyway."

"On what charge?"

Pope found and lit a cigarette while he thought about it.

"Material witness. But I don't think it'll come to that. Check the car first. I'm certain I saw a dark green Mercedes in their garage. And don't mention the Crump thing if you don't have to. Tell her we have a revised deposition for her to sign on her husband's death. Give her some bull about their change of story. I'd like to hit her cold on Crump, but if I go out there, that old lady will be running interference. I want Matilda alone for a change. If the old dame insists on coming, okay. We'll park her aristocratic butt in the lobby with a copy of *Cosmopolitan* or something. We need to get a quick confirmation from the boy if we can."

"That should be easy enough. He's in high school. We can stop by and talk to him on the way to the Carlyles."

"All right, and maybe . . . look, on second thought, if she should get her back up and won't come in, give me a call before you slap the cuffs on her."

Milly chuckled softly. "Cold feet, Ham?"

"No," he said stiffly, "just a little discretion. I get a little carried away. Besides, old man Carlyle is a pretty nice old geezer. So's the old lady, for that matter. Maybe we better play it by ear until we know more about where we stand. Matilda and the Crump woman were schoolmates. Hell, maybe they were buddies or something."

"Maybe," Milly said dryly. "Okay, I'll give Hack your message. It's his case, you know."

"No, it's our case. He's part of the task force. If he disagrees, have him call me."

"All right." She fell silent. He could hear her breathing. "This blows the riddle thing, you know."

"What?"

"Stacy Crump. She was a beautician. There's no way you can get an Indian Chief out of that. She's as German, blond, and blue-eyed as they come."

"That's so," Pope said thoughtfully. "But we'd already decided there wasn't an Indian among the ones left. Well, never mind. What we need to do is get back with Smith and McCormick and Fields and impress on them the seriousness of this thing. They're the only ones left, except Ringley, but he's pretty much out of harm's way."

"And Matilda Carlyle."

"Yeah, and her. We should take them into protective custody."

"Whatever you think. I have to go, Ham. Hack's ready to leave."

"Okay. Remember, give me a call if you hit a snag."

"I think we can manage," she said crisply, and broke the connection.

He replaced the receiver, wincing at the coolness that had returned to her voice. He felt a pang of remorse, wondering if things would ever be the same between them again. He tossed his briefcase on the table and slumped into a chair to wait. Just goes to prove what aggravating creatures women were, their principal function being the frustration and disorientation of males.

CHAPTER
TWENTY-ONE

Hamilton Pope was returning to his office with corrected copies of the Carlyle depositions when the bell on his phone jangled again. He reached across the desk and yanked up the receiver, choking the irritating sound in mid-ring. "Pope."

"Ham, this is Milly again. Matilda isn't here. She flew to Houston this morning, according to the maid. She told the maid she'd probably be home tomorrow. I guess we wait, huh?"

"I guess so," Pope said sourly, "unless you'd like to fly down and bring her back."

"Don't be a wiseass, Pope. I'm inside the house. You want me to nose around a little?"

"No, better not. We don't have a warrant, and if you should find anything, we couldn't use it."

"You're the boss. We talked to the boyfriend of the girl across the street. He confirms what she told us. He said the woman was as big as the side of a house. And he said the car was definitely a Mercedes, but he couldn't tell the exact color—just dark."

"Is the Mercedes there?"

"Yes, it's in the garage. Dark green, just like you said. There's also a snazzy little Porsche. That must have been his. I don't think Matilda would fit in it." She paused. "I guess you may have been right about them being friends."

"Why?"

"The boy said they embraced at the door, that the blond chick laid a wet one on Matilda. I interpreted that to mean they kissed."

"Does that surprise you?"

"Well . . . no. Women friends do hug and kiss sometimes. It's just that she doesn't appear to be . . . well, that warm and demonstrative."

"Why? Because she's fat? I don't know about that. Fat people need love, too, and her and Malcolm were holding hands and making goo-goo eyes at each other all the time I was talking to them."

"Yes, I've noticed that some fat people need more love than others."

He chuckled. "That's not very funny."

"Who's being funny?" she said curtly. "If you have no objection, I'll go with Hack this afternoon. He has some new names from the class of '68 that live out in the country."

"Sure, that's fine," he said hastily. "I'm sure he'll appreciate the help."

"Yes, he will," she said, her voice back to frigid again, reinforcing his firm belief as he hung up the phone that man's worst enemy was no longer himself.

Hackmore Wind dropped Milly Singer off near her car in the parking lot behind Police Headquarters. It was late afternoon, and he decided morning would be soon enough to deliver the meager results of his long day's work. Pope would have gone home to his little blond bombshell without a doubt, and Milly had mumbled something about a date for dinner and a movie, and he had no desire to face surly Sergeant Globe or cynical Detective Kilgarten alone if they chanced to be there.

As he drove, he debated going by Mickey Fields's apartment. He reluctantly counseled himself against the idea because she might well interpret it as irresponsible impulsiveness since he hadn't called as promised and had sneaked off without waking her.

He tried to recall what he had written in the note, tried to remember if he had made reference to the wonderful night, how wonderful she was, how wonderful he felt, how wonderful the whole thing had— Jesus Christ, had he even thanked her? He remembered the terse, businesslike message and groaned. Ignorant asshole! Shit-kicking country bumpkin! Dolt! A simple heartfelt thank-you at the very— And how had he signed it? Jesus Christ! Sincerely, Hack? Yours truly? Something stupid, no doubt.

I'll call her, he thought glumly, *as soon as I get in the door. I'll call her and apologize for being such an insensitive lump, plead total stupidity, throw myself on her mercy, and pray she's as forgiving as she is beautiful, and maybe she'll invite me over for an intimate little dinner for two, and I'll raid the damned garden again and take her a bouquet she won't be able to get through the door and two bottles of wine, and maybe some candy and . . . and oh, shit, what the hell is Wendy doing here?*

The little red Plymouth was parked in its accustomed place, and he felt the muscles in his chest contract as he pulled up behind it and stopped.

A hell of a time to be coming for her things, he thought angrily. *She knows what time I get home from work. The damned least she could do is come while I'm gone. Is she proud of what's happened,* he wondered, *pleased with the ruin of what had been a pretty decent marriage, all things considered? Maybe that wasn't enough for her? Maybe she wanted to rub his nose in it, remind him what he was missing? What he had lost?*

He considered driving around the circular driveway and leaving, waiting until she was finished, avoiding what could only be an unpleasant confrontation. He reached for the key, switched on the motor, then just as suddenly turned it off again. Hell, no! Why should he run and hide? She was the culprit, not he. She was the one who had broken the faith with a milk-white, blond son of a bitch with a fancy damn van and—

He shoved open the pickup door and climbed down, rage threatening to choke him. He slammed the truck door, then opened it again as a thought struck him. What if he had come with her? Surely not? Surely Wendy had more sense than to tempt him a second time? He hesitated, then shook his head and unbuckled his gun belt. He tossed it and the holstered gun inside the truck and closed the door again. Boot heels crunching on gravel, he walked toward the front door. He breathed deeply, feeling the rage beginning to dissipate, to drain away. He felt suddenly empty, a nauseating twitch of apprehension steadily growing, pushing him relentlessly toward a kind of helpless numbness. He sucked in his stomach, tightened up his backbone, and opened the door.

The aroma buffeted him immediately, bringing instant saliva and quivering nostrils as he sniffed the air and caught the familiar, unmistakable odor of the tangy sauce she had learned to make from his mother. And beneath it the more subtle fragrances: roasting pork, faint traces of fresh bread baking, boiling corn on the cob, sweet peas.

''What the hell?'' he said aloud, staring down the hallway toward the kitchen door, listening in total confusion to the ordinary supper-cooking sounds, the off-key whistling that had always made him smile and now made his heart lurch, the cheery rattle of pots and pans, the tap-tap-tap of heels on linoleum, seeing the bright-haired, rosy-cheeked face pop around the doorjamb, wince, smile, then say, "Oh, hi! Dinner in about five minutes. Plenty of time to wash up." Then disappear.

He stood immobile for a full sixty seconds. Stunned. Dumbfounded. Emotions he couldn't begin to analyze chased each other around and around inside his head; he brought a hand to his face and discovered he was trembling, became aware that his throat was dry as a new blotter, a feeling akin to panic breaking loose from all the other emotions and fluttering like a hummingbird in the pit of his stomach.

What in God's name was happening? Could he be hallucinating? No! He could still hear the sounds: the rattle of plates, the creaking of the oven door, the whir of the mixer in the mashed potatoes, the electric knife—only the whistling had stopped, and he walked down the hall to the bathroom, wondering if that was because her mouth was as dry as his, wondering if she was as nervous as he was flabbergasted. He had girded his loins for battle, come in prepared for coldness, contempt, acrimony, and had been presented with the innocuous ingredients of dull routine, a disarming greeting and a cheery, welcoming smile, his very favorites in gastronomical delights. He stared at his befuddled expression as he washed his hands. It could well have been a month ago, a week ago, before Al Judson . . .

He sighed regretfully and dried his hands. But it wasn't, it was now. It was after Al Judson, and no amount of lovely smiles or innocent greetings or favorite meals was ever going to change that. Al Judson *had* happened. It was there in his brain, and it would not go away.

"Granny's Dinner Theater?" Pope stared at her with naked disbelief. "Tonight? My God, that's all the way down in Dallas!"

"But, honey, I have tickets. Free tickets! And it's my last chance to see that new rock group—"

"Rock group?" Pope's look turned to horror.

"Well, soft rock, not hardly rock at all. They play about as much country-western—"

"Oh! Country-western! Why didn't you say so? That makes all the difference in the world. Country western played by a rock group! My God!" He chortled and rummaged in the refrigerator for a beer. "I'd as soon listen to two bobcats making love; at least they'd be enjoying it. Here, this is the last one. You want half of it?"

"No thank you," she said curtly. She turned her back and moved to the kitchen window.

He took a sip, gazing at her profile over the rim of the can. "What're we gonna do about eating?"

Her lips tightened. "I don't know what you're going to do. I'm not hungry."

"Then why did you want to drive all the way into Dallas?" he asked reasonably.

"Just never mind." She flounced into the den and picked up the television guide.

"Are we having a fight?" He watched her from the doorway, amusement warring with irritation.

"What on earth would we be fighting about?" she asked coldly, her eyes flashing.

"Maybe because you didn't get your way, little girl."

"Little girl! Ha! You don't think I'm so little when it comes to fu—making love."

"You're right," he said quietly. "I only think of you as a little girl when you act like one. You're all woman when you want to be."

"I am all woman," she protested weakly, flashing him a sudden smile, changing tactics. "I just thought we'd have a nice night out for a change. Dinner and a little music."

"For a change? We ate out night before last. Saturday night we went to that new country-western place you were dying to see. Sunday night we went—"

"Oh, all right," she said petulantly. She tossed the television guide on the couch and bounced to her feet, undergoing a mercurial change, smiling crookedly, advancing on him. "Okay, I know I'm spoiled and selfish. What do you want for dinner? I'll fix it for you." She wrapped her arms around his waist and squeezed, the top her head even with his mouth. "I'll fix us a nice dinner and we'll go to bed early." She stood on tiptoe and kissed him. "And I'll make it up to you for being so mean." She wiggled her eyebrows and gave him a Groucho leer.

He put his hands on her shoulders and massaged the firm softness, his thumbs in the hollows above her collarbones. He sighed. "Whatever happened to a quiet evening of TV, a good-night kiss, and eight hours' sleep? I think they must have laced your generation's pabulum with speed and you've never recovered."

She laughed and swayed against him. "What's the matter, old man, am I wearing you out?" She tilted her head and watched him with bright blue eyes.

"Not so much out as down. Even stone wears down under running water."

"I guess I am a little hyper sometimes."

"Sometimes, most of the time, it's fun."

"But not all the time?"

"I'm like a grandfather clock. When I run down, I need time to rewind my mainspring."

She smiled wryly. "I think if I looked hard enough, I'd find a message in that somewhere."

"Nothing very significant. I'm a simple man. I say and do simple things, like when I hunger I eat, when I thirst I drink, when I lust I—" He stopped, unable to think of a finish without using the word he had been trying to break her from using.

"When you lust, you what?" she urged, her twinkling eyes acknowledging his predicament.

"I go lay down until it passes." It was a joke and not a joke; it had happened. At forty-six a man could not afford to surrender himself willy-nilly to every vagrant sexual impulse that chanced to come his way. And with an uninhibited twenty-six-year-old flitting about, usually half naked, the impulses were many and varied.

She chuckled softly. "You fret too much. You're like a horny teenager with me."

"I'm just playing catch-up. I've been divorced a long time."

"What about Milly What's-her-name . . . Singer? Milly Singer?" She cocked her head and looked up at him, a small, enigmatic smile curving her lips.

"How did you know about Milly?" There was a trace of annoyance in his tone.

"Oh, I have my sources."

"Come on, Nancy, tell me," he commanded.

"Well, if you must know, it was Hack Wind. But don't blame him. I wormed it out of him."

"Hack? You mean that night out at Fielder's place?"

She shook her head. "No, not then. A few days later. He stopped by here one morning right after you left for work. To see you, he said, but I didn't believe him because he eventually made me go over all that had happened that night. Very casual, but he asked all the same questions again, plus a few new ones. I finally caught on, and I got even by pumping him about you—very casually.''

''Why didn't you mention it to me?''

She ducked her head and made a face. ''It didn't seem important, and besides, he seemed uneasy about it by the time he left.''

''Yeah, he didn't mention it to me, either.''

''Maybe he thought you wouldn't like him questioning your . . . girlfriend!''

''He knows better than that. It's his job.''

''He hasn't been back,'' she said solemnly. ''I guess I'm not a suspect anymore.''

''You never were,'' he said gruffly. ''Hack was being thorough. If a cop isn't thorough, he isn't worth a damn.'' He paused reflectively, his thumbs rubbing his neck. ''I'm surprised he didn't tell me, though.'' He dropped his eyes to her face, blissfully relaxed under his caressing fingers. ''Are you sure you didn't come on to him?'' he asked, intending it to be a light, humorous, joking question, his voice changing of its own volition in mid-sentence, becoming somehow strained, accusing.

Her blue eyes snapped wide, darker suddenly, almost green. Tiny lights ignited in their depths like the quicksilver flash of shooting stars. She wrenched herself away from his hands, her face cold, her jaw set with anger. For seconds that seemed like hours, her blazing eyes flayed him, made him flinch with embarrassment, shame. Then she whirled away, her back ramrod-straight, small fists clenched at her sides, the heavy mass of hair spinning a golden arc, tumbling forward across her shoulders as she stopped suddenly, crumpling, her hands sweeping up to cover her face.

He reached her in one swift stride, gathered her into his arms like a wounded child. He held her tightly, stroked her trembling body, and tried to drown out the racking sobs with hoarse apologies, endearments, promises. He kissed and cuddled and soothed until she was quiet, an occasional sniffle, her face hidden in his neck, cold and wet from tears.

"That didn't come out the way I meant it to," he said apologetically, rocking her in the recliner. "Not that I should have said it at all. Sometimes I let my mouth run away with my common sense." He tugged absently at her skirt, which was now hiked above dimpled knees.

"You don't trust me," she said, her voice low and muffled and faintly petulant.

"Yes, I trust you," he said quietly. "It's just—" He broke off, aware that he was about to venture into dangerous territory, uncharted waters, his common sense warning him stridently to pull back, his honesty urging him on. He sighed. "It's just that there's a way about you, Nancy. A look about you that goes straight to the core of a man. I don't know, maybe you're not aware of it—not entirely. Your eyes promise things, wonderful things, secret things, intimate things and the hell of it is—with me, at least—you delivered all those things and more. You arouse man's most basic instincts. Five minutes after I met you I had an overpowering urge to protect you . . . make love to you. I wanted to *give* you *something* . . . anything." He chuckled uneasily, trying to gauge her reaction from the tenseness of her body, her utter stillness.

"I had this crazy desire for you to ask something of me. To loan you a cigarette, buy you a new car, defend your honor . . . anything. And all the time your eyes and face were promising me things, delightful things that I couldn't believe, wouldn't let myself believe. I dunno. Maybe your size had a lot to do with it. There's something exquisitely illicit about making love to a woman five feet tall.''

"I'm over five feet tall," she protested, and giggled.

"Just barely, squirt," he said warmly, enormously relieved.

"I can't help the way I look," she said. "And I do flirt sometimes. But I didn't with Hack Wind. I don't think he would have noticed, anyway."

"Just forget I said anything," Pope said, his voice more humble than he intended. He cleared his throat. "Do you still want to go to that theater? We still have time."

She lifted her head, her lips quirking on the edge of a smile. "No. Don't be a softy. Don't give in to me because I threw a tantrum. You're a strong man, and I wouldn't want you any other way." Her left hand crept behind his neck and tightened. She pulled his head forward and leaned in close. "Look in my eyes. What do you see?"

"Hmm. Broken blood vessels, swollen lids . . ."

"Not that. All those secrets, wonderful, intimate things . . . can't you see them? They should be there, as sexy as I feel."

He nodded slowly. "Yeah, they're there, all right."

"Well," she said archly, squirming, pressing against him, her lips nibbling at his chin. "Well," she whispered again, "what on earth do we do?"

He rocked back, then forward, then back again, and came to his feet on the forward swing. "I guess one thing we're not gonna do is eat."

CHAPTER

TWENTY-TWO

The dinner went surprisingly well; the conversation polite and constrained, two well-mannered strangers compelled by circumstances to share time and space. Occasionally surreptitious glances collided, ricocheted: small silences burgeoned into deadly emptiness that had to be filled before it became an insurmountable void. They talked of trivial things, inconsequential things in light of their own personal tragedy: the plummeting economy, the murders, joblessness, the latest conflicting signals from Washington, the budget battle.

Wendy was uncharacteristically articulate, her eyes bright, a feverish flush in her cheeks highlighted by the swell of deeply waved, honey-gold hair. Elegant and trim in black Jordache jeans and a moss-green, square-necked blouse, she ate sparingly, tasted nothing, alert to his needs, embarrassingly solicitous.

Hack ate self-consciously, hungrily, hiding his discomfort and an occasional thrill of halfhearted anger behind the mechanics of knife and fork and spoon. Righteous indignation warred with the pleasure of seeing her again, listening to her melodic voice. He felt pangs of sympathy at her obvious nervousness, the next second a stir of resentment with the realization that all his deep hunger was not motivated by the need for food: a moment later a churning emptiness as he pictured her beneath the twisting, sinewy body of Al Judson.

He helped her clear the table, insisted on drying the dishes. He folded the towel, hung it carefully on its rack. He leaned a hip against the counter and lit a cigarette, watching her wipe the counter and sink with quick, jerky strokes that revealed her agitation, her realization that showdown time was near.

"Thanks for the meal, Wendy," he said evenly. "It was great. But you shouldn't have bothered." He puffed on the cigarette and tried not to see the fear in her unnaturally bright eyes as she became motionless except for slender fingers unconsciously mauling the hapless dishcloth. "I've been thinking," he went on quietly. "It would make more sense if you borrowed my pickup to move the rest of your things. I can drive your car for a couple of days."

"No," she said, her voice casual, matter-of-fact. "No, I won't need your pickup, Hack. I'm not going anywhere."

"What?" He stared at her, stunned. "What do you mean, you're not . . . ?"

"This is my home. I don't have anywhere else to go. There isn't anywhere else I want to go."

"You damned sure can't stay here," he said hotly.

She shrugged. "I don't see why not. You're still my husband; I'm still your wife. I made a mistake. A terrible mistake. But not an unforgivable one—not if you love me." Her voice was low and passionate, quivering with intensity, her eyes filled with a dark glimmer of entreaty.

"Jesus Christ!" he exploded. "Jesus Christ! You talk

about love and you . . . you rob me of my pride, my honor, with that . . . that bleached son of a bitch! You break my damned heart and you come prancing in here talking—''

''I said it was a terrible thing,'' she said gently. ''It takes a big man to forgive.''

''Bullshit!'' he yelled. ''Don't try to psych me out with that philosophy crap, Wendy!'' He slammed a fist on the counter, causing her to jump and recoil.

Her lips tightened. She straightened and folded her arms and stared at him defiantly, then took a step closer. ''I'd forgive you. Even if I caught you . . . and I wouldn't try to kill you, either.''

He laughed harshly. ''You know better than that. If I'd wanted to kill either of you, you'd be dead.''

''All right,'' she said evenly. ''I'll concede that. If you'll concede that—''

''This is not a debate,'' he said coldly. ''And there damn sure isn't any room for negotiations.''

''—that a person deserves a second chance. Particularly when you're the only man I ever had. The only one, Hack,'' she added softly. ''Even in high school I knew you were the only man I wanted.''

''You don't get any points for that, lady. You were scared to death of the other boys, the all-white boys. They weren't as patient as I was, weren't awed by your chaste blond beauty. I was so overwhelmed, I was almost afraid to touch you.''

She smiled faintly. ''I don't remember it quite that way. But never mind that. I've had plenty of offers since we've been married, but I was never even tempted—''

''Then why, dammit?'' he yelled. ''Why now? Why this . . . this guy? What kind of excuse do you have all prepared for me to swallow? Maybe he was forcing you? Was that it? Maybe I saw it wrong, heard it wrong!''

"Stop it, Hack!" she pleaded, the high color finally deserting her face, leaving it white and taut, her eyes clenched tightly against unwanted tears. "I—I don't have an excuse. Maybe . . . maybe a reason, or what I thought was a reason." She opened her eyes and brushed angrily at the tears.

"Oh, shit," Hack said huskily. He threw the cigarette butt into the sink and ran water over it. "Why don't you tell me your reason, Wendy?" he said, his voice deceptively gentle. He picked up the soggy butt and tossed it into the trash can beneath the sink.

"Reasons. I . . . I had two.''

"All right, your reasons, then." He folded his arms and looked at her, his dark eyes smoldering, his face impassive.

She took a deep, shuddering breath. "Well, I—I . . . it's going to sound so . . . oh, hell, I wanted to find out what it was like with . . . another man." The words came out in a low, sibilant rush, almost inaudible at the end.

He nodded, his cold face unchanged. "That's one."

"It's not so crazy, Hack. It's only human to wonder. I'm sure you've had other women since—"

"Never," he said flatly. "Not even once. Come on, let's get this over with. What's the other one?"

"Maybe one is enough," she said timidly, thumbing a glistening drop of liquid off her cheek.

"Suit yourself." He pushed away from the cabinet and started around her.

"No, wait!" She grabbed his arm with both hands, dug her fingers into his biceps. "He . . . he promised to . . . there's this story I'm working on. It's good, Hack. Even he said so. He promised to help me get it published."

He smiled mirthlessly. "When I was in Vice, I busted women for that all the time. It's called prostitution."

"It wasn't a . . . transaction, Hack," she protested weakly. "He just mentioned it was good and that he could help me get it published, and then—" She broke off, a trace of color returning to her face.

"And then he started coming on to you," Hack said harshly. "And you let him come on to you. And pretty soon you began to neck a little, grope a little, and then you began to wonder how it would feel with an all-white—"

"Hack, stop." She moaned. Her hands dropped free of his arm and went around his waist. She pulled herself against him. "Stop it!"

"And was it any better?" he went on woodenly, his hands dangling at his sides, his body responding to her abundant warmth even as his mind shrank from the pain of his thoughts, the shadowy, flickering images.

"Oh, God, no," she mumbled against his neck, her arms steel bands around his chest. "It was nothing. My God, nothing at all! Oh, God, Hack, I'm sorry. Please . . . I'm so sorry!" She made a soft whimpering sound. "Please don't . . . don't send me away!"

"I don't know, Wendy," he said slowly, painfully, "I'm not sure I could. And . . . now there's Mickey."

"Mickey?" He felt her body move minutely, her arms tightening even more. "Is that where you were last night?"

He nodded, then realized she couldn't see his head. "Yes. How did you know?"

"I came home last night. I lost my nerve and parked down the road a ways. I saw you leave, then I came in. I spent the night here. I wondered where you were, but I guess I knew you'd have to be with a woman somewhere."

She took a deep breath. "This Mickey, you couldn't love her, Hack . . . not this fast. It's only been a few days."

"What's love?" he asked tonelessly. "I've lost my perspective on love. It seems to mean different things to different people at different times. If wanting to fuck her like crazy is love, then I love her."

He felt her lips on his neck, her warm breath as she sighed. "You're confusing lust with love, darling." Her hands came up and pressed against his cheeks. "I'm sorry. This is all my fault. If you want, I won't mind if you see her . . . for a while."

He stared at her incredulously. "You'd be willing to do that?"

Her thumb traced the curve of his lower lip. "I want you back," she said simply. "Whatever I have to do, I'll do it." Her eyes were moist and shimmering, her face glowing and softly passive. "I love you and I want you," she murmured, swaying forward, her arms sliding over his shoulders and around his neck, soft, devilishly warm lips seeking his.

He could feel himself melting, his treacherous body responding to old, remembered stimuli, an automatic, unconscious reaction to her scent and touch and presence that had nothing to do with his reasoning brain. He felt a slither of self-disgust at his weakness and stiffened in resistance.

"You can't expect me just to forget what's happened, Wendy. And what about the future? How do I know I can ever trust you again?"

"I understand how you feel," she said earnestly. "I'd feel the same way. As a matter of fact, I do feel somewhat the same way. Do you think it's easy for me to accept the fact that you spent the night with another woman, made love to her I don't know how many times? I can't help wondering—'' She stopped, her eyes oddly gleaming. "Even if I hadn't done what . . . I did, you'd have met her. Can you honestly say you wouldn't have felt the same way about her, anyhow? Can you say you wouldn't have wanted to bed her? Can you say you wouldn't have? Can you truthfully say that, Hack?''

"I can say," he said firmly, indignantly, "that I wouldn't have gone to bed with her. I certainly wouldn't have gone over there with flowers and wine—'' He broke off, sensing a tactical blunder of immense proportions.

"So it didn't just happen," she said triumphantly. "You planned it. Flowers and wine! The weapons of seduction." She smiled indulgently and patted his cheek. "How long since you brought me flowers and wine, Hack?''

"Never," he admitted, wondering suddenly why he was the one on the defensive. "We always have a garden full of roses, and you don't like wine."

"That's not the point," she murmured sweetly, "but never mind that. How long has it been since you've told me you love me?''

"Not all that long, but you know—''

"How do I know? Because your deign to live with me? Because you give me a hello and good-bye peck on the lips and maybe a few passionate kisses when we're making love? Maybe I have insecurities too. Just because I'm relatively young and blond and maybe pretty doesn't mean I'm Mrs. Normal-well-adjusted-housewife-of-the-year. I have needs and desires and—''

"You know I do," he said almost humbly, closing his hands around her waist, squeezing.

"Do what?" Her eyes were glowing fiercely.

"Love you."

She shivered and melted against his chest, her face buried in his shoulder, her expression hidden as she ran the gamut from relief to triumph to desire. She shivered again as she felt his response, pressed her groin upward into his rising hardness.

"Show me, darling," she whispered, feeling the sweet thrill of victory, her stomach beginning to flutter, her insides to dissolve. Then came shock and dismay as she felt herself thrust firmly backward.

"No," he said quietly. "I love you, Wendy, and I'm glad you're back home. But slipping into bed is not the answer. There's someone else involved now. How deeply and for how long . . . well, I'm not sure. Maybe when I see her again, I'll know. Right now I'm just confused. But I have to see her again. I know you didn't mean what you said, but unfortunately I may have to hold you to it."

"It's all right," she said quickly. "I did mean—" She broke off as the phone rang, sprang toward it with relief. A moment later she held the receiver out to him, her face pale and taut again. "It's for you." Her eyes locked briefly with his, flicked away, then she turned and went into the family room.

"Hello."

"Oh, hi. Did I catch you at a bad time?" Mickey Fields's voice was carefully cheerful.

"No, it's fine. How are you?" He decided quickly that trying to explain Wendy's presence would be a no-win proposition. Particularly with Wendy listening.

"I feel great," she said softly. "How about you? Were you all . . . tired out today? Or did that good night's sleep fix you up like you said?"

"Yes, I . . . uh . . . I'm fine."

"Can't talk, huh? I take it that was your wife who answered the phone. If you were lying to me, I suppose that means you're in a hell of a lot of trouble, huh? Or did she just happen to come by to pick up her things?"

"Yes, that's right. At least that's what I thought."

She chuckled softly. "Trying to talk her way back . . . oh, damn. Hold on a second, Hack, someone at the door."

He heard the clatter of the receiver on the stand and yelled into the phone, knowing he was too late.

"Mickey! Don't—" He chopped it off, cursing helplessly, jamming the receiver painfully against his ear, smothering his own harsh breathing in an effort to hear.

"Well, hello! I haven't seen you in a long time. Come in." Her voice came faintly accompanied by the sound of a closing door, the murmur of an indistinct voice, a polite laugh, then grew stronger.

"Just a moment, I have someone on the phone. Please have a seat. I won't be a moment. Hi, I'm back."

Hack's pent-up breath exploded in a harsh burst of sound: relief and irritation.

"What's the matter, Hack?"

"Dammit, Mickey, I told you not to answer the door like that. It could have been . . . Who was it, anyhow?"

She laughed her trilling musical laugh. "Oh, Hack, don't be such a worry wart. It's only—"

The rest of it was lost in thunder: a terrible thunder that he recognized instantly for what it was despite the enormity of it, despite the ear-shattering amplification that stunned his brain with concussion, that froze his heart with gut-wrenching certainty.

CHAPTER
TWENTY-THREE

"I was on the phone with her," Hack Wind said dully, telling his story for the fourth time to an attentive Hamilton Pope and Milly Singer. "She said someone was at the door and got away before I could warn— Dammit, I'd already warned her!" His face contorted and he shoved to his feet and strode to the room's only window.

Behind him, Pope and Milly exchanged wondering glances. Milly's eyebrows shot quizzically upward, and Pope shrugged. He dug out his cigarettes, lit two, and gave one to Milly. They sat quietly waiting for the young man to regain his composure.

He came back and sat down, his dark face under control, expressionless. "I heard her let him in, and then she came back to the phone and I—I chewed her out. Then I asked her who it was. He shot her before she could . . . say."

"Did you hear his voice?" Pope asked quietly.

Hack shook his head. "Not enough to recognize. Just an indistinct mutter. Short. Like maybe he said thank you."

"And the gun?"

"Sharp thinks a .32 automatic. They found the casing between the couch cushions. The lab is comparing it with the one found at the Carlyle murder." His lips suddenly twisted in a rictus of hate. "It's the same son of a bitch, Ham!"

Pope nodded slowly. "It's likely." He hesitated. "Mind telling us what you were talking to her about, Hack?"

Hack Wind's eyes came up and met his squarely. "It was personal, Ham."

Pope nodded again quickly. "All right. That's good enough for me."

"It had nothing to do with . . . anything," Hack said. His haggard face turned toward Milly. "You remember I told you I would interrogate her again? I already did that. Nothing new came of it. You have the report."

"Do you think she knew him?" Milly asked. "Could you tell from her voice?"

"Yes, she did. By what she said at the door and again on the phone . . ." His voice trailed off, and he shook himself like a dog emerging from water. "She said 'It's only—' and then the son of a bitch put the gun to her head and killed her." His voice had become dull and lifeless, empty of emotion, his dark, burning eyes revealing the depth of his feeling. He pushed to his feet and stood swaying. "Everything's in the report. I think I'll go home for a while."

"Of course," Milly said, concerned and puzzled at the young man's obvious distress. "Did you get any sleep last night?"

Hack shook his head. "That don't matter. I just need a little time, is all."

"Go on, get out of here," Pope said gruffly. "You're out on your feet. Can you make it okay?"

"Sure, I'll make it fine." He lifted a hand in a brief salute and walked out, the usual springiness gone out of his step, his shoulders slumped.

"What do you think?" Pope asked when the sound of his footsteps had faded.

"I think that's obvious," Milly said. "There was something between them. If she still looked anything like she did at eighteen, she must have been something."

"I wonder," Pope said musingly, trying to remember the last time Hack had mentioned Wendy. The day in his office, he decided, the day he had given him the lecture on the intrinsic value of marital communication.

"If Hack was talking to Mickey Field—personal stuff— I wonder where Wendy was." Milly cocked her head at him, the quizzical look back on her face.

"None of our damn business," Pope said crisply. "It doesn't affect the case any."

"You were the one who was wondering," Milly said curtly, rising to her feet and heading for the door. "I'm going to the lab. They should know something about the gun by now."

Pope watched her leave, grinning, saw her weave quickly to one side to avoid collision with a tall, thin man wearing a long-sleeved sport shirt and faded, ragged jeans.

"I'm looking for Sergeant Pope," the man said.

Milly pointed at Pope. "That kindly old white-haired gentleman over there." She gave Pope a quick glance, and a small mean grin, and disappeared.

The tall man advanced with his hand outstretched. "Sergeant Pope. I'm John Ringley."

Pope stood up to shake hands. He nodded, then frowned at the narrow, handsome face. "I thought you were going to stay another week or so."

"I thought so too," Ringley said, and laughed a short

little sneering laugh. "But one of the kids come down with the mumps. We had to hotfoot it back on home."

"That so?" Pope surreptitiously wiped his hand on his leg under the table.

"You said to check in with the Fort Worth Police, but I live closer to Merriweather than I do the Fort Worth Police Station. Besides, when I called over there, the guy didn't know what I was talking about." He laughed his sneering little laugh again.

"We have a task force set up. You'll have to talk to a Sergeant named Globe. In view of recent developments, Mr. Ringley, I'd advise you to put yourself in protective custody."

"Yeah?" Ringley's eyebrows shot up. "You mean, let them put me in jail?"

"That's about the size of it. It's not exactly the same, though."

"I don't know about that," Ringley said dubiously, absently patting a thin layer of black hair combed across a balding head. "I'm due back at work Monday. I work for the fire department."

"We can't force you into custody, Mr. Ringley, but I'd think about it pretty damn hard. Another of your classmates was killed just last night, a woman named Fields—"

"Aw, shit, no! Not pretty little Mickey Fields." Ringley winced, appalled, his ruddy, sunburned face suddenly an unearthly pink.

"Yes, pretty little Mickey Fields. There are only four of you left, Mr. Ringley."

"No."

Pope's eyes narrowed. "No what?"

"No. There are only three of us left." Ringley watched him intently, shaking his head. "I've been thinking about what you said. You said there were twelve kids. There were only eleven.''

Pope leaned forward on his elbows and clasped his thick hands together on the table. "Look, Mr. Ringley. Eight people have been killed. By actual count. Four are left. That adds up to a total of twelve. You've just forgotten somebody.''

Ringley closed his eyes and shook his head stubbornly. "Eleven. I ought to know, I was the one who got the five couples together. Five couples, ten people, right? Five boys and five girls. I remember the number distinctly because me and Clint Fielder had seen two aluminum boats down on the lake, and each one held five people. Me and Clint rounded up the other eight and went to sign out, and Old Man Stearns put the kibosh on going boat riding. No life preservers. We went on down to the lake, anyhow, and that's where we picked up Teri Smith. So that made eleven. We climbed the cliff right after that.'' He leaned back in his chair and looked at Pope defiantly. "And that's the way it was.''

"Do you remember all eleven people?''

He winced. "No. I've thought and thought, and all I can come up with are nine. But there were eleven. I know that for a fact.''

"Teri Smith, Jean McCormick, yourself, and Matilda Royce Carlyle. Do you agree you are the four survivors?''

Ringley nodded rapidly. "Yes. All four of us were on the cliff.''

"Okay." Hope handed him a sheet of paper and a pen. "Give me the names you remember, would you?''

"Sure." Ringley lit a cigarette-size cigar and ducked his head over the paper, his narrow face bunched in concentration. Pope fired up a cigarette of his own and waited patiently until he finished.

"Did you give any more thought to who you thought Tinker Bell may have been?"

Ringley's face creased with a wide grin. "Yeah. I thought about that. Tinker Bell was Bull's name for fairies." He laughed his sneering laugh, his face pink again.

"Fairies?"

"Yeah, you know." He held out a hand and rotated it in short arcs. "Fags."

"You mean homosexuals?"

Ringley nodded, grinning. "Old Bull was a part-time hustler. He hung out down in the park on South Winslow on weekends. You know, selling it to the queers. I always had a hunch it wasn't only the money, though. Old Bull'd screw anything that moved. He'd've screwed a rattler if somebody pulled its fangs first."

"You got a look at his partner. Do you think it could have been a boy instead of a girl?"

Ringley shrugged. "It looked like a girl. But from up there, it was hard to say. All the guys had long hair, and with that bulky sweater you couldn't tell much about boobs or anything. And, too, we only got one quick look." He paused. "Nobody mentioned they thought it might be a guy that I remember." He shook his head slowly, scowling. "Naw, I think it was a broad."

Pope picked up the sheet of paper and studied the names. No surprises. All familiar. He mashed out his cigarette and looked up at Ringley, his face stern. "I can call Sergeant Globe for you right now, get it all set up for protective custody. I'd advise you to do it, Mr. Ringley."

Ringley rubbed his stubble of beard, frowning. "Naw, Sergeant Pope. I appreciate it, but I don't think so. I gotta go to work Monday. Anyhow, I'm a hunter. I got guns. Some son of a bitch come at me—"

"He's using a gun now," Pope said quietly. "He doesn't have to be close."

"I'll think about it. Maybe I'll call your Sergeant Globe."

Pope sighed and smiled. "Okay. But don't say you weren't warned." He stood up as the tall man pushed to his feet. "Remember, it's entirely possible—probable, as a matter of fact—that our killer is a classmate of yours. So if any old buddies show up out of the blue, let us know, and keep your eye on him—or her."

He nodded vigorously. "I'll sure do that."

"Thanks for stopping in, Mr. Ringley."

"Glad to help, and I hope I have."

"It might just be that you have."

"Good. So long, Sergeant Pope."

"Good-bye, Mr. Ringley. And remember, take care."

Pope walked out through the front entrance of police headquarters. He crossed the wide, divided boulevard and went into a small convenience store. He selected a cold bottle of Pepsi from the glass-enclosed cooler in the rear and brought it to the checkout counter. A slender youth with curly, carrot-colored hair and freckles grinned at him cheerfully.

"How's it going, Chief?"

"Fair to middling, Artie. How're things with you?"

"Great. Are you staying even with the bad guys? That'll be sixty-two cents."

"Sixty-two cents? My God! I thought the cost of living was supposed to be coming down." Pope dug through a handful of change and rattled some coins on the counter. "You charging me for the bottle?"

"Nope. That'll be ten cents extra, you want to take it with you."

"Never mind, I'll drink it here." He took a drink of the tangy sweetened water and shook his head. "I remember when these things were a nickel."

"The olden days, huh?"

Pope grunted and took another swig of Pepsi. "Yeah, when the West was young."

Artie grinned, then leaned his elbows on the counter, his face suddenly serious. "Yeah, but you guys had it made. All kinds of opportunities, man. Everything was cheap. And none of the pressures we have nowadays. Just take the chicks, for instance. They keep scorecards, man, and compare amongst theirselves. You gotta perform, or pretty soon word gets around and you're out behind the barn playing with yourself. Chicks were sweet and innocent in your day, right?"

"Yeah, I guess. How old are you, Artie?"

"Eighteen. Don't look it, right? Everybody says I look like I'm fourteen."

"Tell me something. I overheard my niece talking to her girlfriend the other night. I heard her say her boyfriend had laid a wet one on her. What the hell did she mean?"

Artie grinned widely. "Hey, man, that sounds heavy. That's a kiss, man. A heavy kiss. You know, lots of spit and stuff, a little tongue maybe, depending on what you go for. Didn't you guys do that back in your day?"

"I'm not sure if I remember," Pope said. He put the half-empty Pepsi bottle on the counter. "Pour that out for me, will you? Too many sweets is bad for my arthritis."

"You got it, Sarge. Hey, don't be such a stranger, you hear?"

"I'll see you, Artie."

He recrossed the boulevard, reflecting on the paradox of modern, TV-suckled youth. *Wiser in a lot of respects than my generation,* he thought, *all-knowing in the ways of the world but still naïve enough to believe that they alone had discovered the secret pleasures of sex, that they alone were pilloried by the vicissitudes of life, castigated by the fickle, malevolent hand of fate. The main difference being,* he decided, pushing through the glass doors and walking down the corridor toward the conference room, *we made do with weak beer and maybe an occasional slug of raw whiskey instead of pot and coke and speed and smack and . . . and maybe a hand on a titty stuffed into a bra or a sneaky hand on a thigh instead of grunting and groaning and making babies in the back of souped-up cars—*

"Hey! Ham!" Roscoe Tanner's voice boomed down the corridor. "Wait up, buddy!"

Pope sighed and lit a cigarette while he waited for the lumbering giant, arms swinging, big feet slapping the tile, a heavy scowl wreaking havoc with his normally benign countenance.

"Hey, man," he said, puffing a little, "I just came from meeting with that asshole Chief Durkin and His Honor the fucking Mayor."

"I know. And now your hemorrhoids are acting up." Pope turned and walked the few steps to the conference room. "Sorry, Roscoe, I don't have time to discuss it."

"Huh?" The big man stared after him, speechless, his face slowly turning red. He made an anguished sound and stormed after the stocky detective.

"Dammit, Ham! Don't fuck around—oops, sorry, Milly—don't mess around with me, man. I'm your damn boss! I got a right to know what's going on!"

"And just as soon as I find out, Roscoe, I'll damn sure let you know first thing." He edged closer to Tanner, slouched a little, emphasizing the differences in their heights. "If you'd read your reports, you'd know what's going on. Just because you're big as the side of a house, don't come around trying to intimidate me.''

Tanner sat down abruptly, the color deepening in his round cheeks. ''Come on, man, I'm not a bully.''

Pope looked at Milly and grinned. ''Is he a bully, Milly?''

She shook her head doubtfully. ''I don't think so. He's not bullying me.''

''See there, you wombat,'' Tanner said, smiling reluctantly, acknowledging that he had been nicely handled. ''Seriously, Ham, I need some words for the brass and the damn media. They're both racking my butt.''

''All right,'' Pope said solemnly. ''Tell them we made a breakthrough, that an arrest is imminent.''

Tanner's eyes brightened. ''Is that the truth?''

''No, but it sounds pretty good. Actually, I do have some ideas, Roscoe, but I need a little more time. Milly, what time is Matilda Carlyle's plane due in?''

''Two-thirty.''

''I can't tell them no damn lies, Ham. Dammit, they'd have my ass barbecued for Sunday dinner!''

''Okay, tell them the investigation has . . . oh, taken a turn in a new direction, and that a breakthrough is imminent.''

''Well, is that the truth?''

''No, but it's ambiguous enough that it won't matter.''

''What kind of turn?''

''Just some new things I've found out,'' Pope said evasively. ''I really don't have time to go into it, Roscoe, but we're narrowing it down.''

''You bet,'' Milly said caustically. ''We only have four left.''

Pope gave her a quick, sharp glance. ''What did you find out at the lab?'' He made no effort to hide his annoyance. Milly shrugged. "They can't match the bullets. They were soft-nosed hollow-points and pretty well crumpled up. The two casings match—same caliber, .32, ejector marks the same. Not enough to take to the bench, maybe, but enough to establish the same gun as the murder weapon for our purposes."

"There ain't nothing new about that," Tanner said morosely. "We've known that all along."

"We've suspected it all along," Pope corrected. "There's a difference."

"Another thing," Milly went on, ignoring the interruption. "Roger Sharp says these bullets were hand-loaded. The dumdums homemade. He thinks the powder charge was light, or else the bullets would have exited instead of bouncing around inside the skull. He said they took out too much lead, that the walls were thinner than normal. That's what caused the bullets to flatten so much, lose pieces of lead." She paused for breath. "He said they took out so much that it was likely the walls might crumple in the barrel, come out tumbling. That would account for the larger than usual entry wound."

"Good thinking, Milly."

"It was Roger Sharp's idea, not mine," she said dryly.

"Who the hell would go to all that trouble?" Tanner grumbled. "You can buy slugs all over town."

"Not these kinds of slugs," Pope said. "Besides, there are millions of hand-loaders around. A lot of hunters load their own. Shooting enthusiasts—" He broke off, his face screwed into a thoughtful frown. "Anybody who shoots a lot," he went on slowly. "And it's not always the cost. A lot of times it's the precision loading you can get with a good loader."

Tanner shifted restlessly. "Don't we have any damn idea who it might be, Ham? Any leads at all?"

"Yes," Pope said quietly. "I'm certain, relatively certain, that I know who it is. I just don't have a name handy."

"What the hell does that mean?" Tanner growled.

Pope shrugged and tore the cellophane from a new pack of cigarettes.

Milly leaned back and clasped her hands behind her head, a faint smile on her tanned face. "He means Bull Henderson's . . . loving companion on the beach at Gooseneck Park."

"That's right," Pope said, smoke gusting around the words. "Nothing else makes any sense."

Tanner rubbed his jaw with one massive hand. "Whatever happened to that rich-man, poor-man deal you all were so hot about for a while? That kinda sounded like a nut to me."

"It died," Milly said, "at the same time Stacy Crump did." She glanced at Pope. "Must have been a coincidence, after all."

"Maybe not," Pope said. "Maybe something else."

"What?"

"I'm not sure yet."

"Speaking of Stacy Crump," Milly said, picking up a large manila envelope lying on the table near her left elbow, "I brought this back from the lab. They found it stuck between some records in Crump's closet." She opened the envelope and produced an album-sized rectangle of cardboard. She handed it across to Pope. "It's a blowup of something, Parker's not sure of what. It's been blown up so much, it's lost almost all definition. His best guess is that it might be part of a human face." She got up and moved around the table to stand behind Pope. Tanner crowded in on the other side.

Pope studied the rectangular picture intently, turning it

slowly in his hands in an effort to establish perspective. Seemingly blank at first glance, a closer look revealed faint shadings near the edge that could have been the outlines of a nose and open lips, a dimmer shadow near the bottom that had the upward sweep of a jawline and chin.

"Hell," Tanner said. "It ain't nothing."

"I don't know," Milly murmured. "It has to be *something*. Why would anyone bother to make a blowup of nothing? What do you think, Ham?"

Pope took a pencil out of his breast pocket and used it as a pointer. "I think Parker may be right. See this line? It's definitely the outline of somebody's nose—I think. And here, this could be a chin. And these two curved lines here could be lips, if he had his mouth partway open . . . and here, these three small dots."

Tanner snorted. "They look like pebbles on a beach to me."

"Maybe not, Roscoe," Milly said. "If Ham is right, they're probably moles or skin blemishes of some kind."

"Right," Pope said. "And look here, right at the top edge, this dark smudge could be the beginning of an eye socket . . ."

"Here," Milly said excitedly, pointing to the upper left-hand corner, "this could be hair . . . no, it *is* hair!"

"Okay," Tanner rumbled, unimpressed. "So we've got a section of somebody's face. So what? What does that prove except that somebody went to a lot of trouble for nothing?"

"Maybe, maybe not." Pope trailed a finger across the smooth surface of the picture. "What's the purpose of blowing up a section of a photograph, Roscoe?"

"Well . . . hell, to zero in on something. To bring out something you wanna—"

"Okay," Pope interrupted. "What stands out in this blowup?"

"Nothing," Tanner said triumphantly. "Nothing you can recognize, anyway. They musta lost it in the process or there wasn't anything there in the first place."

"How about your three pebbles on a beach?"

Tanner's eyes widened slightly. "I dunno. They could be anything. Pimples, imperfections in the paper, fly shit on the card stock . . ."

Pope laughed, a not unpleasant tingling in his stomach. "But they're not. I think they're what Milly said they were—small moles." He turned to Milly, his eyes gleaming.

"You don't remember seeing—no, of course, you don't. The only time you saw him he was facedown with his nose in a pool of blood."

Milly stared down at him intently, lips parted, her eyes shining with excitement, a deep crease across her brow disappearing abruptly as her face brightened with comprehension.

"Malcolm Carlyle!"

Pope nodded and smiled. "You got it. He had three small moles beside his nose. Not particularly noticeable, except in good light. Maybe not even moles. I don't remember seeing any hairs or anything like that. Just three small black spots."

Milly frowned. "But why would Stacy Crump have a blowup of Carlyle's face? Why would she want it?"

Pope moved his face wryly. "You've got me there."

"Wait a minute," Milly said. She clamped a hand on Pope's shoulder, the crease leaping across her forehead again. "Hack said something about a camera . . . one of the people he . . . that's right, he said one of the girls on the cliff at Gooseneck Park had a camera."

Pope nodded. "I read that, but I can't see a connection with this."

Milly's hand tightened convulsively on Pope's shoulder. "Listen, this is wild, but . . . but what if she . . . the girl took a picture of . . . of Tinker Bell and Bull? What if—"

"That's not bad thinking, Milly," Pope said, shaking his head. "But aren't you forgetting something? Malcolm Carlyle was up on the cliff also."

Milly's face fell. "Oh, dammit, that's right!"

Pope reached up and patted her hand. "That was good thinking, though, Milly."

She snatched her hand away. "Oh, shut up, Ham. Don't be so damned patronizing." She marched around the table and sat down, her face glum.

Tanner made an exasperated sound. "This whole deal at Gooseneck Park. It sounds kinda vague to me. So some chick gave this guy Bull a blow job—" He stopped, his eyes flicking at Milly, sliding away. "Well, hell, that's no big deal."

"It was a bigger deal in '68," Pope said, "but that's not the point, Roscoe. You're forgetting Bull Henderson was killed. *That's* a big deal."

"Never was proved that way," Tanner said stubbornly. "They got it down as accidental. You told me so yourself."

"The deputy who investigated didn't see it that way. He was overruled by the sheriff for political reasons."

"Okay. You think this sucker who was . . . was—" He stopped when Milly laughed, his face turning pink again. "You believe this girl killed Henderson?"

"I think Bull caught up with Tinker Bell on the steps. Something happened. Tinker Bell hit Henderson in the face with a piece of fallen rock. He fell backward, taking the railing with him. The fall killed him.'' Pope mashed out his cigarette butt, aware of Milly's eyes gleaming across the table.

"Why do I get the feeling you're being evasive, Ham?" she asked quietly.

"Not evasive, Milly." Pope shook his head, his square face moody. "Uncertain. I'm sure of what happened at Gooseneck Park. I'm just not sure what's happened since, recently, to stir it all up again after twenty years, to cause Tinker Bell to decide to eliminate witnesses who could link him to Henderson's murder."

"You said 'him,' " Milly said quickly.

Pope nodded. "Tinker Bell was a man."

CHAPTER

TWENTY-FOUR

Hackmore Wind climbed the steps and walked unsteadily across the porch and into his house. Wendy was running the vacuum cleaner in the living room. She turned it off and came toward him, her welcoming smile dying as she saw his face.

"Hack, honey, you look terrible!" She stopped uncertainly a yard away, anxiously searching his face. "Why don't I run you a tub of water . . ."

He shook his head wearily. "No, Wendy. I just need a little sleep." He unbuckled his gun belt and gave it to her. He took off his hat and ran a hand through tangled hair. "Just a couple of hours."

"I could fix you some eggs and sausage real quick, honey. . . ."

He shook his head again, without speaking, and walked down the hallway to the bedroom. She watched silently while he stripped down to his shorts and stretched out on the bed, belly down, his face turned toward the wall.

She retreated quietly, moved past the waiting vacuum cleaner, and went into the kitchen. She made a cup of instant coffee and took her cigarettes to the small dinette table in the nook at the end of the kitchen that served as a dining room. She opened the bay window's curtains and sat waiting for her coffee to cool, her heart-shaped face reflecting her inner turmoil.

He's just tired, she thought distractedly, *worn-out and naturally upset because a woman he knew has been brutally— Knew? My God, Wendy, face it . . . more than knew! A lot more than knew . . . maybe loved! No! Not that fast! It couldn't happen that fast! A few days only . . . once or twice making . . . But what if she was better? So much better than me, that he . . . but sex is only a part of it, dammit, a small part, a two- or three-time-a-week thing that was sometimes good, sometimes not so good, sometimes only tedious. But maybe that is my fault . . . maybe it was more important than I thought.*

She put her face in her hands and fought down a rising swell of panic, tried to smother a sudden thought that brought a fleeting surge of hope, along with a crawling worm of self-revulsion—Mickey Fields was dead, she was no longer a competitor: an irrevocable fact.

She pushed the thought out of her head and looked guiltily toward the hall that led to the bedroom, her heart suddenly racing, as if by some magical flash of clairvoyance he could know what she was thinking and be disgusted and repelled.

She shoved away from the table and her calamitous thoughts, carried her still steaming cup of coffee out onto the patio. She eased into a chair, realizing belatedly that the bedroom window was half open.

She sipped coffee and listened to the Saturday morning sound of popping, coughing mowers as her neighbors rushed to cut their lawns before the prowling thunderheads in the west fulfilled their promise of another April deluge.

Somewhere in the woods behind their house a chain saw screamed, and she could see the gaily colored helmets and hear the angry hornet buzz of bike riders zigzagging blithely among the trees.

How in the world can he sleep? she wondered, and debated tiptoeing into the room and closing the window. She got up and moved along the patio, wondering if there might be a way to slip out the screen and close it from the outside.

She stopped at the edge of the window, frowning slightly as a new sound penetrated her consciousness; low, muffled, rhythmic, it held her transfixed as awareness dawned, as a spike of pain lanced through her heart, set her bare feet moving in automatic response, sent her flying through the doorway, across the kitchen, down the hall, and into the bedroom to the bed.

He had turned on his back, and in that split second before he brought his arms to cover his face, she saw the wet, shimmering eyes and glistening cheeks.

"Get out of here, Wendy!" It was a plea rather than a command. He tried to turn to the wall again, but she was too swift for him. She caught him with fiercely determined hands, slender arms that exhibited amazing strength and tugged him against a warm, comforting bosom. She brushed aside his arms and smoothed his hair back from his brow, kissed the damp, clammy cheeks, the closed eyes, crooning softly, tunelessly.

"Jesus Christ! This is all I need . . . damned tears!" His voice was hollow, choking.

"Yes," she said softly. "Yes, you do. Cry, honey. Cry for her, cry for yourself."

"How do you know Tinker Bell was a man?" Milly demanded, her expression wavering between belligerence and intense curiosity.

Pope closed his eyes and massaged them with a thumb and a blunt forefinger. "Maybe that's a little strong," he said. "I don't know it for a fact. But common damn sense and some things I've found out tells me it is."

"Such as?"

"Well, first of all, Bull was a . . . a sort of creep from what everybody tells me. From pimples to a foul mouth. None of the young ladies would have been caught dead with him. He didn't have a girlfriend and couldn't get one. On the other hand, I recently discovered that he may have had homosexual tendencies, or to be more accurate, he used homosexuals for both gain and sexual gratification."

"Nice kid," Tanner growled.

"Yeah. Okay, that's a pretty well-corroborated fact. The rest of it is simple logic: I find it hard to visualize a teen-age girl doing that to him in broad daylight. The captain of the football team, maybe, but not Bull Henderson, a lout of a kid with bad breath and a foul mouth, a loner shunned by even the guys who played ball with him. Maybe another kid with homo leanings wouldn't be quite so discriminating." He glanced at Milly and smiled faintly.

She smiled thinly in reply. "My, you seem to have very keen insight into the homosexual mind."

Pope nodded soberly. "I read a lot."

Tanner looked from one to the other. "So where does that get us? If it was a guy, I mean?"

"Maybe nowhere," Pope said. "Except it makes the whole thing easier to swallow. I was never comfortable with the idea that a woman did the first six killings. Women rarely slice the throats of full-grown men from ear to ear. Damn few men, for that matter. Where does it get us? If we go with it, it cuts the suspect list approximately in half. We can concentrate on the male portion of the band in the park that day, dig into their backgrounds, maybe come up with something a little more potent than what they tell us in interrogation.''

"You mean like a fag bust?"

"Maybe," Pope said, and shrugged. "Maybe he's been more circumspect than that. Not all homosexuals have been arrested by any means. Could be he's even bi or heterosexual now."

Tanner's eyes locked with his. "If you believe it, go with it. But for Pete's sake, Ham, get me something. I'm running out of ass." He pressed big fingers on the table and pushed to his feet. He glowered down at Pope for a moment, then turned and walked out.

"He's getting testy," Milly commented.

"Roscoe's okay," Pope said musingly, his eyes straying to the enlarged photograph on the table in front of him. "Why *would* Stacy Crump have an enlarged photograph of Malcolm Carlyle's face? Can you think of a reason?"

"Uh-uh," Milly said, standing up. "No more wild swings from this girl detective. I don't like being talked down to all that well." She moved toward the door.

"Well," Pope said reasonably, "you were wrong. I was simply pointing that out to you. Malcolm couldn't have been Tinker Bell, and that was what you were leading up to. No need to get uptight. You just hadn't thought it through."

Milly turned at the door and gave him a withering look. "You're pompous as hell sometimes, Pope, you know that?"

"I know. It's something I've been working on in my spare time. It's not an easy thing to develop." He watched her face tighten, then grinned.

"Yeah, well, you can kiss my—" She jumped as the phone rang, took a swift, savage step forward, and yanked up the receiver.''

"Yes?"

She listened for a moment, her face slowly flooding with color. "Just a moment, please, I'll see if His Majesty is in." She jammed a finger on the hold button, cradled the receiver, and shoved the phone down the table toward him. "It's for you," she said tersely. She whirled and left the room without looking at him.

"My goodness," Nancy said. "What was wrong with your secretary?"

"She wasn't my secretary. She's one of the other detectives."

"Oh! Well, she sounded mean. I'm sorry I wasn't here when you called. I've been over at Plant Two just about all morning. I found a note on my desk."

"Yeah, I called pretty early this morning. It . . . I . . . uh, it wasn't really anything import— I probably shouldn't disturb you at work, anyhow. Maybe it can wait."

"Come on," she coaxed. "You've never called me at work before. It must have been something."

"Just a moment." He fumbled for a cigarette, a lump slowly forming in his chest, sliding downward toward the pit of his stomach, leaving a slick, slimy trail of uncertainty. He lit the cigarette and breathed the smoke deep into his lungs. It didn't help. He took another breath of clean air and turned back to the phone.

"Nancy," he said. He stopped, then willed himself to go on. "I'm sorry, Nancy." He stopped again, heard a sharp, quick intake of breath, a startled sound, then silence.

He sat waiting uneasily, finally broke the frozen stillness. "Nancy?"

She uttered a low, breathless laugh. "Does that mean what I'm thinking, Ham?" The laugh again. "Of course it does. You haven't been mean or anything, and you haven't had a chance to be unfaithful to me, so I guess I know what . . . it's just that after last night I thought . . . last night was perfectly . . . fine, Ham.''

"That's just it," he said miserably. "Last night was . . . was too fine. That's my point. A few more nights like last night and I wouldn't be able to let you go, and I have to let you go, babe. I have to *make* you go.''

"I don't see why," she said, her voice muted, husky.

"Because," he said, "because—" Then, breaking off as the carefully rehearsed logic abandoned him, leaving a brain bereft of reason, a body slowly numbing with pain. "Because we . . . we're going in opposite directions, little girl. Everything we've done together, everything we do together, represents a compromise for one of us. Last night, for instance, you had your heart set on going to that theater, yet we ended up staying home and going to bed. That was okay. One night don't matter. But we wouldn't always have bed to go to. And each time one of us had to give in, there'd be resentment, a little bit of resentment that would eventually grow into a big resentment. . . .''

"Are you trying to pay me back, Ham? For what I did before?''

"Oh, Christ, no, Nancy! Look, please don't think that. You had every right . . . Christ, the man was your husband, after all!''

"Then why are you doing this?''

"Oh, Jesus, honey, I just . . . Look, Nancy, it's . . . it's like an old plug plow horse hooked in with a young filly. The filly wants to move, to go, to get it done, but the old plug, well, the filly just wears him out, tears him down, frustrates him no end after a while. And in turn the young filly is chomping at the bit, she wants—''

"Why are you talking about horses, Ham? I'm sitting

here bawling in front of everybody, and you're telling me some dumb story about—"

"Come on, Nancy," he said quietly, wearily. "Don't put on your dumb act for me. Not now. This is difficult enough as it is. And I don't believe you're crying. You don't sound like you're crying."

"I am, though," she said just as quietly. "I'm crying inside."

He sighed heavily. "I'm bleeding a little myself."

"Then why do it? Eighteen years' difference isn't so much. Not today."

"Twenty years. And at forty-six, twenty years is a lifetime."

"You'll regret it, Ham. Tomorrow and the next day— you know you'll regret it."

"I know that. I regret it already."

"Then it's just plain dumb."

"Maybe. But tomorrow would be a little bit harder, the day after harder still."

"Don't you love me at all? I thought you loved me . . . some, a little bit."

"Yes," he said reluctantly, "I do. And that's exactly the reason I have to do this."

"You've never asked me if I loved you. You want me to tell you now?"

"Please don't make it any harder than it already is, Nancy."

"I think you're afraid."

"I thought you understood that. If I wasn't a coward, I wouldn't tell you this over the telephone. I can't cope with it any other way."

"But this is so dumb," she wailed, "talking like this on the phone. I need to see your face, Ham. I need to see if you really mean it."

"I do really mean it, Nancy," Pope said heavily. "Please, I just can't handle a one-on-one right now. Look, if you need some money—"

"Don't you dare mention money to me!"

"I didn't mean—"

"If I need any money in the future, I can always find an old man like Clint Fielder. I just may do that, anyhow. I may goddamn well start cursing again too!"

Pope repressed a hysterical urge to laugh. An old man like Clint Fielder? Clint Fielder was thirteen years younger than he was. He could hear the faint, whispery rustling of her breath, could almost feel its warmth on his ear the way it had felt the night before; he closed his eyes for a moment in confusion.

"I have to go now, Nancy. If it still matters, I'm sorry."

"All right, Ham," she said, her voice low but even. "I'll need some time to get my things after work."

"Would eight o'clock be okay?"

"Eight would be fine, thank you. Good-bye, Ham."

"Good—" He broke off, sighed, and hung up the receiver. There wasn't a hell of a lot of use talking to an empty line.

CHAPTER
TWENTY-FIVE

Hamilton Pope sat hunched over the conference-room table when Milly came back from lunch at one o'clock. Eyes closed, his face was tilted downward, supported by a hand pressed against each cheek. A cigarette burned in an ashtray at his elbow, the smoke drifting unheeded across his square, expressionless face, a tiny flicker of eyelids the only indication that he was alive and well and thinking.

She watched him curiously for a moment, then eased quietly into a chair across from him. She lit an after-lunch cigarette and sat silently scanning his quiescent face, stern and forbidding without the mitigating influence of fulgent blue eyes. A strong man, she thought, a hard man when he had to be: a flinty exterior that belied an unexpected sensitivity, a soft core of sentimentality that he went to great lengths to hide from the world. And very successfully, too, she decided ruefully, using cynicism and bullheaded arrogance to hide his vulnerability the way a woman uses cosmetics to camouflage unsightly skin. She felt a tiny inward shiver as she remembered the first time he had kissed her, the first time he had undressed her, burning blue eyes caressing her like warm, subtle fingers, the first time he had—

"You may be right, Milly."

She jumped, startled, dropped the cigarette, then leapt to her feet and brushed wildly as the fireball broke free and fell into her lap. She felt the heat of blood rushing into her face.

"Did it burn your pants?" Pope asked mildly, one eyebrow cocked quizzically.

"No . . . damn clumsy . . . what were you saying?" She sat back down and casually relit the cigarette, slowly, carefully, acutely aware of his eyes.

Pope took in a deep, heavy breath. He picked up a thin sheaf of papers and held them up. He fanned them like a hand of cards and selected one. "These are the lists of names we got from the survivors of the Gooseneck Twelve." He paused and smiled faintly. "That's Roscoe's name for them." He held out the sheet of paper. "Tell me, what do you see?"

Milly scanned it quickly, then looked up, her eyes puzzled. "I see twelve names. What else is there to see?"

"All right. That's the master list I compiled from the others. The thing is, John Ringley swears there were only eleven people on that rock. He tells a pretty convincing story, Milly. I'm inclined to believe him."

Milly shook her head slowly. "But how can that be? You have the names of twelve people, Ham. And you took them from the statements of all the others. I've gone over these lists a dozen times. All the names appear on at least two lists, sometimes three. John Ringley must be wrong."

"I thought so too," Pope said. "At first. And you're wrong about one thing. All the names appear at least three times—except one." He stopped and grimaced ruefully.

"I knew that a long time ago, but it didn't seem to matter."

"I can't see that it matters now," Milly said, an edge to her voice. "I don't understand what you're getting at. What's the difference? Two lists are enough corroboration, and anyhow, we're talking about the victims, not the killer."

"Are we?" Pope's eyes gleamed.

"Aren't we?" she asked uncertainly, meeting his bright gaze, feeling a faint pulse of excitement, a discernible acceleration in her heartbeat. She wet her lips. "What did you mean a while ago, when you said 'You may be right, Milly'?"

Pope shook his head sadly, grinning suddenly, a fiendish, devilish grin, she thought; realizing that he wasn't going to tell her, that he was in one of his pompous jackass moods, one of his 'I figured it out and now, by God, you can too' moods, and she could consider herself lucky if she didn't get a lecture on top of that.

And she was right.

"We screwed up, Milly," he said solemnly, his grin fading. "Mostly me, but all of us to a degree. You and me because we didn't go with our instincts. All of us because we cut corners, we didn't ask the right question at the right time. We relied on paperwork. We're becoming a damned paperwork world, and the worst part is that we tend to believe what we see written down. The more often we see it written down, the more we believe it. It becomes gospel. Unquestioned truth. I knew that, dammit. And yet I moseyed blithely on my way while people were dying all around me. Smothering my instincts, reading and rereading damn paperwork—I'm getting too old, Milly. Maybe Roscoe's got the right idea, after all. Become an administrator, let the young bucks handle—"

"You're not going to tell me, are you?" Milly said tightly.

"No," he said curtly, shrugging into his jacket. "I may be all wet. If I am, I don't want you taking the heat with me." The grin came back, a ghost of its former self. "Anyhow, you know as much as I do now. Use that intelligent brain of yours. Think a little. Consider your hunches. You've had several that I squelched. Consider what John Ringley said." He was at the door. He lit a cigarette. "Consider the atrocities of mankind that have been committed in the name of honor, pride . . . and love." He smiled sardonically. "Especially that last one."

"You can't go after a killer alone, Pope. Dammit! It's against the rules."

He chuckled. "Who knows? Maybe I'm not. All I've got are bits and pieces and a couple of hunches I've been denying too damn long. I may be joining Roscoe on a hemorrhoid ring, or if worse comes to worse, ten million other people in an unemployment line." His face smoothed, sobered. "Don't worry, Milly. I'll be as safe as the pope in a nunnery."

"At least take a gun, Ham. Please."

"Sure thing." He winked and slipped out the doorway.

"Dammit, Hamilton Pope," she yelled at his disappearing back. "You're a stupid, stubborn—" She broke off, not because he couldn't hear her but because everyone else in the building could.

Matilda Carlyle stood in the doorway, staring at Pope silently. She blinked her eyes once, twice, then turned and walked down the hall.

He stepped inside, closed the door, and followed her broad back and buttocks through the dimness, reached the door of the game room in time to see her settle onto the tan couch, the butter-soft cushions accepting her bulk with a soft sigh, slowly giving way until her elbow on the arm canted upward.

He crossed the room and sat down in the chair he had sat in twice before. He looked automatically for the room's single ashtray, found it, happily, on the end table beside his chair.

"We need to talk, Matilda," he said conversationally. He lit a cigarette and settled himself comfortably. He studied her emotionless face, the pudgy white hands crumpled in her lap like dead birds. Her hair was slicked back with its accustomed severity, her huge body encased in billowing black with touches of white lace at the collar and cuffs. She wore sturdy, sensible black shoes with ankle-high tops and heavy, square heels. Her face was downcast, berry eyes hidden behind swollen lids.

"We seem to keep missing you," Pope said apologetically. "We just missed you the other day when you went to Houston."

She remained motionless, silent.

"That was the day after Stacy Crump was killed—you did know about that?"

Her head came up. "Yes. I heard . . . about that."

"Of course. Were you and Stacy good friends, Matilda?"

"Yes."

"Did you visit each other a lot, would you say?"

"Yes."

"The night Stacy was killed—between nine o'clock and midnight, according to the coroner—did you see Stacy that night?"

"I left a few minutes after nine. She was fine when I left, Mr. Pope."

Pope nodded, pursed his lips thoughtfully. "Did Stacy seem upset, nervous, agitated in any way?"

Matilda sighed. "No, Mr. Pope. Stacy was . . . happy."

"Were you happy, Matilda?"

Her eyes came up and locked with his. "Yes, I was very happy."

"Why were you happy?"

The corners of her mouth lifted in a meager smile, and she rolled round shoulders in a shrug. "I believe you know why, Mr. Pope. It doesn't matter anymore. She's dead."

"Were you lovers a long time?"

Her head bobbed minutely. "Ever since high school. It really began even before that, I think."

"How about the three years she was married?"

"That was a . . . an attempt at breaking away for her, an attempt at straight life. She was miserable."

"And your marriage, Matilda?"

She moved her shoulders again and remained silent.

"And your marriage, Matilda?" Pope prodded gently.

"It wasn't a bad marriage."

"Was it a marriage at all, actually?"

"Yes, we were legally married."

"Oh, I know that. I mean, wasn't your marriage pretty much a farce?"

She lifted her hear, her face composed, serene. "If you mean did we have sex . . . no, Mr. Pope, we never had sex." The ghostly smile drifted across her face. "Technically, Mr. Pope, I am still a virgin. A thirty-three-year-old virgin. That must be something of a record."

"Oh, I don't know. A lot of people never have sex for one reason or another."

Her eyebrows lifted. "Married people?" Her lips curved upward, and for a moment he thought she might laugh.

It was Pope's turn to sigh. "I'm having a little problem

with this. Was Malcolm aware when he married you that there would be no sex? Or was it just something that happened—or rather, didn't happen?''

Her hands moved in an expressive half circle. "Look at me. I weigh almost three hundred pounds. I weighed one hundred and eighty-five when I married Malcolm. Does that sound like he married me for sex?"

Pope shrugged. "Some men like heavy women."

"Not Malcolm. His mother is his idea of an elegant woman. Slender and tall."

"Speaking of your mother-in-law, where is she?"

"She stayed over to attend a luncheon with the mayor's wife. I'm expecting her at any time."

"All right. You keep giving me the reasons why Malcolm didn't marry you. Why don't you tell me why he did."

She sighed again, lifted one hand to her cheek in an unconscious gesture of distress. "It doesn't matter anymore. Malcolm's dead now."

"It matters. Believe me, it matters. Why did he marry you, Matilda?"

Her eyes danced around the room, as if looking for aid, came back fleetingly to his, then dropped to her hands.

"He had no choice. He didn't want to marry me, but he had no choice."

"Why not?" Pope asked softly. "Did . . . someone force him to marry you?"

She nodded minutely.

"Who?"

"I can't tell you that."

"Why not?"

"I—I may get into . . . trouble."

Pope's mind was racing. "Did his parents, his mother, make him marry you?"

Her head jerked upward. "Oh, no! My goodness, no. She threw a fit."

"Who, then?" He felt a familiar cool tingling at the base of his spine.

"I . . . can someone get in trouble after fifteen years?"

"It depends. It would have to be something pretty terrible after fifteen years."

"How about . . . blackmail?"

Pope expelled his breath in a low, gusty sound. "Not after fifteen years. There's a statute of limitations on blackmail."

She nodded without speaking, refusing to meet his gaze.

"Well?" he prodded quietly. "Was that how you got Malcolm to marry you?"

She nodded again, he small mouth a tiny red line.

"Why did you blackmail him?"

"I wanted a husband. Stacy was married then, and I thought . . . I knew about Malcolm . . . I wanted a good husband, a rich husband."

"Let me rephrase the question. What did Malcolm do to enable you to blackmail him?"

Pope suddenly realized he was on the edge of his chair. He settled back and lit another cigarette. He consciously relaxed his muscles, regulated his breathing to a slower, more normal pace. He could feel the tension dissipating, a return of vital forces, a slowly budding elation. His mind raced feverishly, fitting her small revelations into the giant hole in the middle of his puzzle. Still not enough to form any kind of picture.

"What did you mean 'I knew about Malcolm'?"

She averted her face, her sleek head moving back and forth.

"All right. Fair enough. I'll tell you. I'll tell you a little story about some teenagers who went on an outing to a place called Gooseneck Park. Okay? You told me about it once, you and Malcolm. And that was smart. Really smart. Smarter than I would have given either of you credit for being. It put you right up there at the head of the list of helpful, cooperative, open witnesses. It also laid the groundwork for a scam you laid on me from the very first. I saw it written down twice, and it became a fact in my mind. I saw it on your list, and on Malcolm's list, and it never once occurred to me that both of you were lying. It should have. After all, you were man and wife. Why wouldn't you lie for him?'' He stopped and studied what he could see on her face. He mashed out his cigarette and went on, his voice low and harsh and accusing. ''Malcolm wasn't on that rock with you that day. Oh, he was there, near, thirty-five feet below, down on his knees to Bull Henderson.'' He paused again, his eyes blazing, commanding her to look at him.

She turned hesitantly, her face pale, eyes slowly widening. ''You're guessing,'' she whispered.

''No, I'm not guessing, Matilda. I have the photograph, the blowup of Malcolm's face. The blowup from the picture you or Stacy took that day up on the rock. I'd guess Stacy, since she was the one who saw them first. I have the picture and the small fact that no one else listed Malcolm as being on the cliff with you, another small fact that there were only eleven kids instead of twelve. Malcolm was the nonexistent twelfth. The only thing I don't quite understand is why you waited so many years before using what you knew to blackmail him into marrying you.''

''I—I didn't know,'' Matilda said, her voice dull, resigned. ''It was my camera. Stacy was taking pictures of the lake, she . . . she saw them, I guess, and snapped a picture. She doesn't—didn't—remember doing it, either. We saw it when we had the pictures developed, but it was just a . . . a giggle, and it got mixed in with all my other snapshots. I didn't see it again until a long time later." Her voice faded and she sat immobile, staring at the intricate pattern of the deep-piled carpet.

Pope waited quietly with difficulty, impatience gnawing at him. Solving a twenty-year-old riddle was fine, but there were still a few jagged pieces missing from his own puzzle.

"What happened a long time later? What made you decide it might be Malcolm? I assume that was the reason for the photo enlargement."

She took a deep breath. "Stacy got married. I was crushed . . . heartbroken. We were so . . . so close. But it was after that, even. She had already realized her marriage was a mistake, but she was pregnant, and for family reasons she had to keep on with it. We were seeing each other again. Not often, not often enough. I was still hurt, resentful. And then one day I came across the picture in a bunch of old snapshots. I started thinking about it, about Bull being killed and all. About the deputy believing he was pushed or hit. I began to wonder who the person was, remembered something one of the guys said that day . . . that he thought it was a guy, that no self-respecting girl would be caught dead with Bull. Everybody laughed, but I thought about that . . . it kept coming back to pester me. I guess I was intrigued. I studied the photograph with a magnifying glass, but I still couldn't recognize who it was. But even then I think I had a feeling it was Malcolm."

"Why?"

"When you're gay, you develop a kind of intuition about other gays. I think I recognized subconsciously that Mal was gay a long time before I consciously thought about it. And then there's a kind of an underground . . . a grapevine. Back then there was . . . now it's more out in the open.'' She stopped, her hands fluttering aimlessly. ''God, I admire them, marching in broad daylight, in front of TV cameras.'' She gave him a horrified look. ''I could never do that.''

''It takes a lot of guts,'' Pope admitted.

She shook her head wonderingly. ''A lot more than I have.'' She glanced at him. ''Just telling you this . . . it's difficult.''

''I can understand that,'' he said quietly, ''but it's necessary, Matilda.''

She nodded absently. ''Where was I?''

''You were trying to decide if the—''

''Oh, yes. The photo. I took it and had it enlarged. But it still didn't do any good. I had forgotten about the moles on Mal's cheek, you see. And, anyhow, they looked like tiny gray smudges on the enlargement. It was Stacy who finally realized what they were.''

''Then Stacy knew about this from the beginning?''

''No, not exactly. She was the one who remembered about the moles on his face. We got out our old yearbook, and there they were, right in a dimple in his cheek. We were really excited . . . after five years we were the only ones who knew who Bull's lover was.''

''And his killer,'' Pope reminded.

She shook her head quickly. ''We talked about that, but nobody knew for sure. He could have fallen, you see.''

''But you still decided to blackmail him?''

''No, no! Not then, not for a while, and it wasn't like that—exactly.''

''What was it like—exactly?''

''It was a few months later. The first time I heard anything directly, about his being gay, I mean. The grapevine I was telling you about. I heard that he had been involved in a . . . well, a fight, I guess, over a man in Dallas. It was hushed up, of course. I'm sure Mother dear saw to that." She stopped and made a face. "I suppose that was what started me thinking . . . about Malcolm, his father being so important and all . . . about their money. And it was a very bad time for me. Stacy wouldn't leave her husband. I was getting fat by leaps and bounds. I lost my job as a private secretary and had to start over as a clerk typist somewhere else. It was a terrible time. I was terribly depressed. I thought about things like overdosing, jumping off tall buildings, crazy stuff like that. But I didn't have the nerve."

"And so you looked up Malcolm and blackmailed him into marrying you?" His patience was creaking and groaning under the weight of her rambling. But she was talking; that was the important thing.

"No," she said, giving him a reproachful look. "It didn't happen like that. It was a five-year reunion party— just for band members. Mitchell Dolan and Barbie Mc-Clune organized it. Band members only, no wives or husbands or anybody like that. We—I got a chance to talk to him, and it just sort of drifted around to Gooseneck Park and Bull and what happened and that I knew who it was and that I knew he was homosexual but that it didn't matter because I was gay, too, and I thought it would be a fine idea if we . . . got married." She sighed and shook her head regretfully. "Poor Mal was always so weak. He was so scared, he got sick and threw up."

"But he went for it, obviously."

"Yes. But we had to run off and get married—we went to Las Vegas. He said his mother would never allow it. He was sick all the time on our honeymoon. He was worried about facing Mama." There was a caustic edge of acrimony in her voice. "And he was right. She threw a fit. Not in front of Mr. Carlyle, of course. She was sweet

as apple cobbler until he left. Then she blew up at us. Bu
in the end she couldn't do anything about it. She knew al
about Malcolm being gay and what had happened a
Gooseneck Park, you see.''

Pope stared at her intently. "You're sure of that?''

Matilda smiled. "Of course I'm sure. And even before
she forced it out of Malcolm, she had it all figured ou
about us. Only I don't think she ever knew that I wa:
gay.''

Pope found himself on the edge of his chair again. He
stayed there, lit a cigarette with hands that were trembling.
his throat dry and scratchy.

"Three weeks ago, Matilda, about three weeks age
something happened. What?''

She stared at him, her eyes squinted in perplexity.
"What? I don't understand.''

"I think you do. Clinton Fielder was killed. That's wha
happened.''

She nodded, still puzzled. "Yes. You talked to us about
that.''

"But you weren't telling the total truth that night, remember?''

Her eyes widened in shock. "But only about Malcolm
being on the cliff. There was a reason for that. You know
that.'' Her eyes blinked, bounced off his cheekbone,
flicked around the room.

"Yes, I know that,'' Pope said harshly, feeling her slip
away, frustration boiling up in him like acid. He lurched
to his feet, strode around the coffee table, and stood over
her. "Something happened, dammit! Something that
started someone on a rampage of killing. Eight people,
Matilda, including your own husband! Eight people dead!
And you know something! You have to know, and dammit,
you're going to tell me.''

She shrank away from his rage, his narrow, blazing eyes, pushed back into the marshmallow-soft cushions and closed her eyes. "Please . . . I—I don't . . . unless it was . . . unless it was the money."

"What money?" His voice was instantly back to normal, quiet and casual, conversational.

"Please go sit down. I'll tell you."

"Sure," Pope said genially, resuming his seat, his face bland and innocent. "Tell me about the money, Matilda."

"It was Stacy. Oh, I can't put it all on her . . . I was involved too. The money came from Malcolm, his mother—" She broke off and swallowed noisily, her hands trembling violently.

"It's all right," Pope said soothingly. "Just take your time and tell me. How much money?"

"Almost three hundred thousand s-s-so far."

Pope eyebrows shot upward. "Three hundred thousand dollars?"

Matilda nodded jerkily, pinched her nostrils with a tissue. "But it was almost six . . . six months ago when we started."

Suddenly Pope felt lightheaded, was aware of the coolness at the base of his spine again. "It gets to be habit-forming, blackmail." Light-headed or not, his brain was clicking along in high gear.

"We wanted to . . . to just go away somewhere together."

"And you decided the Carlyle family should finance your independence, your future."

"They have plenty—millions. A half million was all we wanted. I thought that was fair after ten years."

"So you went after the last two hundred thousand. When was that?"

"About—about a month ago, I guess. Stacy handled all that part of it. I didn't do . . . anything."

"Except set your own husband up for blackmail."

"He wasn't a real husband," she said, her voice sullen. "It wasn't a real marriage."

"You sure fooled me. That first night you held hands like newlyweds."

She sighed. "We were scared to death. Both of us. For different reasons, I guess."

"Oh! What reasons?"

"I was afraid it would somehow come out about . . . you know, the money. He was scared about Gooseneck Park, I guess, about his father finding out that he was gay."

"But his mother knew."

"Oh, yes, she's always known, I suppose. About Malcolm, but not about me."

"You're very wrong, Matilda, dear." There was a penetrating quality about the voice, a husky resonance that Pope remembered, though not as well as the lilting, melodic laugh that punctuated it. She walked across the carpet soundlessly, shorter without her shoes but with the grace and carriage of visiting royalty. She was wearing a simple gray dress with a small white bow at the neck, a tailored jacket with large patch pockets and silver buttons the size of Susan B. Anthony dollars. She wore white gloves to match the bow, and her hair was carefully arranged in whorls and spirals just below the nape of her neck. Simple, understated elegance. The only jarring note was the small black gun that clashed not unpleasantly with the white glove on her right hand.

"I've always known about you, my dear," she said, her voice velvety smooth as she crossed behind the couch and stopped beside the shrinking fat woman. "That you were a pervert," she went on amiably, flashing Pope a small, genial smile. She reached out with her left hand and stroked Matilda's sleek head. "But I'm afraid I underestimated you, my dear daughter-in-law. You and your pervert lover. That's a failing of mine. I always tend to underestimate my inferiors." She smiled again and wagged a finger gaily. "I credited you with small ambitions only, my dear. A beautiful place to live, all the food you could stuff into that monstrous gut of yours . . . and, of course, my son as your husband." Her hand came out and settled lightly on Matilda's head, began slowly to dig into the slicked-down hair, to twist. "It simply never occurred to me that you would have the courage to blackmail me. You and your slut lover. I'm very glad to find that out, my dear. It simplifies matters no end." Her hand was filled with Matilda's hair, lifting, pulling backward. She looked over the stricken woman's head at Pope and smiled.

She placed the barrel of the small black gun against Matilda's head and pulled the trigger.

Matilda's head jerked, rolled grotesquely, lolled forward, and slowly slid sideways when Marsha Carlyle released her.

Pope yelled. He lurched to his feet and took a step forward. He saw the gun come up and the still smiling face above it, saw his fate in the crazily shining eyes, felt his heart slip downward, and then a trip-hammer blow to his chest; he staggered backward and heard the faraway thunder again, the second blow not so much a shock, somehow not so violent as the first. He staggered again, fell backward into his chair. He watched her with disbelief, unable to hear the words her moving lips were saying. Then a loud pop in one of his eardrums and her voice came through faintly.

"Sorry, Mr. Pope. I had no wish to bring you into this.

But as you can see, I have no choice. This cow had to die. This entire mess is her fault—my son's death, all the others—her fault.''

''Your son.'' Pope coughed and removed one hand from the fire in his chest to wipe bloody froth from his mouth. ''Suicide . . . like I—''

''Yes, Mr. Pope, my son took his own life.'' She came and leaned forward, stared intently into his face. ''It won't be long, Mr. Pope,'' she said almost kindly. ''You're dying.'' She turned and moved back to Matilda. She stripped off her right glove, began tugging it onto the fat fingers. ''She shot you, then turned the gun on herself. You see, I learn quickly. I remember about the gunpowder tests.'' She dropped the gloved hand and reached for the left one.

''You? You killed all . . . ?'' He gagged, swallowed convulsively, the sickening taste of salty blood thick in his mouth.

''Oh, my, no!'' Her laugh was deep and musical, the sort of laugh that would carry across a crowded room, penetrate the aimless chatter of a cocktail party, turn heads. She straightened and looked at him. ''Oh, no, Mr. Pope,'' she said chidingly. ''Only the last two.''

''Who . . . who, then?''

She made a wry face and shook her head reprovingly. ''You are dying, Mr. Pope. What does it matter?''

''Pl-please!'' The numbness was going away; he began to shake with the incredible pain.

''Oh, very well,'' she said, then smiled as if indulging a recalcitrant child. ''It was Malcolm, of course. Not that he could have done it without me. He was such a . . . a baby. I had to hold his hand all the way. Tell him what to do, how to do it. I even had to help him with Clyde Burns. . . .'' Her voice trailed off as she squatted gracefully and placed the gun carefully beneath Matilda's dangling right hand. She rose to her feet and surveyed her handiwork. "Very good," she said musingly, giving her hands a slow, symbolic brush.

"Why . . . for God's sake?" He could feel turgid movement inside his chest, a hot seepage as his life juices drained and gathered in the dark cavities of his body.

"I told you once, Mr. Pope." Her voice was chiding again, a rough edge of impatience. "I should think that would be evident. My husband, his work, his life—my life—all for nothing if . . . I had to protect that, don't you see? I still must. My husband, my son . . . both weak men. Each in his own way. Someone in the family had to be strong. I am strong, Mr. Pope. I have always done what was necessary to protect my family. Even as long as twenty years ago, I protected my family. My son. When that terrible boy forced him onto his knees on that stairway at Gooseneck Park, even then I protected my son. I hit him. I beat him in the face with a rock. I wanted to scream with joy when he fell and I saw that he was dead. Retribution, Mr. Pope, can be most satisfying." She looked down at Pope, her eyes shining, her face expectant. "Do you understand now?"

Unable to speak, Pope closed his eyes and shook his head.

"I had to be sure the blackmailing stopped once and for all. Fifty thousand. Then a hundred. The last demand was two hundred thousand dollars! How long could it go on without my husband finding out? And if he knew about the blackmail, then he would want to know why. He wouldn't stop until he found out . . . about Gooseneck Park . . . about Malcolm all these years . . . about me." She stopped, her face ugly, twisted. "I should have killed this fat cow when she made my son marry her!" She turned and started out of the room.

Pope slid forward to his knees onto the carpet. He screamed with pain, watched helplessly as a dark wall-cloud swept toward him. Then the scream turned to a cry of savage rage. He threw himself across the coffee table, his hand scrabbing for the small black gun, his insides exploding with agony; thick, bloody mucus dribbling across his chin.

He felt the cold metal at the same instant he saw her meticulously coiffed head come into view, her face blurred and melting behind the black spots that distorted his sight.

She tried to stop, tried to reverse direction when she saw he had the gun. She was nimble and she was quick: a fake left and going right in a try for the chair he had just vacated, the knowledge that he was almost gone spurring her on.

But it wasn't enough when balanced against cold determination and burning anger, and Hamilton Pope shot her through the stomach. And again on her way down.

"Hello, you damn big dummy," Milly said cheerfully. She dumped a wilted bunch of chrysanthemums from a tall, slender vase and replaced them with a riotous bouquet of roses. "These are from Hack and Wendy," she said, coming to the bed and leaning to kiss him lightly on the cheek. She remained leaning over him, her eyes moist. "It's good to see you among the living again, old man. It was touch and go there for a while. They pumped enough red stuff in you to feed a whole colony of vampires for a week."

"I feel bloody awful," Pope said weakly.

She cocked her head appraisingly. "You look bloody awful too. But not half as awful as you looked when I got to the Carlyles'. Jesus, you're a dumbass, Pope. If I hadn't figured out what you were talking about and chased on out there—'' She stopped and shivered. "You'd sure look a lot more awful right now.''

"Mrs. Carlyle . . . ?''

"Hush. They said for you not to talk. Yes, she was dead, Ham. You—the bullet cut a main artery . . . but all that can wait until you're better.'' She patted his hand and tugged his sheet a quarter of an inch higher. "Oh, by the way, everyone's been up to see you. Hack and Wendy, all the guys, Roscoe a couple of times, and . . . well, she only came once, but she asked me to tell you she'd been here, said you'd know why she wouldn't be back, not unless you got worse or something. She said you weren't . . . together anymore.'' Her eyes were holding steady, but there was a faint trace of a quiver in her voice. "She boot you out, old man?''

Pope nodded, smiled faintly.

She sighed, wrinkled her face in mock exasperation. "You lie, Pope. You'd rather lie than eat. She told me what happened. Okay, that's between you and her.'' She turned and walked to the window, looked out, her expression bemused.

She came back and leaned over the bed again, picked up one of his hands, and pressed it between hers.

"I've been thinking, old buddy. This relationship of ours. There's not enough of it. No, don't try to talk. Just lay there and keep your mouth closed for a change. Okay, maybe up to now it's been all right, this on-again, off-again affair we call a relationship. But no more. Like I said, I've been thinking. My lease is up at the end of the month, and you're going to need someone to take care of you, anyhow. Well, I've decided I'm going to move in with you. And I'm bringing a new way of life. I'm not going to be a slave to your old bones. Two, three times a week, you're taking me out to eat, at least once to a movie or maybe dancing. A play now and then, picnics, fishing, and rodeos . . . I love rodeos. And I may even learn to deer-hunt.'' She broke off and looked down at him, her face flushed and smiling, eyes sparkling. She leaned down and gave him a butterfly kiss, lowered her voice. ''And in between times I'm going to screw you blind.''

She straightened and folded her arms under small, round breasts, her eyes glinting.

''Did you get all that down, old stud?''